To Michael & Ann —

Enjoy the ride!

Rebel Heart

Jannine Corti Petska

Highland Press

High Springs, Florida 32655

D1732804

Rebel Heart

ISBN: 978-0-9746249-8-3
PUBLISHED BY HIGHLAND PRESS

Dedication

To my own hero, my husband Ken,
who is always there for me and who,
along with my children,
encourages me to continue on.

Acknowledgements

Senior Editor – Patty Howell

*Senior Copy Editor –
Monika Wolmarans*

CHAPTER ONE

April 1873

The ride to the train station had been delayed by a loose carriage wheel, forcing Courtney Danning to search for a seat on the overcrowded train. She moved down the aisle, tightening her mouth as she entered another car and discovered it as full as the first two.

Tiny beads of perspiration trickled down the small of her back and between her breasts. Other women fanned themselves with whatever they had nearby, while men blotted the sweat from their brows with fancy handkerchiefs. Why hadn't she chosen a more appropriate dress for traveling? The blue silk poplin was much too heavy for this time of year. At least the heart-shaped neckline gave her skin breathing room.

At last Courtney spied an unoccupied seat in the crowded train. A ray of hope lifted her spirits until she noticed the man sitting on the aisle side of the bench seat. His arms were folded across his chest, his head bent, and his hat covered his face. Perhaps he was asleep.

Searching up and down the car at the sea of people pressed together, Courtney felt renewed despair. Apparently no one wanted to sit next to the savage.

Curious, she perused him. Ash blond hair came midway down his neck and he had an eerily untamed appeal about him. His buckskin pullover was unlaced down his chest where a fair amount of dark blond hair poked through the crisscrossed leather ties. The shirt fit him nicely, hiding nothing of his wide shoulders and brawny arms. She swallowed the dryness in her throat and dropped her gaze. She had never been this close to a man wearing dual guns. Certainly, she'd never in her life seen one wearing a knife strapped to his right calf. The gentlemen she'd known often carried a concealed derringer, but never a weapon in plain sight.

"You gonna stand there all day, lady?" the man grumbled.

Courtney bristled at his pestered tone. She narrowed her eyes. At her continued silence, he lifted his head. Not enough for her to clearly see his features, but she had the distinct feeling his eyes were roaming up her skirt to her waist and breasts. Suddenly she wished she'd worn a different dress. Only moments earlier she'd thought the dress had been too hot. Now she wished for a higher neckline, the heat be damned.

"I can't very well climb over your legs," she said, perturbed by his lack of manners.

At first he didn't move. Then, slowly he straightened and tucked his feet beneath the seat to give her just enough space to pass. Courtney slipped by, unaware her backside closely neared his face. As she lowered to the seat, she shivered. Drawn to the stranger, she peered at him. Though his eyes remained shadowed, she was able to see his square jaw and a faint scar on his right cheek. Her eyes darted to his hands, then back to his face. His dark skin looked bronzed from the sun.

Scooting over as far as she could, she left a proper amount of space between them. She gazed out the window, thankful to have scenery to occupy her journey. Deep down, she had the awful feeling it was going to be a long one. Oddly, the brute stirred her curiosity.

Every muscle in Beau's Hamilton's body pulled as tight as a gate spring. Since the train pulled out of the station, he'd remained tense. He hadn't expected to be sitting beside Courtney Danning throughout the entire trip. Was it only yesterday he'd stood in the study with her father? Sinking lower in his seat, he remembered the scene all too vividly.

"I have another job for you. My stubborn daughter thinks she's in love. I'll pay you twenty-five hundred dollars to follow her to Santa Fe. And another six-thousand to keep an eye on her for a year following her wedding to that no-good scoundrel who wants to marry her."

Beau had schooled his shock. It had been a damn generous offer and he would have been a fool to turn down easy money. How hard could it be to keep track of a spoiled, rich girl in Santa Fe? The job description seemed too simple, had made him grow leery. The simple things ended up costing him more than he bargained for.

Still, that amount of money was damn hard to resist. "I'll do it."

Now here that woman sat, stiff as a board next to him.

She smelled clean and wore a hint of flowery perfume. Honeysuckle or jasmine, he couldn't be sure. Mixed with the glistening perspiration beaded on her upper breasts, the scent was driving him to distraction.

He shifted slightly, cursing his body's swift reaction to the woman's nearness. From her expensively tailored dress—with folds of blue velvet on it, for God's sake—to her gloved hands, he couldn't stop his eyes from roaming. He glimpsed her profile, strong, yet refined. She had a small nose and high cheekbones. In them he saw the stubbornness her father had spoken of. When her lips pursed, he had the sudden urge to taste them, to appease his curiosity. Were they as soft as they looked?

Damn. He should have said no to this job. Should have walked away the instant he saw her from her father's study window and gone back to doing what he did best–tracking down men with insidious reputations. No matter what he'd told Danning, he was nobody's nursemaid. He had no business wasting his time on a spoiled woman who'd decided to go traipsing off to the West for love.

But that first image of her wouldn't leave his mind.

"Step over to the window, Mr. Hamilton," Leif Danning had said. *"My daughter is all I have left; I need someone to protect her. Not that worthless Burgess. But she's too head-strong, needs a man who will tame her."*

Beau crossed the room. When he glanced down at the woman talking to a stable boy from atop her horse, his breath jerked in unexpectedly. He narrowed his eyes, keenly studying her from head to toe. Her carriage bespoke money. No doubt about it, this filly was used to the finer things in life, to luxuries most women only dreamed of.

From that distance, he'd perused her waist-length hair, the silkiest and finest he'd ever seen. And the straightest, not a curl anywhere. It swirled about her upper body when she moved, glistening brightly beneath the afternoon sun. Her riding habit clung as though painted on her feminine curves. His breath had lumped in his throat, and a familiar stirring crept through his lower belly.

So now, fool that he was, he sat beside her on a train to Santa Fe.

Settling back into the seat, he tipped his hat forward to cover his face. With any luck, he'd sleep through the entire trip.

Santa Fe, New Mexico Territory

Courtney shielded her eyes from the late afternoon sun as she scanned the Plaza for Stanley. The profound heat was almost suffocating, yet the first thing she noticed was the clear blue sky. It was an artist's canvas compared to the debris-littered streets leading away from the Plaza.

She took a deep breath and regretted doing so. The smells of the town differed greatly from those in New York City. Most notable was the foul scent from hogs, goats and dogs roaming freely.

People dressed rather poorly. The whites wore plain prairie clothes, while Mexicans dressed in unusual colorful garments and Indians dressed similar to the savage she'd shared a seat with on the train. The pace seemed slower, too. Mosey, she'd heard several men say when they disembarked. Glancing around, she assumed the word meant to walk like the dead.

"Need a hotel?"

Courtney startled at the smooth, deep tone of the stranger's voice. She spun around and tilted her head back to glance under his hat brim. He held his head at just the right angle to shield his eyes from her view. After the long, silent journey by train, followed by the jostling, uncomfortable coach, this was the first time he'd spoken since he'd asked if she was going to stand all day on the train.

She swept him with an assessing look. From what she'd seen of the other men roaming the Plaza, his rustic clothes fit in perfectly in Santa Fe. "Thank you, but I'm certain my fiancé has taken care of my lodging."

Tossing his saddlebags over his shoulder, he touched his forefinger to the brim of his hat and ambled off without another word. Courtney might have taken offense at his rudeness if he hadn't given her the courtesy of bidding her goodbye. Watching him walk away, she indulged herself and let her eyes skim his wide shoulders and broad back. His gun belt hung low around his hips, the leather ties hugging the inside of his thighs. She found his panther-like walk intriguing. Courtney swallowed hard, perplexed by her attraction to the man. She didn't even know his name.

"Hello, Courtney."

She tore her eyes away from the physically appealing stranger to face Stanley. Fearful she was as red as the kerchief sticking out of Stanley's coat pocket, she pretended to dab her hot cheeks with her gloves. Guilt wrung her heart twofold. She'd been so enthralled by the stranger, she'd momentarily forgotten all about Stanley. Daring a quick peek over her shoulder, she saw the man enter the hotel across the Plaza.

"You're as beautiful as ever," Stanley complimented.

Courtney floundered for words.

"Don't you have anything to say to your soon-to-be husband?"

"I'm sorry, Stanley. It's been a long, tiring journey." She presented her gloved hand, and he placed a kiss on top of it. Courtney tried not to frown. Where was the giddy feeling that used to tickle her stomach when he'd kissed her in New York?

"Show me your bags and I'll have them taken to the house."

"The house? We're not—"

"Don't worry. You're staying at the Exchange Hotel until this evening. I'm glad you sent the telegram to let me know when you were arriving. Everything is arranged for the ceremony and the celebration. I think you'll be extremely pleased."

"I'm sure I will." A year had changed Stanley. It wasn't simply that his once neatly cropped brown hair had grown to his jaw. She could get used to that. Yet something seemed— different. "I'll take the floral bag with me to the hotel."

"Sure thing, honey."

After instructing a Mexican boy to load her bags and trunk onto a wagon, Stanley hefted the only piece of luggage she would need for the wedding and started off toward the Exchange.

Courtney balked.

"Is something wrong?"

She glanced at the same hotel the stranger had entered. "Is this the only hotel in town?"

"It may not be Fifth Avenue, but it's a nice place. Come on, now, let's get you settled."

Once she and Stanley entered the lobby, Courtney wondered if she might come face to face with the stranger.

The mere thought jolted her into examining why she would even care if she saw him again. Just because they'd traveled together from New York to Santa Fe didn't mean they were acquaintances.

"Are you sure you're all right?" Stanley asked.

"Yes, I'm fine." She hoped her forced smile was convincing.

Stanley escorted her to a room that opened onto a courtyard landscaped with rocks and desert plants. She sighed, much preferring flowers and lawn.

Stanley set her bag on the plank walkway outside her door and gave her a quirky smile. "This is where I leave you. Wouldn't want anyone thinking I'm taking advantage of a lady." After a quick kiss on her cheek, he left.

Courtney observed his jaunty walk, as if he were a man without a care in the world. She expected him to be a little nervous on their wedding day; she certainly was. She eyed his gray suit and the way it fit his slender body. Charming, and handsome in a cultured way, Stanley wasn't a rugged man, by any means. The complete opposite of the savage.

She compressed her lips in self-castigation. Now why had she thought of him? No other man had the right to take up residence in her head. She was in love with Stanley.

The door next to hers opened and out stepped her unwanted distraction. He still wore that damned hat. Courtney snatched her bag and hurried into her room. She prayed the deliberate sound of the turning lock would keep the wolf at bay.

CHAPTER TWO

In the cantina Beau nursed a beer and mulled over the turmoil wrestling with his gut. He hadn't had a decent minute's peace since laying eyes on the Danning woman. She was trouble. He knew it the instant she sat beside him on the train. But he'd endured that part of the journey better than he had the stage ride.

Thinking back, he clenched his fingers tightly around his mug. The stage had been full. Jammed inside with six other people, their legs bumped and their shoulders had been wedged into a space built to fit three to a seat. His gut remained unbearably coiled the entire way. Worst of all, her enticing scent baited his overworked senses.

"Dammit," he gritted through clenched teeth.

Gulping down the rest of his beer, Beau slammed the mug on the table and stood. Four beers couldn't deaden the confusion in his mind or the roiling low in his belly.

He walked across the cantina, barely noticing the sultry heat of the late evening. He'd lived in Santa Fe long enough to have grown accustomed to it. It was the heat of another kind he couldn't ignore –his body's burning need for a woman. But not just any woman—that woman! Truth was, he'd lost interest in the females in Santa Fe. And those in New York had turned up their aristocratic noses at him.

He looked across the Plaza at the woman dressed in expensive white silk. Unlike any other in Santa Fe, she was conspicuously beautiful and snobbishly well-bred.

Beau lifted one corner of his mouth in a sneer as he stared at Courtney Danning, now Mrs. Stanley Burgess. He ducked the low entry of the cantina and leaned his shoulder against the wall. Mulling over her father's words, Beau doubted if any man could ever tame Courtney, though trying might be worth the challenge. Her fiery nature seemed cooled only by her social upbringing.

He'd be a damned liar if he didn't admit wanting to ride and master a pure bred like her.

She was married now. By his own rules, he didn't mess with married women. Besides, he'd already seen how the high and mighty eastern fillies reacted toward him. Courtney would probably be no different.

Two arms snaked around his middle and hugged him back against small, firm breasts. Beau's gaze remained trained unerringly on Courtney.

"Do not think you will share that white woman's bed, *querido*," the Mexican woman said. Sidling beside him, she tried to fit herself under his arm. When he wouldn't let her, she bared her teeth at the bride and spat harshly, "*Puta.*"

"Afraid of competition, Celina?" he asked, fully aware of her overflowing jealousy.

"Celina is afraid of no woman, especially that *gringa*."

Glancing down at the glower on Celina's face, Beau warned, "Careful, honey. The new Mrs. Burgess might have claws as sharp as yours."

Celina was a beauty in her own right. But the little whore packed too much spit and punch for his taste. Her spiteful nature didn't sit well either. Another glance at Courtney, and Beau realized how much brighter her beauty shone in comparison to Celina's.

"You've got nothing to worry about. Burgess won't give you up just 'cause he's got a wife."

Celina grew pensive. After a short spell, she stepped in front of him and ran her long, painted fingernails seductively along his arm, across his chest and along his jaw.

"What about you, *mi amor*? Do you not have an eye for the *gringa*? Or do you prefer a woman like me who can pleasure you into forgetting any other woman exists?"

Beau arched a brow. Wildcat that she was, Celina could make a man forget his name in the throes of passion. But she couldn't make him forget what he didn't want to forget. "You know my rule, Celina."

"I do not believe you are faithful to it," she pouted. "There must be many women you have taken to your bed more than once."

"Don't bet on it, honey. You can forget trying to get me into yours again." She fixed her mouth with a hurtful pout. It lasted one very short minute and soon she was scanning the Plaza, searching for Burgess, no doubt. Beau laughed scornfully to himself. Right from the beginning, he had told her flat out, he never bedded a woman more than once. He should have known she wouldn't leave it at that.

Celina swayed to the music. "The celebration is *grande*, no? Señor Stanley knows how to throw a *fiesta*."

"Sure he does," Beau said, his tone bitter, "on his victims' money."

"Take me out with the others to dance."

"I don't dance." Beau narrowed his eyes on Courtney again. Look at her, pretending to enjoy herself, he scoffed privately. She didn't belong here. Probably realized that by now. It showed in the way her eyes darted over the dark-skinned faces and in the stiff way she moved among the guests—mostly Mexicans and Indians. Strong-willed or not, the woman wouldn't last the full year. Regardless, he had every intention of collecting all Danning had promised him.

The Plaza was awash in color, with lanterns hung across the underside of the portals and from the few trees in the square. White paper streamers were strung everywhere—all for her and Stanley. She should feel honored the townspeople went to such lengths. But all she could think was she'd made the biggest mistake of her life. After a year apart from Stanley, she foolishly believed she still loved him. Too late she realized the idea of marriage had been more appealing than the man she'd traveled across the country to marry.

A cold spear of uncertainty shot straight up Courtney's neck, tingling at the back of her head. Surreptitiously she skimmed the Plaza to validate the strong feeling that someone watched her. The thought ruffled her nerves. Taking a deep breath, she turned toward Stanley as he rejoined her.

"How's married life so far?" he asked jovially.

Courtney glanced at her husband, bedecked in a plain navy suit and crisp white shirt with ruffles down the front similar to what the Mexican men wore. He was clean shaven and tidy, much like a respectable gentleman in New York. Too bad her heart no longer swelled with love when she looked at him. She wondered if it ever had, even a little.

"I haven't any complaints."

"I won't give you any cause for complaints," he promised, running the back of his finger across her cheek.

The promise sounded empty, his gesture meaningless, the touch of his flesh against hers ineffectual. She noticed the black-haired woman walking seductively toward Stanley.

When she looped her arm through his and leaned into him, it was a little too cozy for Courtney's peace of mind.

The woman turned her painted lips into a pout. "Do you have room for a dance with Celina?"

"Let me check with the missus here." He flashed Courtney a dazzling smile.

Glancing from her husband to the woman, then back to Stanley, Courtney wished he had the decency to appear ill-at-ease. She held back a glare for the petite woman.

"Go ahead, Stanley." At least he remembered to ask for her permission. "I believe I'll stroll around the Plaza, perhaps greet our guests." She heard Celina's snicker just before Stanley whisked her off to the portable, wood dance floor.

As the mariachi band played, Courtney hung back, tracking her new husband and his spirited partner. They glided to the music as if they'd danced in each other's arms many times. Celina clung to Stanley like a cub to its mother. He didn't seem to mind the woman's closeness or the indecent proximity of her hips pressed into his. He was too busy nuzzling her ear.

Courtney turned away abruptly. She weaved throughout the large gathering, nodding at guests, trying repeatedly to engage in conversation. When she realized few spoke English, she gave up and wandered to an unlit boardwalk.

Drifting farther from the festivities, Courtney snuck a peek over her shoulder. Stanley and Celina were lost in a slow song, clearly a love song. Looking away, she meandered down the boardwalk, feeling slighted. A newly married man simply didn't intermingle with loose women in public. She should be angry with Stanley, but couldn't find one reason to blame anyone but herself for bursting her dreams. Missing from what should have been the happiest day of her life was the grandeur she'd grown up with. What she got instead was a raucous party, glares from the women and leers from men.

Courtney chomped on her lower lip as she moved to a deserted area of the Plaza. Searching the sky overhead, she glimpsed the many stars. "I *will* make this work," she muttered, fighting tears of regret.

She detached herself from the mariachi's sound and lifted the hem of her wedding gown. The *poult-de-soie* was ruined, and her white kid shoes were covered with dust, neither worth keeping after tonight. She'd left her white tulle veil somewhere, she couldn't remember.

Her father's warning replayed in her head. *"The man is a lecher, a womanizer...and scum!"*

Thank God he wasn't here to witness her foolish mistake. She could see his face now. When his I-told-you-so expression jumped out of the dark, she flinched.

"A long way from the party, aren't you?"

Frightened, Courtney gasped and whirled to find the dark outline of a man.

"You sure don't look like a happy bride after traveling all this way to marry the man of your dreams."

Her breath gently whooshed out the instant she realized it was the man from the train. *The savage.* Her heart pounded fiercely, and her nerves tingled beneath the surface of her warm skin. She tried to glance under his wide-brimmed hat. As he'd done before, he angled his head, depriving her of satisfying her curiosity. It was as if she might see into his soul if he exposed his eyes to her. Indignant, Courtney straightened, too perturbed with the turn in her life to give in to caution and run.

"You are happy, aren't you?"

He stepped out of the shadows then. He wore the same buckskin clothing and black hat, the same dual guns, the same knife strapped to his calf. And the same grim expression he'd worn during their long journey together. "My happiness is of no concern to you." She was unnerved by his skulking. "Are you lurking in the dark for a reason?"

"Could be."

"Join the festivities," she invited offhandedly, then added with sarcasm, "everyone else in town has."

"I don't care much for parties."

The man wasn't much for socializing civilly either. When she turned to leave, she found her wrist caught in a grip as strong as steel. She yanked back, but he held her firmly, burning her skin where his fingers banded. She jerked her head aside, about to scream. He hauled her against his rock-solid torso and covered her mouth with his warm lips.

He was rough, powerful, and the possibility that he might rape her flashed across her mind. Then something changed. His hard kiss eased, turned almost tender. He released her, and she stumbled back against a hitching rail. She pressed the back of her hand to her stinging lips and gaped at him. His manly smell lingered, teasing her scattered senses. A hitch

17

caught in her throat. The jaded excitement invading her body from his improper behavior didn't quickly subside.

Pulling herself together, Courtney squared her shoulders. "Why did you do that?"

"Isn't it customary to kiss the bride?"

"Customary?" How could he justify a kiss that nearly curled her toes as customary? How could she justify the thrill it gave her?

"If I got in line again, could I have another kiss?"

"Kiss?" Courtney started to tremble. The idea of another kiss was too inviting. Confused by her unladylike reaction, she tried desperately to recall what she would have done in New York had a man kissed her without permission. Then she reminded herself she wasn't in New York anymore. Here in Santa Fe, the liberties this stranger had taken might be considered acceptable.

Courtney held her breath and pressed her hand flat against her fluttering stomach. She knew it would be awfully difficult to forget that bold, stirring kiss.

CHAPTER THREE

As she hurried toward the safety of the Plaza, Courtney glanced back over her shoulder. The stranger was gone. A shiver raced down her spine, chilling her to the bone. She took a deep breath to calm her wildly galloping heart, but her hands refused to stop trembling. The man's dangerous appeal didn't frighten her, but his kiss had taken her off guard, shocked her to the deepest corner of her soul and stirred something in the pit of her stomach. Worse, it had piqued her undying curiosity. Honestly, she should have been appalled. Instead, she found herself intrigued.

Touching her lips once more, Courtney felt their tenderness, the tingling left behind, and tasted the beer from his lips. Her heartbeat slowed to a canter and her hands finally stilled, but the fluttering in her stomach held the dangerous reminder of the savage's rugged kiss.

Courtney shook the stranger's brazen behavior from her mind and walked toward a wagon where a temporary bar had been established. Stanley was hoisting a glass of whiskey and talking to two men she hadn't noticed before. One was burley with long scraggly dark hair; the other was thin, his skin leathered like an old saddle.

"Well, there's my beautiful bride."

Stanley clamped his arm around her shoulders, displaying affection Courtney knew wasn't genuine. Worn out, she barely smiled. "I'd like to go home now, Stanley."

He produced a lopsided grin. "Sure thing, princess." To the two men he apologized. "Sorry boys. You'll have to win back your money some other time. My lovely bride and I are going home to our conjugal bed."

Beneath a blush of humiliation, Courtney's nerves prickled with questionable concern. She couldn't tear her sight away from the two mean-looking men.

Stanley gripped her elbow, pulled her back with him and turned her toward their wagon, an older rig some of the locals had decorated with paper streamers and strands of chili peppers. He tossed her onto the seat, forcing her to grab hold of the front board or she would have fallen between the wagon and the horse.

"Was that necessary?"

"Sorry, sweetheart. I got carried away."

Quickly guiding them out of the main part of town along San Francisco Street, Stanley seemed nervous. He glanced back over his shoulder more than once before they headed north toward open range. The sound of revelers faded to a murmur, then silence – a silence broken by the occasional howling of a wolf and the melodic chirping of insects. The combination was eerie.

"I'm sorry if I embarrassed you," Stanley said.

"You should have thought before you spoke."

"Let's not start our marriage off with a spat," he cajoled.

Courtney agreed. She was too tired to argue, anyway. "Why didn't you describe Santa Fe in your letters to me?"

"Would you have joined me if I had?"

"Yes, I think I would have." She couldn't be sure, though. Maybe for love alone she would have. Now, with that emotion no longer part of their equitable future, she had to be careful about her honesty.

Which brought to mind a most distressing thought. With their wedding night looming, she glanced at Stanley. Heat crept up her cheeks when she tried to imagine lying naked in his arms. The truth of the matter was, not even in her wildest dreams had she ever conjured wedded bliss with Stanley. More precisely, the idea of giving up her virginity to him had never crossed her mind. She had only his chaste kisses to remember him by, though she recalled now how they had never left her breathless. Certainly not the way the stranger's kiss had. She closed her eyes on a low moan.

"Are you all right, Courtney?"

"Yes, I'm fine, Stanley." It was a terrible lie. Not until she rid her memory of *that kiss* would she be convinced.

Bewildered, Courtney stared at the small adobe. It wasn't much larger than the parlor in her father's house. Not that she'd expected to live in a huge mansion from the start. But she had expected Stanley to provide a home with more style, not some mud adobe a good distance from the main part of town.

Hiding her disappointment, she waited for Stanley to come around the wagon to help her down. He swayed as his arms reached for her. Too much whiskey finally caught up with him. She was about to tell him she'd get down on her own when he closed his fingers around her waist and pulled her off. Amazed they both hadn't tumbled to the ground, Courtney reprimanded him with one very stern look. All he could muster in his defense was a sloppy grin.

"I'm gonna take care of the horse and wagon. You go on in and make yourself ready for me. A lantern's hanging on a nail to the right of the door. At the back of the house, the door to the left is our bedroom. The right door leads to the kitchen."

Incredibly, he kept his drunkenness from his speech. She watched him climb back into the wagon, flinching when he missed the narrow step on his first try. His inebriation left her with one consolation to celebrate. Stanley would probably fall asleep as soon as his head touched his pillow. Her father always did when he drank too much.

She entered the house and removed the lamp hanging beside the door where Stanley said it would be. When she turned up the wick, the flame pranced, creating eerie shadows over the room. Shocked by what she saw, Courtney balked. Except for a massive fireplace against the left wall, the room was furniture bare.

Regretting her rashness all the more, she started across the floor. The unfamiliar quality beneath her soft-soled shoes gave her pause. She lowered the lamp, stunned to find earth everywhere – hard packed, but nonetheless, earth. Her heart plunged to her stomach, and she had to force down the sick feeling trying to wiggle upward to her throat. What had she gotten herself into? Married to a man she didn't love, living in a strange part of the country with a reputation for lawlessness...

"No point feeling sorry for yourself now," she admonished aloud. "You wanted to be married. You wouldn't listen to Father. You insisted you were following your heart."

Feeling about as low as any woman could, she entered the bedroom. Too weary to lament her meager new home and her self-made predicament, she set the lamp on a dresser and immediately removed her wedding gown, tossing it over her trunk at the foot of the bed. In her chemise, pantaloons, stockings and filthy shoes, she hugged her arms around her waist. Despite the hot night, a chill spread over her body. She abhorred the thought of Stanley touching her like a husband had the right to. She couldn't very well deny him, even though making love with him seemed repulsive now. Lying with Stanley would be akin to lying with a brother, if she had one.

"What a disgusting thought," she chided. Unfortunately, it was the truth. Before it went too far, she should face Stanley with the honesty of her feelings. It wasn't fair to either of them to be stuck in a loveless marriage.

The bedroom door suddenly crashed open. Courtney jumped with a startled cry and gawked at the rag-tag men standing there. Her heart trapped in her throat and her eyes grew large with disbelief when she realized they were the same men Stanley had spoken to in the Plaza. The bear-sized one dragged Stanley into the room and dropped him to the floor.

"Get the money," he ordered.

"No," Stanley rasped, struggling to get to his feet.

Courtney grimaced when she noticed the gash above his left eye. Blood streamed down his cheek and over his nose, leaving red splotches on the ruffles of his shirt.

"Give them what they want, Stanley," she begged.

"Stay out of this," he warned angrily.

"Listen to the lady, Burgess. 'Sides, that money ain't yours, leastways not fairly. We know you cheated," the same man accused.

"You cheated these men out of their money?"

"Shut up, Courtney."

She gawked at her husband, seeing a side of him she wasn't aware existed. Sickened by the wild, greedy glow in his eyes, she turned her attention to the pair of cowpokes. Without warning, the burly one drove his meaty fist into Stanley's midsection, dropping him to his knees in agony.

"For God's sake, Stanley! Give them the damn money."

"No!" he shouted. "I don't have it. I lost it in another card game."

"You ain't too smart Burgess. I hate to ruin your weddin' night, but I'm gonna kill your bride if you don't quit lyin' and hand over our money." The man leveled his gun at Courtney's chest. She froze.

"Don't shoot her." Stanley gasped as he fought to regain his footing. He stumbled to the dresser and leaned on it, carefully drawing in a deep breath.

"Don't go gettin' a notion about pullin' a gun, Burgess," the same man warned. "I'll shoot your woman before you can cock any pistol."

Stanley glared at him. "The money's not here."

"You're lyin'. Pete, get the girl."

"No!" Courtney screamed. The wiry man leaped for her and slammed her against his body. Real fear gripped her entire being, surging bile to her throat. She swallowed repeatedly, forcing down the awful taste, all the while praying these men would leave them unharmed after they got what they came for.

"What're we gonna do with her, Tully?" Pete asked, his foul breath making her gag.

"Kill her." His matter-of-fact attitude heightened Courtney's fear.

"Don't touch her!" Stanley shouted, rushing Tully. Another hard drive of the man's huge fist to his stomach crumbled Stanley in an instant.

"Come on," Tully ordered Pete. "We'll turn this place upside down 'til we find the money. First I want the girl outta here before she goes hysterical on us."

He pulled a bandana from his neck and tied it around her mouth. Courtney gagged from the stench of sweat and the taste of dirt. Her stomach lurched frighteningly.

Tully yanked her hands behind her back and tied her wrists with a length of rope he'd carried in his back pocket, then shoved her back at Pete. "Take care of her."

Courtney resisted at first, but Pete, as wiry as he was, jerked her through the main room with little trouble. She didn't feel the full weight of panic until he tossed her onto his horse and mounted behind her. Tully stepped onto the porch, holding Stanley by the scruff.

"Let her go and I'll take you to the money."

Tully laughed gruffly. "You'll take us to the money no matter what we do to her."

Stanley twisted and wrangled himself free, knocking the gun from Tully's hand. Grimacing, Stanley leaped for the loose weapon and whipped it toward the man's huge chest.

"I said let her go. Now!" Stanley demanded.

In the next instant, a gun barked and echoed into the night. Horrified, Courtney watched helplessly as Stanley's body jerked and stiffened. His head turned slowly, his glazed eyes finding her atop the horse. Through the stunned

23

expression on his face, she recognized his silent apology. He took two steps, then collapsed like a rag doll.

Tully toe-kicked him. "Dammit, Pete. Why'd you have to go and kill him for? Now we'll never get our money."

CHAPTER FOUR

Courtney slid her wary gaze from Tully to Pete. As they went about making camp for the night, it seemed they had forgotten about her. But they did remember she was there, and she colored hotly when Pete leered at her prone form.

Four stakes had been hammered straight into the ground, her wrists and ankles secured to them with leather strips. She was spread open with only her chemise and pantaloons to protect her. That wasn't any comfort, though. The fine material would rent easily if either miscreant had a mind to rape her. Pete's intentions clearly hedged toward that ghastly crime. He practically drooled each time he sought her out with his mawkish eyes. As hopeless as it seemed, she wouldn't give up fighting for her life.

Pete glanced at her again, scratching his crotch in plain sight. Repulsed, Courtney would have turned away, but she didn't dare take her eyes off either man. Knowing what they were about made it easier on her nerves – no surprises that way.

"You know, Tully, I ain't hungry just yet. I think I'll work me up an appetite first." Pete smacked his lips together, turning Courtney's stomach inside out.

Tully squatted and poked at the campfire with a stick. "Do what you want, just don't mess her up. I want her awake when I take her. We'll kill her before we move out."

Pete tossed his bedroll down. "I'm only gonna relieve myself between them pretty legs. But first I gotta relieve myself of a different nature."

Courtney tracked Pete until he disappeared into the brush. She returned to Tully, narrowing her eyes on his large back, wishing she could shoot bullets with her glare. She tugged on her restraints, wincing when the unforgivable leather bit deeper into her skin. It was useless. She'd have to saw clean through her flesh and bones before she'd be able to pull free.

Out of nowhere a bare hand clamped over Courtney's mouth. She tensed. Her heart thundered painfully. She feared Pete had come up behind her. The smell of beer from the man's warm breath beside her ear pulsed dread through her veins. She lay perfectly still.

"Keep quiet, lady. I don't intend to lose my life over some hair-brained female." He removed his hand slowly. "Good girl," he praised, a small amount of relief rimming his words.

Courtney recognized the smooth voice instantly. It was *him*. The him who had given her *that kiss*.

Oh, God, why did it have to be *him*?

She craned her neck, but all she could see were moccasined feet. The rest of him remained hidden in the spiny shadows from surrounding trees. Looming above her like a nightmare, he was all she had at the moment to protect her from those two murdering rovers.

Beau grasped his rifle firmly in one hand and waited, breathing calmly as he observed the man hunched beside the campfire. Damn, he was a big son-of-a-bitch. He glanced down and spoke barely above a whisper. "How many? Two?" She nodded, the uncertainty and fear in her eyes pricking his heart.

Careful Hamilton. Feeling sorry for her will only get in the way of your judgment, could damn well get you killed.

As he moved toward the woman's feet, out of the shrub ambled the other man, fastening his grungy denims. He raised his eyes and dug his heels into the dirt.

"What the hell?"

The bear beside the campfire jumped to his feet, surprisingly agile for someone so large.

Before either could reach for his weapon, Beau cleared leather and fired his six-gun and rifle simultaneously. When the smoke cleared, both men lay sprawled on the ground.

A remorseful sigh passed between Beau's pursed lips. "God, I hate doing that."

He checked each man for a pulse even though he knew he wouldn't find one. He trusted his accuracy. The bullets hit his intended victims clean through their hearts.

Without hesitation, he lifted the leaner man, throwing his lifeless body over one of the horses and tying him to the saddle. He did the same with the other man, grunting from his dead weight, and almost dropped him halfway to the horse. Grimacing at the painful pull in the curve of his back when he bent to retrieve his rifle, Beau swore to himself. He set his hardened sight on the woman. She was the reason he'd probably lie awake all night suffering from a sore back.

Courtney met his icy cold eyes, fearful yet curious. He had killed Tully and Pete in a heartbeat, and she wondered if he realized what he'd done. She swallowed hard as he approached and stood at her feet. The brim of his Stetson hid his eyes. Instinctively, she knew they were measuring her length. She swore she could feel them inching up her legs and torso.

Boldly, Courtney returned the assessment. Her carefully trained eyes roamed up his buckskinned figure with as much thoroughness as her humiliating position allowed. He wore a bandoleer across his chest and held a rifle at his side. All those weapons and ammunition, she thought. He was outfitted to face an army of thieves. One thing was certain: His ruggedness bewildered her and at the same time excited her senses. She couldn't help fidgeting from the strange sensation turning circles in her lower body.

When the stranger pulled the knife from its scabbard and squatted near her head, Courtney's breath sucked in on a gasp. He held the sharp weapon over her face, watching her eye the blade glistening in the firelight. When he brought the knife down, she squeezed her eyes so tightly she saw stars behind her eyelids. Instead of the expected searing pain from the blade imbedded into her flesh, she felt a tug at her cheek and an uncomfortable shift in her facial muscles as the bandana fell away.

Relief washed new warmth and life into her body. She was so grateful to be rid of the disgusting bandana she didn't think about the stranger's motive for coming to her rescue. He moved to her feet, his eyes raking over her in a way that made her feel naughty for exposing too much of herself outside the privacy of her bedroom. Courtney licked her lips to restore the moisture to her mouth while keeping her eyes steady on the man. His continued silence made her nerves dance with trepidation. Had she been saved from one evil and tossed into the pit of another?

She cleared the dryness from her throat and attempted to speak. To her dismay, her voice came out like a frog's croak. Clearing it once more, she asked tentatively, "Are you going to untie me?"

A lazy smile brought up the corners of his mouth. "I don't know if I want to. You owe me for saving your life. And since you're in the right position..."

Courtney stiffened with indignation. "If raping a defenseless woman will make you feel manly, go ahead."

He stooped, setting his rifle on the ground, and sliced the ties at her ankles. Leery, afraid he might take her up on her foolish challenge, she kept a guarded eye on him as she raised her knees, restoring life to her stiff joints. She caught a glimpse of his eyes, though it was too dark to see their color. Their shine settled over her, following the movement of her legs. He lifted a hand to her calf, stilling her in an instant. His fingers stepped up her leg, pressing into her flesh through her snagged and torn stocking. When his hand drifted to her thigh, Courtney froze. Then his hand snapped away, as if it had been branded by a red hot poker. Without another word, he cut the ties from her wrists and pulled her up to sit.

Courtney immediately rubbed at the chafed skin around her wrists. The stranger frowned. He removed a blue bandana from the waist of his pants and handed it to her. As she wiped away the spots of blood, she kept her eyes steady on her rescuer while he sheathed his knife and retrieved his rifle. A minute passed, then another. Realizing he wasn't about to offer her a hand up, she stood on her own. Unsteady, she prayed she wouldn't embarrass herself by falling. She had already suffered enough humiliation. A shiver wracked her body, and she hugged her arms. She wasn't cold, but she was flooded with a spate of emotions: relief, fear, uncertainty and...desire.

Baffled, she wondered why that particular emotion would surface now. After coming so close to death – knowing she had to return to the adobe she was supposed to share with Stanley, who lay dead because he'd tried to protect her—why would anything but bereavement overcome her?

She cleared her throat gently. "Thank you for saving me, Mr..."

He watched her a moment before responding. "Beau."

Peeved by his clipped tone, Courtney raised her chin a notch, lengthened her spine and stood tall. "I realize you had to kill those men to save me, but the least you can do is respond like a gentleman."

"I'm no gentleman, lady."

"I have gathered as much." She continued staring down her nose at him. "Do you have a last name?"

At first she didn't think he would answer. Then just as rudely as he'd spoken before, he replied, "Hamilton."

Courtney squared her shoulders, unintentionally jutting her breasts higher above the low neckline of her chemise. She couldn't begin to understand the look that flashed across his face and settled into his eyes.

"Son-of-a-bitch," he muttered and stomped over to the fire. He promptly scooped the bedroll from the ground and shook it out, scattering its contents. He thrust it at her. "Wrap this around yourself."

She shook her head. "It smells awful."

"Lady, either you wrap this around yourself, or I'll rip your underwear off and take you right here in the dirt."

She snatched the wool blanket out of his hand and made a face at its foul odor as she wrapped it securely around her shoulders. "Do you always try your damnedest to intimidate others?" she snapped.

"I don't have to try." He left her for a moment, but returned shortly with his horse in tow. "I'll take you back to your ranch," he said abruptly before he mounted. He glared down at her. "What? You'd rather walk?"

She held her ground.

"Lady, if I had wanted to harm you, I would have already done so."

Still she hesitated.

He narrowed his eyes. She tried to figure out what he was thinking, but she suspected that would be harder than hitting a pea from twenty yards away with a hand gun. For now she had to trust he wouldn't harm her. He hadn't so far. No matter, she wasn't willing to put herself at his mercy, so she trounced around his horse and started for the copse of trees.

"Dammit, don't be an idiot. You won't make it back to the ranch alive." He nudged his horse alongside her, easily keeping up with her hurried strides.

Courtney kept moving. "And I would if I rode back with you?"

He leaned down, took a firm hold of her upper arm and yanked her up to his saddle. "Lady, I'm all you've got right now. And don't say another word or I'll gag you."

She bristled, but kept a tight grip on some sense. The ruthless set of his jaw and the stern sound of his voice gave her reason enough to believe he would indeed gag her.

After a while, Courtney gave in to exhaustion and slumped back. She rested her head on his shoulder, a solid shoulder. The muscles were thick and strong, by no means an uncomfortable pillow for her weary head. She closed her eyes and unknowingly sighed. He smelled like a man should, she supposed, his natural scent undisguised by cologne. Stanley had worn cologne. Sometimes he had reeked from it. But not Beau Hamilton.

The bullets from his bandoleer pressed into her cheek. Courtney hardly noticed. The steady gait of his horse and the even rise and fall of his chest lulled her into a pre-slumber state.

"It was one hell of a wedding, lady," he commented. "A wife and a widow all in one day."

She sensed he was holding his sarcasm at bay. She glanced up anyway, studying his features, giving him the chance to study hers.

Beau liked what he saw.

"I can't feel anything," she revealed. "Am I a terrible person?"

"Not so terrible." The moonlight drew sad shadows on her pretty face. "It's hard to mourn a low life like Burgess."

As he expected, she jerked upright and fixed him with a hostile glare. "That was uncalled for, Mr. Hamilton."

He regarded her coolly. "It's the truth."

"How is it you knew my husband?" she asked, suspicion evident in her tone.

Beau hardened his features against the repercussions answering her question could bring. Somehow he had to end her curiosity about his acquaintance with Burgess. "We sat in on a card game occasionally. Shared a beer now and again. Went to the local cathouses together."

If she tightened her body anymore, she'd break in two, Beau thought as he watched her features twist with rage. When her hand came up to slap him, he turned his eyes as hard as flint.

"Go ahead, strike me if it'll make you feel better. I'll even be fair about it and give you my cheek. But I'm warning you. The last woman who slapped me lived to regret it."

30

She took his threat to heart and dropped her hand to her lap where it balled into an angry fist. Then she surprised him again by losing steam, her fire sucked into some black hole. Oh, he didn't doubt it would flare up again the instant he mentioned a truth about Burgess.

"Stanley's unfaithfulness was to be expected. We had been separated a year, after all. He would have ceased his errant ways if he were alive."

"You're so damn naïve," Beau said quietly. "You best go back home. Leave Santa Fe and Burgess far behind."

"I won't, Mr. Hamilton. This is my home now, and I'll take over the ranch and the business Stanley worked hard to build."

"You go right on believing that, lady. It may be all that'll get you through life out here."

A short time later, they reached the adobe house. Beau dismounted, taking the woman down with him. Setting her on the ground, he made sure she was awake enough to stand on her own before moving off to the barn to fetch a horse to carry Burgess' body to the cemetery. He cursed himself for holding her protectively while she slept. He could have sat her behind him, could have forced her to lean against his back to stay on the horse. Instead, he had cradled her in his arms like a man who really gave a damn about her. He didn't. She was another job, that's all.

Twenty minutes later, Courtney stood on the porch in her nightgown and robe, in time to see Beau Hamilton replace his hat and mount his horse. He wasn't much at conversation and was rude and unrefined. But he had saved her life and safely returned her to the adobe. She couldn't fault him for that. Neither could she blame him for speaking the truth about Stanley. Coming to her senses, she realized the signs of Stanley's infidelities had been there all along.

Married life wouldn't have changed him one bit.

She glanced at Stanley's lifeless body slung over a horse. No matter how unfaithful he was, he didn't deserve to die a violent death. She gave her rogue savior an appreciative smile.

"Thank you for seeing to my husband's burial, Mr. Hamilton."

He gestured with a curt nod. "You're in no condition to do it yourself."

"Still and all, you are kind to help me."

"If you say so."

Courtney dropped her arms to her sides and took up a combative stance. "Yes, I say so. I'm trying to be friendly. Can't you accept that?"

"Little old ladies are friendly. So are whores. Be careful which friendly you want to be." He tugged gently on the reins. "You might want to lock your doors, Mrs. Burgess. I'm not killing any more men because of you. Unless I'm paid to."

CHAPTER FIVE

Courtney straddled a bay gelding, one of only two horses she found in the barn, which doubled as a stable. The other was a beautiful gray mare. At least Stanley had the good sense to obtain well-bred horses. He certainly had little wisdom for much else.

As she steadied the horse on a sloping hill overlooking her land, she tried hard to imagine what a city boy like Stanley had seen in this place. Pastures were abundant as far as the eye could see – some plush grasslands, others eaten down to the trampled dirt. A river flowed in the distance, providing water for the stream that passed close to the back wall of the adobe. The barn appeared new, as did several corrals. A short distance behind the barn was another adobe, perhaps for the hired help. In a way, the setting was almost perfect. Almost, but not quite.

She looked out over the far range at the scattered sheep grazing in peaceful silence. What in God's name did she know about sheep ranching? Why hadn't Stanley had the insight to warn her she'd be helping him raise sheep? She'd have been better prepared when she awoke this morning to the shocking discovery. Raising cattle, she could understand. Or breeding horses. But sheep? God, they smelled awful.

Tugging on the bay's reins, she urged him down the slope and headed for town. She could have easily packed up and taken the first stage out, but her last conversation with her father still rang in her ears. She wouldn't go back to New York if he begged her on bended knees. Besides, it still goaded her that he'd been right about Stanley. What did it matter now? Stanley was dead, and she was left to prove she didn't need her father's help to survive.

A short while later, she reached the main part of town. She wondered if she'd ever see Beau Hamilton again. She owed him for having the courage to help her. An ordinary gentleman might not have gotten involved. In some small way, she felt indebted to him for his bravery.

"You must still be in shock, Courtney. Beau Hamilton is a man you have no right being indebted or attracted to. He's trouble," she said aloud.

Oh, but *that kiss*. It had haunted her throughout the night. She had tossed and turned, burning with the memory of it. It had almost obliterated her sorrow over Stanley's death.

"Stop it!"

The horse pulled up abruptly. He flicked his ears back and forth and turned his head toward her. Courtney lifted her brow in awe at the animal.

"I don't believe it. You thought I was telling you to stop, so you did." When the horse bobbed his head, her eyes widened. "Did Stanley teach you –?" She shook her head. "No, he couldn't have. Stanley wasn't good with horses." The animal bobbed his head again, as if agreeing with her. "I'll be damned. You do understand. I suppose you couldn't tell me your name?"

Heading up San Francisco Street, Courtney looked ahead to the Plaza. Scattered decorations and loose trash blew across the wide open area. No one paid any mind to the debris. They simply side-stepped anything blowing in their path. Remnants of last night's celebration were trapped along the low slung adobe buildings that framed the square. Beneath the portal of the Palace of Governors, she noticed burros using the thatched canopy for shelter from the hot morning sun. She gawked at the sight, disbelieving a place of government would permit such an implausible use of the building.

Life flourished in the Plaza. Peddlers hawking their wares appeared to enjoy the friendly competition among one another. Almost everyone was of Mexican heritage or from one of the many nearby pueblos. Their lifestyle seemed impoverished in comparison to the Anglos. She glanced down at the expensive clothes she wore: a royal blue split leather skirt, a white long-sleeved shirt buttoned down the front, and a black soft-leather vest that fit closely to her small waist. Even her knee-high riding boots spoke of elegance. Suddenly she felt conspicuous, so much more with her long, straight blonde hair. And one more thing made her different from the others. She was the only person not wearing a hat.

At the First National Bank, she dismounted and draped the reins over a splintered hitching post. Before entering the building, she observed a Mexican climbing into his mule-driven *carreta*. Inside, Courtney immediately sought out anyone who seemed important and was grateful when a slender Mexican wearing a suit approached.

"*Buenos días,*" he greeted in a soft-spoken voice. "Señora Burgess. I deeply regret your misfortune."

She was taken aback by his fluent English, but not more than she was by his condolences. His kind face and the fatherly look in his brown eyes bespoke of genuine sorrow for her loss.

"It is so tragic," he added.

"Yes, it is. But how –"

"News travels like wildfire in Santa Fe. After Señor Hamilton brought in the bodies–"

"Yes, well, I'm grateful to Mr. Hamilton, though I'm not sure how he knew I was in trouble."

The man grinned. "Señor Hamilton knows everything that goes on in Santa Fe."

"Does he?"

"*Sí, señora.*" He grasped her hand and held it a moment. "Please excuse my forgotten manners. I am Mr. Garcia, manager of the First National Bank. What can I do for you, Mrs. Burgess?"

"I would like to discuss my husband's ranch."

The banker's head swiveled from side to side. He acted as if she'd said something secretive. He appeared suddenly uncomfortable and whisked her to his office at the back of the bank. Confused and a little curious, Courtney accepted the hard mahogany chair he offered and waited while he took his seat behind a matching desk.

"Now, what is it you wish to discuss?" He fussed with papers on the desk top, his smile as uncomfortable as if he'd sat in a puddle of water.

"My husband and I never had the chance to discuss our ranch. I thought I'd start by going over the business ledgers." She thought he was going to spring from the chair. His lips twitched, seeming indecisive about whether to smile or frown.

"I am sorry, *señora.* Your husband ran out of money and was forced to list the ranch as collateral for a loan. His account with us was closed months ago." He lowered his voice to a whisper. "The bank was ready to foreclose at the time of his death."

"That can't be. Stanley owned a prosperous business," she insisted. He'd said so in his letters, she wanted to add, but the genuine sorrow in the banker's eyes told her he had spoken the truth. Her heart slipped into icy disdain. "How much did Stanley owe the bank?"

"Two thousand dollars. But do not worry about it now, *señora*," Mr. Garcia added in a rush. "Because of the circumstances, the bank will hold off on foreclosure and extend a new payment deadline. Will two months be sufficient?"

Courtney inhaled to clear her head. Mulling over the offer, she realized she had no other choice and accepted the new terms. "I don't know why or how Stanley got himself into debt, but I *will* make the ranch profitable again," she promised.

Her mind whirled as she made her way through the bank, too preoccupied to notice how the patrons and employees alike gaped at her. Outside, she mounted her horse and wondered what she should do next.

"Señora Burgess," she heard and glanced down at a stout Mexican man beside her right leg. He wore baggy pants and a white shirt with garters cinching the wide sleeves at his thick upper arms. Deep down Courtney sensed he hadn't sought her out for a social visit.

"Señora Burgess, I am José, owner of the cantina. I apologize for burdening you so soon after your husband's death."

Impatient, Courtney spoke bluntly. "How much did Mr. Burgess owe you?"

"Three hundred dollars, *señora*. The tab –"

"Will be paid," she interrupted, grimacing at the audacity of her late husband. "I'll need time to gather the money, but I assure you, you will have it."

Courtney was livid. How could Stanley leave her with so much debt? She tugged on the reins and absently let the horse lead the way. With the unexpected responsibility on her mind, she failed to notice the boy who imitated the bleating sound sheep made. If she dwelled on her financial woes, it would only make her sick and further aggravated. She must get over the dreadful disappointment she harbored toward Stanley and deal with the knowledge that she had married a first rate bastard.

Courtney looked up with a start. The horse had brought her to Seligman's General Store. It was uncanny how the animal knew her mind. She planned to purchase the proper clothing to work the ranch. The wardrobe she brought from New York was far too expensive and elegant for working with sheep. She could only hope the proprietor of the store would be a gentleman and allow her to open an account.

As she dismounted, she shuddered from the prickly sensation of fingers stepping along her back. She squeezed her shoulder blades together to rid herself of the uneasiness gripping her like a vise. Without solid reason, she turned her attention down the street to the Exchange Hotel. What she saw gathered her breath into a formidable lump within her chest. Beau Hamilton leaned casually against the building. He tugged down on the brim of his black Stetson with its two rows of colorful beads circling the crown.

She acknowledged his guarded scrutiny by lifting her chin, then turned sharply and entered the store. The sudden silence was indescribable. All the people in Seligman's, including the small children, stopped. She must be getting used to the impolite attention, she assumed, because suddenly they didn't ruffle her feelings anymore. Unfortunately, the store was at its busiest during the morning hours before the high temperature drove the Santa Feans indoors. With her head held high, she wove through the crowded room toward the counter.

The proprietor immediately stepped through faded blue curtains hung over the door to hide the back room. He wore the same expression of regret as had Mr. Garcia and Jose. Rankled, Courtney arranged her mouth into a stern line and blatantly engaged the man's eyes.

"I'd like to open an account. I will not be able to pay you on a regular basis until I get the ranch–"

"I'm sorry, Mrs. Burgess."

Of course he would know her name. Everyone knew who she was. No one wanted to be her friend, though. Her composure fled. "Sorry I lost my husband? Or sorry you cannot extend me credit? How much was Stanley in debt to you?"

The man pinched his lips together and glanced at his nosey customers. He leaned over the counter and whispered,

"I'm sorry for both, Mrs. Burgess. Your husband's account is already close to twelve hundred dollars. I can't extend –"

"I understand," she said curtly. "You'll have your money. It may take a little time, but you'll have it."

Damn that philandering, inept bastard! If Stanley wasn't already dead, she might kill him herself.

Bursting through the door, Courtney leaped from the boardwalk to the stirrup, hoisting herself into the saddle with ease. She glanced over at the Exchange and was unnerved to find Beau Hamilton still there, his position unchanged. She tried her damnedest to fight the strong pull of the man's eyes and wheeled the horse in haste. She couldn't trust herself to remain in town, couldn't trust her temper to restrain itself much longer. Tapping her knees to the bay's sides, it was all the urging the horse needed to get her the hell out of town.

CHAPTER SIX

Filth. Everywhere Courtney turned she saw layers and layers of dust and dirt. It appeared the hand of a cleaning woman hadn't touched the inside of the adobe in months.

She started in the bedroom, taking an old cloth to the pine furniture. By the time she finished, the heavy wood gleamed. In the kitchen, she scrubbed and chipped away at the grease for hours until her stinging muscles couldn't take any more. Thank God the adobe only had three rooms, two that were furnished.

As she stretched her stiff muscles, Courtney smiled. Housecleaning wasn't so difficult, merely tiring. Doing it all herself gave her a genuine appreciation for the servants who worked for her father.

Sitting on the bed, careful not to mess the pretty calico quilt, she released a well-deserved sigh. The bedroom wasn't as sparse as it seemed at first sight. All she needed was there: the bed, the night table and the chest with four drawers. Amazingly, they matched. A chair sat beside her trunk, which she had cleaned out. She'd even removed Stanley's clothes and her wedding dress, throwing them outside the back door until she decided how to dispose of them. It wasn't the comforts of her father's home, but it was her home now.

Her glance grazed the dresser, and she huffed in frustration. Dust already settled over the furniture from the damn earthen floor. Although it was packed as solid as cement, it wasn't enough to keep the dust from flying every time she walked on it. All her efforts seemed fruitless.

Regardless, she made a mental note of what was left to do. The blue checkered curtains begged to be washed, but she was too tired to tend to them now. As it was, it had taken hours to remove the wood shutters from the entire adobe. She hadn't been able to figure out why they'd been put up when glass panes and curtains dressed the windows.

The clopping of horses' hooves brought her to the fore of the box-style adobe. Through the sparkling window pane she saw three men on horseback. Two wore ranchhand clothes.

The man in the middle bore a regal posture. He wore an expensively tailored suit. She glanced at his russet brown hair, then his face. A man of means. Thank God. She promptly flung back the door.

"Good afternoon, ma'am," the well-dressed man greeted cordially. "The name's Jared Stover. I own the Bar S ranch to the west."

"A pleasure to meet you, Mr. Stover." Courtney suddenly felt the heat rise to her neck and face. She wore an old pair of Stanley's trousers rolled up at the ankles and cinched in with a belt too long for her small waist. She'd tied off the oversized cotton shirt above her hips and rolled the sleeves to her elbows. She was so happy to see another Anglo face that she forgot all about her scrub woman's appearance.

"I apologize for coming unannounced," he said, his eyes raking over her.

After smoothing back the wayward strands of hair that had slipped from her single braid, Courtney waved aside his apology. Feeling awkward, she shoved her hands into the pockets of her trousers and attempted to smile. "Please don't tell me my husband was in debt to you, too."

"Not at all, Mrs. Burgess. And please accept my condolences. I'm simply here to let you know you can come to me if you need assistance." His gaze flickered over her breasts, then her lower body, and the green of his eyes glazed over. "Anything at all, I will be happy to oblige."

Courtney stifled a shiver and accepted his offer sweetly. "Thank you, Mr. Stover. I'll keep that in mind."

He smiled politely, looking every bit like a man who'd been triumphant in a quest of some kind. "Do you intend to work this ranch?" he asked.

"I'm certainly going to try. You wouldn't happen to know anything about sheep, would you?"

"No, Mrs. Burgess. I'm a cattle rancher. Isn't Manuelo here?"

"Manuelo?"

"Your husband's...hired hand. Manuelo, his wife and two sons worked the ranch. They live –" He lifted his eyes briefly to the adobe behind her, then twisted in his saddle. "They live there," he said, nodding at the smaller adobe beyond the barn. Stover returned his questioning stare.

"I haven't met them yet. But it relieves me to know someone is here to guide me."

Stover's smile twittered. "Well, be careful out here. It's not safe for a woman by herself. Good day, ma'am."

The sun beat relentlessly on Courtney's back as she knelt in the dirt, tilling the garden beside the main house. Many varieties of cacti, herbs, roses, and colorful flowering plants surrounded a fragrant piñon tree. The soil was overrun with weeds, but once she began clearing them out she noticed the garden had been thoughtfully laid out.

On her feet, Courtney stretched from one side to the other to relieve the stiffness in her sore muscles. Two days of hard work had taken its toll. Painful knots formed in her shoulders and across her back. Her legs ached, and her hands had lost their softness. She could have lamented their redness and rough texture, but casting an appreciative eye over the garden, she wasn't sorry for all she'd done. It felt good to get her hands dirty. But at the moment, a bath would make all her hard work feel much better. Because the hip tub in the kitchen was rusted, she decided the next best thing was the river.

She gathered a towel and soap and followed the narrow stream to the point where it widened into a mild-tempered river. Among the cottonwoods on both sides, firs and other trees grew thick along the banks and deep into a forest. She carefully scanned the rocks and boulders that, in some areas, resembled roofs protecting secret hiding places. The water lapping gently against the rocks and fallen branches had a calming effect. It was beautiful here, the serenity mesmerizing. She instantly fell in love with the birds singing from the trees.

A shameless thrill spiraled through Courtney. What she was about to do was entirely improper. In New York, she never would have removed her clothes outside the privacy of her *boudoir*. It would have been scandalous. But Santa Fe was a far cry from New York, she reminded herself, and a wicked smile edged the corners of her mouth. She kicked off her shoes, loving the soft feel of the grass beneath her bare feet. Because of the heat, she no longer wore hose. With an exaggerated flair, she removed the oversized pants and shirt and plunged into the water, shrieking from the unexpected cold enveloping her body.

The peaceful respite drew out all her problems and floated them down the river. For the moment, she thought of nothing and no one. Suddenly, something frightened her. She floundered in the water and sat up. Scanning the trees, she found nothing out of place and saw no one watching her. Although alone, she didn't feel like it.

With the exception of her head, every inch of her body remained underwater. She hugged her knees to her chest. Once she convinced herself she was alone, she would leave. Anxious, she searched the two sides of the river banks and the trees again. The feeling of unease refused to dissipate and for some reason she glanced at the taller rocks.

"Oh, my God!"

He was there, sitting atop a boulder like a vulture stalking its prey. Would he swoop down, scoop her out of the water and devour her? A violent shudder ripped through her body. The reality of what he could do to her in their secluded hideaway intensified her fear. She thought about screaming, but what good would that do? Sheep weren't created to rescue humans in trouble.

"You're on private property, Mr. Hamilton," she pointed out. "Do you mind?"

"Not at all," he replied in a lazy drawl.

"Threatening you would be futile. I'm certainly not in a position to carry out any threat. But if you don't leave at once, I'll report your trespassing to the sheriff."

Unmoved, he offered, "I'll ride you into town."

His arrogance tripped her anger, and it couldn't have happened at a more inopportune moment. "Don't think I'm bluffing. I've made friends in this town who will come to my aid, if necessary."

"Like Jared Stover?"

"Why...yes." How did he know she'd spoken with the rancher? "He's offered me his protection," she lied.

"And what have you offered him?"

Appalled by his defaming insinuation, Courtney pulled her mouth into a tight line to keep from blurting out an unwise retort. Soon, she pressed her lips in earnest to still her chattering teeth. He must have noticed her dilemma.

"You should finish washing and get out of the river before you catch a chill." He held out his hand. Courtney's eyes rounded with shock when she saw her cake of soap lying on his open palm. "Don't you want it?"

"Throw it to me."

He jumped down to the grass.

Realizing his intent, Courtney panicked. Her eyes tracked him as he moseyed along the river's edge toward the spot where she'd undressed. He must know she wouldn't leave the river in his presence. Was she doomed to a watery death?

He squatted, haunch to heel, his forearm resting across one knee. "Are you always so stubborn?"

"Yes," she bit off, giving credence to his observation. "It gets worse, Mr. Hamilton."

He chuckled. "I'll bet it does."

Her body trembled fiercely now. She didn't know how much longer she would last. "Mr. Hamilton, this water is freezing."

"Come out and dry off."

Courtney clamped her lips together, though it did little to stop their incessant chattering. "Will you at least throw me my clothes?"

He wagged his head, and an unconvincing frown pulled down the corners of his mouth. "Can't."

"Why not?" Warily following his direction, she glanced at the cottonwood. The bastard had tossed her clothes onto a branch, along with her towel. "That...that was a rotten thing to do!"

"Come now, Mrs. Burgess. It's not like a man's never seen you naked before." He smiled wickedly and reached for her towel. "Come on out now. I'm not going to watch you freeze to death because of false modesty."

A wave of panic rose to her chest and her heart hammered mercilessly. "Please," she whispered, despising him for making her grovel. "Drop the towel and leave."

"Stand up," he demanded.

Obey him or freeze to death. Either way, he'd see her naked. Courtney drew in a deep breath and slowly shed the protection of the water. Flames of humiliation licked across her cheeks. Her long hair clung to her like pale tentacles, but neglected to cover her embarrassment. She couldn't believe this was happening to her.

"Come here," he commanded.

"Please –"

"I said, come here." If she didn't do as he said, Beau was afraid he'd lose control of the lust she made him feel. As it was, he'd tortured himself over her for days, his mind battling his body over the right and wrong of wanting to delve into that enticing body of hers.

He shouldn't have followed her after she'd finished working in the garden, but he couldn't resist one peek, like a boy sneaking up on his sisters and her friends playing innocently in the river. He hadn't intended to stay. But when the fool girl had stripped naked, he hadn't been able to turn away, to leave her unprotected. *Try convincing a judge of that, Hamilton. Her father sure as hell wouldn't buy it.*

Beau's eyes riveted to her. She was willowy, yet curvy where a woman should be. Her full breasts stood proud, golden like the rest of her skin. But it was her shapely legs that captured his direct attention. The muscles in her thighs shifted gracefully with each step, cording and relaxing, showing their strength.

When she stopped on the grassy bank, Beau suddenly couldn't move. It was a good thing, too. He would have taken her in his arms, kissed her lips with the promise of what was to follow. *Idiot! What the hell are you thinking?*

He reached up and yanked down her garments. Tossing them at her feet, he ordered, "Get dressed."

He cursed the lingering gruffness in his voice, chastised the meanness of his behavior. He wasn't about to apologize, though. Not when he couldn't rid himself of the tantalizing images of her attractive limbs wrapped around him as he rode her to heights of pleasure he'd bet she had never experienced before.

She dressed in a hurry. In fact, he'd never seen a woman dress that fast. Her head didn't raise once, not even after she was completely clothed. Taking the towel to her hair, she vigorously worked down its length. As if suddenly remembering he was there, she pinned him with a glare that didn't let up until she bunched the towel and tossed it angrily to the ground.

"You don't have to continue proving to me what you said the other night. It's obvious you're not a gentleman. Your manners are loathsome and unacceptable."

"Do you prefer gently bred sissies like Burgess?"

"He was not a sissy! Stanley may not have been callous and cold, but he wasn't weak. He was a good man."

Beau's mouth quirked upward, but he stopped himself short of a smile. "Your eyes flash with fire when you're angry."

Her jaw dropped open. Clearly, she didn't understand him. Hell, he didn't understand himself sometimes. He knew she was off limits. The truth was, he didn't care for her type—

the snobbish, spoiled daughter of a wealthy businessman. So why couldn't he stay away from her? Why couldn't he stop wondering how she would feel lying naked in his arms or how it would feel losing himself inside of her?

His sexual need grew swiftly. He wanted her. Now.

Rebel Heart

CHAPTER SEVEN

Courtney's heart pounded relentlessly as she tried to stave off the building anticipation of his touch. His hand floated toward her. Would he kiss her as excitingly as he had on her wedding night? She couldn't distance herself from the tingling sensations bridling her mind and body. She prayed he wouldn't come any closer and implored him with her eyes to stop, but he seemed intent on a mission to overpower her confused senses. The air closed in, surrounding her. When his hand clamped over her wrist, her chest rose and fell raggedly from the palpable current of awareness awakening her yearning desire for the man.

"Mr. Hamilton, please don't do this." Her voice warbled like a frightened child's. She pulled back, but his grip was iron strong. One look into his eyes and she seemed to be irrevocably drawn to him. It was the first time he let her see under his hat brim to his smooth gunmetal gray eyes and the danger lurking in their depths. There was more to Beau Hamilton than the rough quality that had first intrigued her. He had a survivor's instinct, perhaps a cold-hearted way about him. And as usual, her poor judgment might just have gotten her into the kind of trouble no woman ever wanted.

He brought her hard against his body, knocking the air from her lungs. She fought to breathe as he pressed her tightly to his soft buckskin, then tighter yet until she felt every hard ridge of him. She would have protested his unfair imprisonment if her own body hadn't betrayed her, reacting like a ship in a violent storm and tossing her good senses out of reach.

"Don't–" Courtney managed, not a second before his mouth swooped down and claimed hers, stealing a kiss with a savagery that for some ludicrous reason didn't frighten her. She breathed in his scent–an appealing mixture of man, leather and horse–felt his body tense, heard his low groan.

He seized her buttocks, pushing her deliberately into the stiff line of his masculine bulge. Courtney's breath sucked in sharply, forcing him to release her mouth, if for only a moment. When he recaptured her lips, his kiss deepened. She clamped her hands over his taut shoulders and held on in case the earth fell away from beneath her feet. He tipped her over his arm, forcing her head back. His warm lips coursed across her cheek and along her jaw to her neck, leaving a trail of heated flesh in their wake.

"God, you smell good. Not like the cheap perfume the whores wear."

Courtney tensed. Had he just compared her to a whore? Her senses hurtled back just as he started unbuttoning her shirt. She pushed at his chest and managed to redo the buttons before he realized what she had done.

"I am not a whore, Mr. Hamilton." He gave her a strange look, as if he didn't know what she was talking about. After a few seconds, he shrugged his wide shoulders and smirked. "Bastard."

Impulsively lifting her hand to slap him, in that split second before she did, she caught the dark warning in his eyes. She snatched her hand away and angrily scooped her towel from the grass. Moving to stand behind him, she glared at the straight line of his shoulders. She should have taken his knife and plunged it into his cold, insensitive heart. It was what he deserved for stirring her woman's desires and passions and for making her forget she had recently lost her husband.

"Don't ever do that again, Mr. Hamilton. The next time, I just might shoot you."

Courtney leaned her forearms on the top slat of the corral fence and shielded her eyes from the blinding morning sun as she watched the mare and the bay prance energetically. Her thoughts drifted back to the day before at the river. Admittedly, she hadn't really exhausted all her efforts to rid herself of thinking about Beau. In truth, she'd thought constantly about the passion he'd aroused in her, how he'd made her yearn for his touch and for something more she knew she shouldn't want. She couldn't help herself. After his commanding kiss yesterday, her desire for the mysterious man had grown stronger. He wasn't the kind of man she needed, not now. Not ever. In fact, she saw him as an intrusion in her life at a time when she already had enough on her mind with the ranch and Stanley's debts.

The pounding of horses' hooves over the dirt pulled her away from delving further into her disturbing attraction to Beau. She glanced down the road leading to the adobe. Jared Stover and the same two men who had accompanied him two days earlier rode toward her. The cattle rancher's face was dark, threatening. Courtney stepped away from the fence and faced the three as they approached.

"Mrs. Burgess," Stover greeted with a terse nod. He gave her a sweeping assessment, the kind a man saved for a woman like Celina.

Realizing what had captured his attention, Courtney frowned. It wasn't that she was a trifle overdressed in a low-waisted dress made of pink silk and black velvet trim. She doubted he even noticed. He was too busy leering at the square neckline pushing her breasts upward.

She cleared her throat to distract him. "This isn't a social call, is it, Mr. Stover?"

"My men found some of your sheep on my property. They moved them back to your pastures. You'd best find your two sheep dogs and do something about their straying."

"Dogs?"

"Mrs. Burgess, it's obvious you aren't cut out for ranching. Before your husband died, I made him an offer for this ranch. He agreed to sell to me. Perhaps you'll honor the agreement."

"Stanley never mentioned any such agreement. Besides, I haven't decided what I'm going to do with the ranch."

"Then keep your sheep away from my land. Trespassers are usually shot in this part of the country. That goes for man or animal." He nodded curtly before he and his men rode off at a hard gallop.

"Aren't there any gentlemen out here?" she shouted.

Intending to go back to the adobe, she caught a movement on the hill. She squinted for a clearer view, though she knew exactly who it was. Beau Hamilton sat astride his horse, watching her again. The man was a bad itch that couldn't be scratched.

Courtney started for the adobe just as an idea popped into her head and she pulled up short. As crazy as it was, she gave it some serious thought. Lifting her mouth into a calculating smile, she aligned her chin along her shoulder to look at him.

"Soon, Mr. Hamilton, we will meet again."

Courtney emerged from Seligman's General Store, grinning like a little girl with a new doll. She hadn't been pushy, but she was persistent, and the proprietor finally agreed to give her a small amount of credit. She bought herself a pair of Levis, two shirts, work boots, gloves, and several pairs of heavy wool socks. She flung the laden saddlebags over her horse and unconsciously glanced at the Exchange Hotel. Her breath caught in her throat at the sight of Beau Hamilton leaning casually against the building. She compressed her lips tightly. He disappeared into the hotel then, unwittingly stoking the fire under her quick-draw curiosity.

Leaving her horse in front of Seligman's, Courtney marched over to the Exchange. The repercussions of her going to a man's hotel room entered her mind, but she'd had enough of his loitering about, watching every move she made. It was time to put an end to it. She passed under the arched doorway of the hotel. Thankfully, the inner courtyard was deserted. Most of the town was taking their afternoon *siesta*.

At Hamilton's door, Courtney paused to give some thought to disturbing the enigmatic but arrogant man. She pulled her blouse away from her damp skin and dabbed a hankie at her neck, all the while talking herself out of knocking. But like a rabbit jumping into a pot of boiling water, she rapped her knuckles on the door.

"I know you're in there, Mr. Hamilton."

In a heartbeat she was yanked into the room and shoved against the slamming door. He pressed into her, his knee intimately parting her legs, and seized her lips in a searing kiss she had come to recognize. There was nothing gentle about the man, but he never raised a hurtful hand against her.

"Is that what you came for?" he growled beside her ear. He nipped the tender lobe and traced its outline with his tongue. She shivered involuntarily.

Yes, Courtney would have answered, but she didn't dare bait the lion in his own den. His tongue laved across her jaw and plunged between her parted lips. The intoxicating taste of his warm intrusion jolted her senses. He wasn't making this easy for her. Finally, she pressed her hands flat to his chest, ignoring the heavy hammering of his heart against her palms, and pushed. He reluctantly released her from his arresting kiss. Now if only he would move back a few steps. She couldn't think clearly with him so whispering close.

"Actually, I came here to talk to you about following me."

"What makes you think I'm following you?"

"Don't play games, Mr. Hamilton. Whatever your reasons, I don't want to know. However, I am willing to offer you a job."

She thought she saw a spark of surprise in his eyes, maybe amusement. Then he schooled his features.

"What can you offer me in return, lady?"

Courtney deliberately fidgeted, hoping he would understand that she needed space between them. She simply couldn't talk to him with any rationality as long as he remained so damn close. "I'm prepared to pay you for your protection."

His light brows arched in question. "I thought Jared Stover handled that end."

"Not...exactly."

His brows lifted higher.

"Mr. Stover did offer his help, but he's suddenly changed his mind. Apparently my sheep wandered onto his property."

"Cattle and sheep don't mix."

"Why not?" She figured it was a valid question, so when he laughed dryly she took offense. "It was a simple question, Mr. Hamilton. Why not?"

"Go home, lady," he said, evading her question. "Go back where you came from and leave ranching to men."

"That is such a predictable answer and just what I expected from you. However, I will not leave. I can handle almost anything a man can."

"Then why do you need my protection?"

"Because I don't know the first thing about sheep and cattle, or ranching, or Santa Fe. Or the people here. And where the hell are the two sheep dogs I'm supposed to have?"

"Easy, lady. Don't get so worked up."

"I-I guess I am a bit overwhelmed. It's just that I don't know where to begin," she admitted quietly, dropping her gaze.

His crooked finger under her chin lifted her face. Only then did she realize he wasn't wearing his Stetson. His wavy hair fell recklessly to the edge of his squared jaw. The color reminded her of a field of pale wheat. She also noticed a small bump on his nose, just like the boxers at her father's club sported from a broken nose.

"Just what kind of protection did you have in mind?" He reached behind her, lifting her single braid over her shoulder.

"I need someone to watch over my land. To protect my sheep and make sure they're taken care of until Manuelo returns."

"Protect your sheep?" His features twisted strangely, turned dark and foreboding. Courtney reacted by pressing her back to the door. "It's not a hired gun you want, is it?"

"Hired gun? N-No, of course not."

"I'm not what you need," he said flatly.

"But I want to hire you."

"To protect your sheep? Not on your life, lady. If you hired me to guard your person, that's one thing. But I draw the line at dying for stinking sheep."

Courtney flinched. "You don't have to get so hostile, Mr. Hamilton."

"You don't get it, do you, lady?"

She ignored his question. "I want an answer, Mr. Hamilton. Will you accept my offer?"

"Only a fool would accept what you're offering. Everyone in Santa Fe knows the debts your husband incurred."

"But I *will* pay you."

"How?" he demanded harshly.

"I don't know yet. No!" she cried when he leaned into her again, pinning her to the door. He lowered his head, balancing his lips mere inches away from hers.

"If I accept your offer, I expect to be paid in cash. I don't take trade." His hand roughly inched along her waist to her breast. "Although I might consider taking it from you for a week's work."

She slapped at his arms. "You'd have to work a year for the trade you want." She could have died from that thoughtless remark. Then she caught his subtle smirk and the way he appraised her as if she'd made a fair offer. "Mr. Hamilton, either you want the job or you don't."

He eased back. "All right, lady. I'll take the job. But on my terms."

"Now look here—" Before she could chide him for his assuming attitude, she found herself sitting under the portal outside his room. Courtney was too stunned to move. He had thrown her out like yesterday's trash. She was insane to think she could strike a working relationship with the man. "Brute," she spat.

She got to her feet and brushed her hands free of the dirt that littered the boardwalk. She glared at the closed door, hoping her anger penetrated the wood.

"You should do something about your manners, Mr. Hamilton. When you work for me, you'll show some respect."

He snatched the door open. Courtney jumped back with a start. Lord, but he wore the most ferocious expression.

"You didn't hire me to be polite. If you want me to protect you and your damn sheep, then you'll accept me as I am. *Comprende, señora?*"

She slowly backed away. "We'll discuss the terms of your employment tomorrow."

He flung the door back and stepped menacingly onto the boardwalk. He looked as if he wanted to strangle her. Courtney didn't stay long enough to give him the chance.

Rebel Heart

CHAPTER EIGHT

Beau noticed the Burgess woman from a distance and stopped to observe her working in the garden. She jabbed at the soil with a short hoe and had already cleared away three-quarters of the greens. It began to resemble the old garden once again, with even rows of flowers and cleanly turned soil. He'd lost track of how long he'd been sitting atop his horse on the hill. He figured at this distance, his body wouldn't tighten with carnal need for the woman. He was dead wrong.

Urging Paco into a lazy gait, he rubbed the animal behind his left ear to signal silence. The woman was completely absorbed and had no idea he was coming close to her. Beau scowled. He could have been Stover or some other miscreant intent on harming her. He would make it his business to teach her how to be attuned to her surroundings, no matter what she was doing. For now, though, he'd simply enjoy the view.

She was on her hands and knees, her sleeves rolled up her slender forearms and her new chambray shirt secured around her small waist. She had elegance, an aura of richness bred into her from birth. He'd noticed it when he'd observed her from the window in her father's study. She was no mutt, any fool could see. Only pedigree blood flowed in her veins.

Beau stopped his horse a few feet from the garden. The woman was crawling backwards as she rotated the soil. His eyes rooted to the inviting sight of her denim pants pulled snugly across her attractive behind. A powerful surge of lust launched through his body, spreading like wildfire through his blood. He closed his eyes and counted to ten, hoping to alleviate the fullness in his Levis. It didn't help.

He shifted in the saddle. "I don't think this is the proper greeting from a boss to a newly hired hand."

She whipped her head around too fast and lost her balance. Beau couldn't believe his eyes when she toppled onto one of the flowering plants.

"Ogre," he heard her mutter.

Mesmerized by her beautiful green eyes shining at him and the rosy hue on her cheeks, he didn't realize she was glaring. Then her eyes shifted and slowly roved downward over his blue striped pullover and black vest, perusing his body almost too thoroughly. He wondered at the blush spreading over her face, thinking it was embarrassment over his comment. Or maybe she remembered the scene at his hotel room the day before. It was enough to get his blood boiling all over again.

"You'll kill that plant if you don't get up."

She sprang to her feet and glanced down at the flattened flowers. Her mouth twisted into a frown. Vexed as all get out, her eyes turned to him.

"Now see what you've done by sneaking up on me. You could have warned me."

How the hell was he supposed to know she'd get so frightened that she'd fall on the plants? "I'll start wearing a cow bell around my neck," he remarked dryly, then surprised himself by grinning. "I guess I couldn't take my eyes off that rear of yours."

"Mr. Hamilton..." The woman was clearly affronted. He liked the way her chest puffed out when she let off steam. "Let's get one thing straight. From now on there will be no more immoral insinuations, and you will keep your hands, body and mouth to yourself. Is that clear?"

"Very." He tugged on the reins, turning his horse.

"Where are you going?"

"I quit."

"But you can't!"

She ran after him. He listened to the quick padding of her footsteps and her small chirps of frustration. She was easy to provoke, and his go-to-hell attitude probably rubbed her like a burr under her skin. Too bad she used that superior high and mighty tone with him. He never did take to anyone giving him orders.

"Mr. Hamilton, if you don't stop this minute I'll...I'll find some way to make your life miserable."

He continued at an unhurried pace. "You already have."

"What is that supposed to mean?"

Beau finally stopped and urged Paco around. He crossed his forearms on the saddle horn and leaned forward. "Do you think your threat scares me?" he asked casually.

"I'm sure it doesn't."

"I don't take kindly to threats, Mrs. Burgess. Neither do I like being told what I can or cannot do. When I'm hired to do a job, I do it my way. Have I made myself clear?"

"Very," she responded, imitating him. "Now, if you'll tether your horse to the post, I'd like to discuss my terms with you."

"Is that an order?"

"No," she huffed, fire radiating from her eyes. When she spoke again, her lips drew taut. "*Please,* come into the house where we can discuss your employment."

After a spell, Beau nodded.

She'd already entered the adobe by the time he stepped onto the porch. He could take a real liking to annoying the hell out of her. Her reactions were predictable, and that was fine with him. He'd seen to making sure she wouldn't slap him, a gesture haughty women resorted to when they couldn't outsmart a man. So far, she hadn't forgotten his threat.

"Pick out the furniture yourself?" he asked as he walked across the main room.

"Your sarcasm is not appreciated," she informed him bluntly. "I suppose Stanley never got around to furnishing this room."

He followed her into the kitchen. Just inside the door he surveyed everything with a thoroughness he'd learned over the years when his life depended on his keen awareness of his surroundings. Though he tried, he couldn't stop a frown of discontent. At least the kitchen still had furniture, if not much else.

"Please, sit. May I offer you a glass of water?"

Beau declined and perused her as she poured herself a glass. He backed up to lean against a pine cupboard. In the corner beside it stood a rusted hip bath.

"Please, sit," she repeated.

"I'll stand." He glanced to his right at the aged iron stove, then to his left at the sink and cabinet. Without a word, he opened cabinet doors.

"What do you think you're doing?"

Beau moved in her direction, but she refused to step aside. He pulled her away and flung open the cupboard doors. Inside were a few canned goods and a bag of flour that was half gone.

"What the hell have you been living on?"

Slamming the doors shut, she faced him boldly. "How I live does not concern you, Mr. Hamilton."

"Like hell, it doesn't. If you can't afford to feed yourself, how are you going to pay me?"

"I'll find a way."

He scrutinized her—from the fervor in her eyes to her belligerent stance. She believed money was the issue here. But he had something more on his mind. What would Leif Danning say about the poor conditions his pampered daughter lived in? Now Beau had to find a way to remedy her situation without raising her suspicions. He didn't want her thinking he did it out of real concern. Once a woman started thinking that way...

He stifled a shiver.

"Dammit!" He slammed his fist on the counter, rattling dishes and drinking glasses. He saw her jump, noticed her widened eyes. He frightened her, but he wasn't about to console her fears. "I'm not a goddamned nursemaid," he muttered to himself.

The protective wall surrounding his patience crumbled, and he rambled in Spanish. If he was going to lose his patience, better she couldn't understand a word.

"You needn't get so upset, Mr. Hamilton."

Beau gave her a sharp look. He realized then, she truly believed she'd be able to pay him. It wouldn't be with her father's help. Her powerful pride wouldn't allow it. He meant to walk around her, to put distance between his temper and her pigheadedness. But when he moved, she backed up all the way to the heavy pine table. He pinned her to the edge. Her cheeks wore a healthy glow from working outdoors, and her skin was the smoothest he'd ever seen. Her long, ebony lashes were tinged with blonde tips that shadowed her cheekbones when she blinked. He hadn't taken the time before to notice the little details that combined to make her face the most beautiful he'd ever laid eyes on.

"If you're thinking about kissing me, Mr. Hamilton, I'll be forced to fire you. I don't want to, but you can't work for me if you don't behave."

"Is that a threat, Mrs. Burgess?"

She slipped under his arms and moved across the kitchen. Was that a challenge swirling in her green eyes? Was she daring him to kiss her, to break the first rule of his working agreement, though he hadn't agreed to anything yet?

He closed the space between them in two strides. She didn't cower away this time. On the contrary. She welcomed him, lifted her lips to his. Losing his precarious grip on his senses, he gathered her to his chest, taking greedily what she generously offered. Unless he'd sorely misjudged her, she wanted him as badly as he did her. He would have carried her off to bed if she hadn't abruptly chilled his ardor by emptying her glass of water over his head.

More vexed than startled, Beau broke away instantly. Rivulets of water dripped off his hat to his vest. He dropped his hands to his side – better there than around her precious little neck – and tightened his jaw to restrain his unstable temper.

"Real slick move, lady."

"I warned you to keep your entire person to yourself."

Beau remained stock still or he would have ignored her warning and kissed her again. "I was just seeing what kind of payment I'd get if you didn't have the money to pay me."

"My body is the one thing you'll never have."

Beau yanked her against his length. "Lady, that's the one thing I'd have no problem getting." He released her and dropped heavily onto one of the chairs. His eyes trained on her, he shook the water off his hat, then raked his hair away from his forehead. "Tell me your terms or I walk outta here."

All business now, she complied. "I need someone to protect my investments. The sheep are all I have on which to survive. If I can sell a few, I'll have the money to pay you. But I don't know where to begin or how to go about–"

"The sheep are Manuelo's job. His two sons help him."

"In the five days I've been here, this Manuelo person hasn't shown his face."

"He's in Taos visiting family."

Astonishment adorned her features. "How do you know?"

"I overheard someone talking in the cantina." The lie rolled off his tongue easily. He too had wondered where the Mexican sheep herder and his family had gone. He was afraid harm had come to them, so he'd asked questions around town. "They'll be returning soon," he added, knocking down that suspicious look she gave him.

"In that case, until Manuelo returns, I'll need your services."

Beau's brow arched.

"For heaven's sake! You know what I mean."

He rose and stood before her. "What if I won't accept money in return for my...services?" He traced her jaw with the tip of his finger.

She brushed his hand away. "You'll have to."

"Then I'll take twenty-five dollars a week. If there's any trouble, I'll be asking for more."

"That sounds fair. Will you begin right away?"

Beau stole another kiss, then plucked his damp hat from the table and set it on his head. "I'll start when I'm ready." As expected, he riled her again.

"I'm the boss here, Mr. Hamilton. I hired you, and you'll start when I say, and I want you to start now!"

He casually walked into the main room, smiling to himself when he heard her aggravated sighs followed by her hurried footfalls over the earthen floor. Outside, he mounted and was about to ride off when she emerged from the adobe.

"You can't ignore me, Mr. Hamilton. Not if you want to get paid."

"You'll pay me if you want my protection. I'll be back when I'm ready. Good day, Mrs. Burgess."

CHAPTER NINE

Courtney rode out to the northwest pasture to investigate the two gunshots she'd heard earlier. She wouldn't have bothered if it hadn't been for the unusual silence of the sheep, who were always bleating. Skittish about riding among the flock, she was afraid she'd crush the smaller animals beneath her horse's hooves. Fortunately, the bay seemed accustomed to the sheep and calmly made his way across the huge pasture. When she reached the borderline, she discovered long portions of wire fence lying in a twisted mess on the ground. Two sheep lay on Stover's side of the fence, a single gunshot to their heads.

"Your troubles have begun," said a familiar voice.

Courtney's heart pounded fiercely. Why did the man persist in sneaking up on her? "If you'd been here this morning, these poor sheep would still be alive."

"They would have been slaughtered soon anyway."

Something tugged at Courtney's heart. It never occurred to her that the small, innocent animals would be slaughtered. She simply couldn't bear the thought. There must be a mistake. "Why?"

"For the meat. Why do you think you're raising sheep?"

"I told you, I don't know the first thing about sheep ranching." She glanced down again at the dead sheep and truly felt saddened. "Shouldn't we bury them?"

Beau's eyes widened. "You don't really mean that, do you?"

"Yes, Mr. Hamilton, I do." She thought he rolled his eyes, although she couldn't be certain with his hat brim so low.

"Sheep aren't people. You don't bury them when they die. You shear the wool to sell and the meat will go to market." He grinned. "Then you can start paying me my wages."

Perturbed with his preoccupation over his wages, Courtney snapped, "You'll get paid when you've earned your money. And stop grinning at me!"

"Whatever you say, Mrs. Burgess," he drawled.

"I should have thought this out better," Courtney muttered. Why did she never learn that impulsive decisions ended in disfavor? "Since you're here, you might as well earn *your wages*. After you take care of the sheep, mend the fence."

His features swiftly lost the smile lines. "I don't shear sheep."

"Then find someone who does." She attempted to ride off, but he tangled his gloved hand in her reins.

"You should learn how to ask politely."

"I would, Mr. Hamilton, but you don't take to politeness very well."

He released the reins and Courtney immediately rode away.

Courtney reclined on her bed reading last week's newspaper when a knock at the door cleaved the silence. She hesitated, afraid of who might be calling on her at such a late hour. It approached ten, well past bedtime for most people. After another knock, she slipped her feet into soft slippers, picked up the lamp and left the bedroom.

"Who is it?"

"Hamilton."

Her nerves danced beneath her skin, and her heart pounded fiercely against her ribs. "Whatever you have to say can be said in the morning."

"I'm not leaving, so you might as well open the door."

She heard something odd in his voice, as if he were too tired to pronounce his words clearly. Was he exhausted? Or drunk? All the more reason to keep him on the other side of the door. "Just say your peace then and be on your way."

The door shook beneath his heavy pounding. "Open this damn door or I'll break it down. That will make me very angry, Mrs. Burgess, and you won't like me when I'm angry."

"I don't like you now," she retorted, flinching when he resorted to kicking. The wood creaked and groaned. "All right! I'll let you in."

Against her often lacking better judgment, Courtney lifted the wood slat and jumped out of the way just as the door crashed open with a loud boom. Beau Hamilton filled the doorway like an ogre from a child's fairytale. The flickering flame from her lamp cast fiendish shadows over his dark features. He looked evil, like Satan himself.

"This isn't proper, Mr. Hamilton. Can't we talk in the morning?"

He stepped into the adobe and swung the door behind him. Courtney backed across the room, hoping to make herself less conspicuous. But with the lantern in hand, she had nowhere to hide. He tossed his hat to the floor without losing sight of her. Determination filled his eyes. As he moved forward, his swagger gave her fear good reason to rise.

The rough adobe wall bit through her nightdress at her back. Ignoring the discomfort, she tried to determine what exactly he wanted. Was he here to quit again? She'd save him the breath and fire him if only she could. But the closer he came, the more difficult she found it to think clearly. The man's rugged appearance did something to her she probably would never understand. His animal grace made her desire him, even though she considered it terribly wrong. The fact he couldn't walk a straight line paralyzed her limbs. He wasn't tired; he was drunk. Her father often turned unruly in that condition. What would Mr. Hamilton do? If only she could get to the gun in the dresser drawer.

When he stopped a breath away, her heart beat with an unusual rhythm, pounding like the distant wild drums she heard at night while lying in bed. He was going to kiss her again. She held her breath, waiting for the familiar feel of his lips. Instead, confusion filled her head. He removed an envelope from his vest and handed it to her.

"Your money, Mrs. Burgess."

Relief flooded her entire being, yet her heart still hammered her chest. "From the dead sheep?"

His lips formed a grim line as he nodded. His eyes met hers for several long seconds before he spoke again. "I rode the northern most section of your property. I found your dogs. They're dead."

"Dead? First the sheep and now the dogs. Why would anyone want to frighten me into leaving Santa Fe? That *is* what is happening, isn't it, Mr. Hamilton?"

"Some people in these parts hate sheep. There'll come a time when they'll stop with the warnings and go after you."

"Are you saying I'm in danger?"

He nodded ever so slightly. He took the lamp and the money from her hands and set both on the floor. She should have made her move, should have darted around him for the door. Without reason, she stayed. "I'll fight whoever is behind the malicious attacks."

"I buried your husband. I don't want to bury you, too, Mrs. Burgess. The sheep ain't worth it." He removed his gloves and dropped them to the floor. His bare hands caressed her arms.

Courtney shuddered. "Please, don't."

His face floated closer, his lips ever so near. His breath mingled with hers, but she was too frightened by her unwanted reaction to notice he reeked of stale whiskey. The instant his lips touched her neck, she tensed.

"Easy, lady. I'm not gonna hurt you."

She smelled it now, that awful drift of old liquor. But there was more. He also smelled like sheep and...cheap perfume!

"No, Mr. Hamilton." She spoke with conviction and backed it up by attempting to push him away. Her palms were a meek barrier to his formidable chest. "I will not allow you to—"

He silenced her with a solid kiss. Before she completely lost her senses, she knew she must gain his attention. She was probably making a huge mistake, but there was only one way to stop him.

The crisp sound of flesh against flesh reverberated in her ears. His head popped up. A savage glow leaped into his eyes and a snarl curled his lips. *The last woman who slapped me lived to regret it,* he had told her. What had she done?

He wrapped her unbound hair around his fingers and yanked her head back, forcing her to meet his wild eyes. Courtney held herself stiff, boldly daring him to throw a punch.

"That was a stupid thing to do, lady."

"You wouldn't listen to me," she said, trembling now, not from fear but from the intense feeling of desire, of longing for his touch, of his lips moving on hers.

You've finally lost your mind, Courtney. You have no business desiring a man like Beau Hamilton. He's no good for you.

"I didn't know of any other way to make you listen to me."

"Now you're sorry?"

"No," she whispered.

He lowered her to the floor. It was futile to fight him off, considering his strength and size. Given the force behind his desire, she might not have minded what he was about to do—if he wasn't drunk. Worse, the smell of another woman's perfume clinging to him boosted her righteous anger. She'd not allow him to treat her like the whore whose bed he'd just left.

"You can't do this, Mr. Hamilton. You can't leave one woman's bed and expect to share mine." Confusion knitted his brows. "You smell like a whore!"

She could have slapped him when he grinned broadly, outright boasting he was as fit as a stud in mating season. Accusations and anger only ignited his fury, so she found another way to reason with him.

"Mr. Hamilton. You've been drinking. You'll regret this in the morning."

"Lady, I may be drunk, but I won't regret anything come morning."

She turned her head aside to avoid his kiss. He squeezed her cheeks between his fingers, forcing her eyes to his smoky ones.

"Tell me you don't want me," he said hoarsely. "Tell me you haven't been giving me those looks lonely women give to men. You can't, can you?"

She opened her mouth to deny him, if for no other reason than to convince herself she hadn't given him inviting looks of any kind. But he was quick, his tongue striking like an angry rattler, plunging into her mouth before she uttered one dissenting sound. Her fight fled in an instant, along with all the denials she tried to conjure. It was so very wrong to want him, but deep down she already knew it was too late to deny what her heart truly desired.

When their lips parted, Courtney gasped for air. He nibbled her neck, kissing and drawing his tongue along her heated flesh. He pulled her nightdress down her shoulder, trailing kisses over her collarbone. Courtney moaned from the delicious sensations. Unknowingly, she lifted her hips off the floor, pressing into him, making him reckless with need. She sensed his urgency, felt it in the hurried way his hands slid up and down her arms, then her waist and hips. He tugged at her nightdress, but she was too lost to her own building passion to notice...until her bare backside touched the cold, damp floor.

"Beau, we shouldn't," she moaned unconvincingly.

He pulled the garment over her head, and Courtney shivered. When he covered her body with his, she instantly felt enveloped in a warmth no amount of blankets could ever offer. She held his head between her hands to guide his lips back to hers. He wouldn't take her lead. Instead, his mouth closed over her breast, shocking her naiveté. She curved her hands over his shoulders as shiver after shiver raced up and down her body at an incredible speed. His mouth slid to her other breast, and she cried out from the unimaginable pleasure squirming throughout her body. He captured her hard nipple between his teeth, relentlessly flicking his tongue back and forth until she could take no more and begged him to stop.

It was no use. He was too far gone, and she wasn't far behind. He reached between them to unbuckle his gun belt and unbutton his pants. She sensed his reluctance to release her breast while he sat up on his knees. In a haze, she searched his features as he pushed his pants down his thighs. His impassioned gaze never strayed from her face, holding her prisoner while he lost his vest and almost his shirt. In his present state, he was clumsy and unable to get the pullover off, getting tangled in it instead. Giving up, he lay on her again, their bare bodies coming together in an explosion of fire.

Once again, the voice of reason echoed in Courtney's head. "Mr. Hamilton, please, we shouldn't do this."

"Why not?" he rasped. "No one cares, if that's what's on your mind."

"You don't understand. Stanley and I–"

He placed a silencing finger to her lips. "I don't want to hear about you and Burgess. As much as I've avoided virgins all my life, I find myself wishing you were still pure as Montana snow." He dug his elbows into the dirt floor and laced his fingers through her hair. "Wrap your legs around me," he commanded gruffly.

Courtney hesitated. She'd tried to tell him she *was* that virgin he wished for. How could he possibly know the truth? Like everyone else, he assumed she and Stanley had consummated their marriage.

The very tip of him teased her innocence. But she was too nervous to enjoy his mentoring her into womanhood. She tensed, making it difficult for him to push into her. He didn't swear in anger or force himself inside. Instead, he touched her where no man ever had before, stroked her with his bold fingers, coaxed her into relaxing. His gentle caresses brought forth a strange moistness, unlike anything she'd ever experienced in her life. It wasn't long before she opened up and invited him into her secret place.

Intense pain drove her hands to his arms, and she dug her fingers into his dense muscles. Through her tears she saw his eyes widen as he slowed his strokes. Did the fact he'd just ripped through her womanhood pierce through his drink-muddled mind? Or was he so drunk he didn't even realize she was a virgin?

When her nails quit digging into his arm, he moved slowly within her, groaning with each undulating stroke, lost in an ecstasy she had yet to attain. Amazingly, the pain subsided, and she let go of the grueling hold on his arms. Her hands molded more intimately to his upper arms, feeling the beauty in his shifting muscles. Soon, he glided in and out with ease, luring the ultimate response from her body. She was unable to control a staggering shudder. Mortified, she gasped as he groaned in her ear. He pumped faster, harder and seized her buttocks, elevating her to his powerful thrusts. Her body's unfamiliar response forgotten, Courtney gripped his arms tighter and pushed upward with a sudden urge to meet him halfway. She forced him deeper, matching his excited movements thrust for thrust, moan for moan. All of a sudden something inside her exploded. His guttural sound contrasted sharply with her high-pitched cry. She felt him pulse repeatedly until finally it subsided and his hips stilled.

It was over.

Her induction into womanhood hadn't been the romantic event she'd anticipated, yet it was more than she ever imagined it could be. One thing was certain, she felt betrayed. Not by Mr. Hamilton. She'd expected him to try seducing her into bed. Had known it would happen from her response to his kisses. The betrayal was of her own doing. She simply wasn't strong enough to resist his coarse personality and rugged charm. Neither was she capable of telling him no. Now how would she face him and be his boss after allowing him to take her virginity?

He rolled off and lay beside her, breathing raggedly. His chest heaved from his effort; hers glistened from sweat. She was ashamed to just lay there without attempting to cover herself, but what was the point? He'd already seen her naked—and knew her most intimately.

After awhile, Courtney sat up and hugged her knees to her chest. Confusion reigned in her mind. Emotions bounced tumultuously, but she didn't give in to crying. There was no point lamenting what had just happened. She would have changed only one thing—losing her virginity to Beau Hamilton on her bed instead of on a cold earthen floor with him drunk and neither of them in love.

He moved her hair aside to kiss her shoulder. She tensed. His heavy sigh fanned out over her skin. Thankfully, he rose and moved about getting dressed.

"I should report you to the sheriff." Ice formed around her threat.

"Why? Because you enjoyed lying with a real man?"

She pressed her lips together to stop from denying what was a lie. She wouldn't tell him there had been no other man to use as comparison, though she suspected none would get her blood flowing like Beau did. No, not Beau. Mr. Hamilton. If she allowed herself to think of him in familiar terms, it would undermine her position as his boss.

"You forced yourself on me."

"Did I, Mrs. Burgess? Your cries of ecstasy seemed mighty obliging to me. And the clerk at the hotel saw you come to my room willingly."

"Bastard," she spat, hating him for speaking the truth.

The iciness in his eyes caused her to shiver. "I wear that title with pride, lady. Don't think you're hurting me with it."

CHAPTER TEN

Thunder erupted in Beau's head. He clutched his temples and struggled to sit. Iron bands tightened insufferably around his skull, squeezing like a snake with a death grip. Carefully moving his legs around to sit on the edge of his bed, confusion angled his brows. Where did it go? He forced his eyelids upward, flinching when a ray of sunlight pricked his eyes. All of a sudden his stomach twisted and gurgled then lurched sickeningly. He closed his eyes and swallowed hard, forcing back the awful urge to heave his guts. Between his throbbing head and roiling intestines, he knew he'd finally descended into the pits of hell. But how did he get there? Beau felt his chest and belly. Nothing indicated he'd died by the bullet. So what was making him feel like an animal hide hung out in the hot sun to dry?

His hands fell heavily to his sides. It was then he realized he was sitting on hay. Slowly lifting his lids again, he kept his movements minimal and searched his surroundings through his blurred vision. Just how in blasted hell did he get into a horse's stall?

He staggered to his feet and supported himself against one of the wood-slatted walls. He fought the lightheadedness threatening to topple him back to the hay when a huge, wet tongue licked the side of his face. He startled and jerked his head, regretting it in an instant. Cursing the downright cruel pain, he found himself staring into the culprit's large brown eyes.

"You damn near scared me to death," he scolded Paco in a gravelly voice. "Don't ever sneak up on me when my head's about to roll from my fool neck."

His throat felt as scratchy as sand. He reached for his canteen and cursed again. He'd been so drunk he'd forgotten to unsaddle his horse. Taking a long guzzle of water, Beau thought he'd never slake his thirst. After drinking the canteen dry, he wiped his mouth with the back of his hand. Bits of the past evening started coming back. Through the fog in his head he remembered sitting in the cantina drinking whiskey instead of beer. A huge mistake. He and whiskey never mixed well. Celina wiggled her way into his lap and fondled him. Her persistence angered him so badly that he dumped her to the floor. Furious, the whore cursed the blonde *gringa* for his disinterest. Then she took up with a hired hand from the Bar S.

Beau rubbed gingerly at his temples. What happened after that? *Think.* If only the persistent pounding in his head would stop.

Vaguely recalling finishing off a full bottle of the rotgut before leaving, there was something he had to do. Something to deliver. He remembered now. He saw the rising sun in the black of night. No, not the sun. It was hair the color of pale...

"Shit!" The harshly spoken word ripped through his head like a flaming arrow. But the excruciating pain paled in comparison to the knowledge of the insufferable thing he'd done. How could he have bedded Courtney? For Christ's sake! He worked for her father. He was supposed to protect her.

Just how the hell was he going to get himself out of this mess?

Beau gripped Paco's mane and let the horse guide him out of the barn. The radiant sun blinded him, crushing his skull with its intensity. "God, I swear I'll never touch another bottle of whiskey again."

At the trough, Beau dropped to his knees and immersed his head into the water. He came up for air only when his lungs felt close to bursting. He submerged his head again. He was being punished for every indiscretion in his miserable life.

He came up for the second time and gently shook off the water. As he slicked back his hair, he wished he could remember what he'd done with his hat. Jesus, he felt wretched. Maybe if he lay down again, rested his head on a soft pillow.

"I should charge you for sleeping in my barn last night."

He lifted his head sluggishly. Courtney had planted her feet to the dirt and folded her arms sternly across her chest. She sure as hell looked none too happy. He balanced on the edge of the trough and whispered, "Do you have to speak so damn loud?"

"I should shoot you."

"At the moment that would be a blessing."

70

"I hope you're suffering like the devil you are," she spat, causing him to flinch from the force of her irritation. "I have no sympathy for drunkards, you lecherous bastard."

Beau would have scowled at her verbal attack if his head wasn't in so much pain.

"Sober up, Mr. Hamilton. Make yourself presentable and join me in the kitchen."

"I don't take orders from anyone."

"So you say."

He cocked a wary eye at her when she marched right up to him and placed her hands flat against his chest. Thinking she was going to slap him, he tensed. After what he'd done last night, he deserved to be slapped. To his utter amazement, she shoved him hard into the trough. He came up splashing and sputtering, cursing the whiskey that put him in this condition.

"Like I said, sober up. If you want to keep your job, you'll behave like a gentleman should."

Beau glared at her retreating back. She wouldn't be so haughty if he wasn't incapacitated. "Aw, hell," he moaned, gripping his stomach. He was going to be sick.

Courtney removed the biscuits from the oven and dropped the pan on the counter. She tossed a towel over it and checked on the coffee. She couldn't believe she was making breakfast for a man who crassly took her virginity on a cold, dirt floor. After he'd left another woman's bed, for God's sake. She should hate him, despise him with every ounce of her being. But how could she without hating herself as well? No matter how she rationalized last night, all roads of blame led back to her and her inability to stop her body from responding wantonly.

Just as she finished pouring two cups of coffee, the object of her irritation entered the kitchen. Courtney pulled back abruptly, struggling to keep hold of the pot. "You call that presentable?"

He glanced down at the towel wrapped snugly about his lean hips. It was all he wore. "Somehow my clothes got wet. And my guns," he added, his tone a mixture of disgust and disbelief. "You'd better pray the water didn't ruin them."

Courtney wasn't listening. She was lost in the breathtaking sight of his near naked body, fascinated by the little dark blond hairs covering his long legs. Her perusal paused at the corner of the towel tucked in just below his navel. Darker blond hair speared up his stomach and fanned out over his chest. When her eyes rested on the breadth of his shoulders, she gasped softly. In the gilded light of the lantern last night, she hadn't noticed the scars.

"My God. What—?" She stifled her curiosity when his features transformed to stone. "I'm sorry, it was rude of me to stare." She tried not to gawk at the scars riddling his upper torso. She'd never known a man could survive so many bullet holes. She discovered more of the same on his arms and...legs. "I'm sorry," she repeated, but couldn't retract her reaction.

He sighed as if he'd received the same reaction a hundred times and was tired of it. "I was caught in an ambush. Got fourteen holes in all."

He sat at the table and said nothing more. She served the biscuits and slipped into the chair across from him, but her appetite was gone. The simple biscuits must have been edible because he ate three, drank two cups of coffee, then devoured two more biscuits piled with butter and the jelly she'd found in the cupboard. He certainly recovered quickly from his drinking binge.

He leaned back in his chair, his third cup of coffee in hand, and studied her. The awkward silence lengthened. Courtney felt terribly uncomfortable. Not only from his lack of proper attire, but also from her undying curiosity. She wanted badly to ask about the ambush and his wounds, but she didn't want to dig up his bad memories. However, her curiosity was something she'd never been able to control and she asked, "Was the law after you?"

He nodded.

"Did you kill a man?"

"No." One corner of his mouth lifted slightly. It could have passed for a smile. It also could have been a gesture of arrogance. "I've killed eight men, counting those two drovers when I rescued you."

Courtney scraped her chair back across the floor and rose rather abruptly. She gathered the plates and set them in the basin with a clatter. With her back to him, she was able to hide her sudden distress. He'd spoken about killing as if it was as much a part of his life as breathing and eating.

"Not bad eats for a spoiled filly."

72

"Thanks...I think." Unable to leave well enough alone, she faced him and asked outright, "Are you wanted by the law?"

He held up his empty cup for a refill. "Does my past bother you?"

"Just answer the question."

He set the cup down with deliberate calm, she noticed. "No, Mrs. Burgess, I'm no longer wanted."

She carried the coffee pot to the table, praying her hand wouldn't tremble when she poured. "It doesn't actually," she answered and returned the pot to the stove. "As long as you do the job I hired you to do, then there will be no more questions asked about your past."

"But you're curious, aren't you?" He half-grinned. "All right, Mrs. Burgess, I'll appease your curiosity, only so you stop looking at me like I'm a no good killer."

"I was not–"

He inclined his head, silencing her.

"I was shot seven years ago. Only twenty-two and dying. But I knew the mountains better than most bounty hunters and made it to Mexico where a friend took me in. I spent a year there recuperating."

"And you're not wanted now?"

"Nope."

His chair scraped along the floor as he stood. He walked around the table, and that same flittering feeling returned to Courtney's stomach.

"My friend is an important man in Mexico. He has friends in the United States who owe him favors."

His smile melted her heart. "But you were a criminal."

"That's a matter of opinion." He looked over her shoulder. "Got anything else to eat?"

She accused him of being a criminal and all the man could think about was food? "No, I don't. I intend to go shopping with the money you gave me..."

"Last night?" His expression soured. "I was wondering if you'd bring that up."

Courtney bit the inside of her cheek to keep from blurting out how she truly felt about the previous night. How his rugged passion excited her, ignited her own desire. But she refused to ply him with praise for the rotten scoundrel he was, taking advantage of her when she was at a most vulnerable point in her life.

"I wish I could apologize," he said, "but I don't rightly know if I should. I mean, the whiskey really got to me. But it won't happen again, Mrs. Burgess."

Courtney threw him a scathing look. "You're damn right it won't. The next time I *will* shoot you."

There was that grin again, that half-hearted, nonplussed grin that both aggravated her and made her heart skip a beat.

"I'll remember that." He reclaimed his chair. "So, what did you want to discuss?"

"Perhaps you should dress first. This is highly improper, Mr. Hamilton."

"You could undress and wrap yourself in a towel, too," he suggested.

"Certainly not!"

"Then it seems we have two options. We talk now, or we sit here until my clothes dry, and that could take hours. So which is it, Mrs. Burgess?"

Wait, she almost said, but the thought of him hanging around the adobe wearing only a towel wasn't only perplexing, it was utterly tempting. "We talk now."

She joined him at the table, doing her best to keep her eyes from straying back to his muscular chest. Not even the scars made him any less appealing. "I want to learn about the sheep business. Can you teach me?"

"'Fraid not. I know nothing about sheep."

"Then perhaps you know someone who can guide me."

"Don't you think you're already in debt enough?"

It always circled back to money with him. She didn't understand his obsession. Maybe the fact that she never had to worry about money had something to do with it. "Don't you see? If I can make a go of this ranch, I can pay off all of Stanley's...my debts."

"You don't belong here, Mrs. Burgess. Take the money you got and buy a one way ticket home."

Vexed, she rose and leaned her palms on the table, locking her elbows. "Don't tell me where I belong. I hired you to protect me, not give me advice."

He left his chair, too, imitating her stance, though she was positive he looked a sight meaner. "Lady, the advice is free."

It would be futile to argue with him, so she calmed her ire...or was it resentment of his authoritative manner. In some ways, he reminded her of Father. "You, sir, are quite impossible."

"I was thinking the same about you," he returned with subtle arrogance.

"Mr. Hamilton..."

He molded his hand to the back of her head and eased her closer. "Beau," he whispered before engaging her in a brief but tender kiss.

Courtney removed his hand from her head and stepped away from the table. The mere touch of his lips elevated her senses. She felt frightfully exposed, more so now that he gave her permission to call him by his first name. Really, how could she not address him by anything else. Even though it bred familiarity, it seemed inane to stand on formality. Well, at least in her mind it did.

"I am capable of running this ranch," she insisted. "All I need is someone to teach me about sheep."

He straightened and finger combed his semi-dried hair. She wondered if he was trying to get rid of her, like Jared Stover had. But then he relented. "You don't need to hire anyone. When Manuelo returns, he'll help you. In the meantime, I'll arrange for the sale of several hundred head of sheep. That'll get you enough cash until you decide if ranching is what you really want to do."

A small smile of victory rippled across her lips. "Fair enough, Mr. Hamilton. But who will buy the sheep? And can I afford to sell off several hundred?" She liked the way the sides of his eyes crinkled when he smiled.

"I know some ranches between here and the far north. Up Cheyenne way there's John and Tom Durbin. They're always looking to buy. There's also the Bar H. And yes, you can spare several hundred sheep. Apparently your husband forgot to tell you he owned more than two thousand head."

"Two thousand?"

"Two thousand."

She never would have guessed. At best she estimated about five hundred or so. "What will I do with so many?"

"Sell them for slaughter."

"No, I can't. That's cruel."

"Do you think the meat you eat grows out of the ground?" He shook his head. "I don't understand you, lady."

"They can't be killed," she insisted. "They're so...so sweet."

"Jesus! What kind of reasoning is that?"

"It's my reasoning," she shot back defensively.

Consternation cut across his handsome face, creating new lines. Dark blond stubbles covered his upper lip and jaw, and for a fleeting moment she wished she could caress his cheek, run a soothing finger over his firm lips.

Courtney headed off the turn in her thoughts and broached the matter of her sheep in a different light. "You mentioned selling the wool."

"If you can't raise sheep for the meat, then shearing is the next best thing. A shearing crew comes this way once a year, working from Mexico to Canada. They hit all the sheep ranches, stay a few days to a week, longer if the ranch has a larger number to shear. A small crew can do your sheep in three days. They're fast and efficient."

"Does it hurt the sheep?"

He rolled his eyes and drew in a deep breath. She sensed he was trying to be patient.

"The animals don't feel a thing." The smile in his eyes contained a humorous shine. "I'd best get out to the barn. I can make myself useful until my clothes are dried."

She looked past him and gasped. Instinctively, he pushed her out of harm's way and went for his gun. Apparently, he'd forgotten he wasn't wearing any weapons. Suddenly he grinned broadly at the man standing near the open door.

"Manuelo! You're a damn good sight, *amigo!*"

CHAPTER ELEVEN

Manuelo clutched a worn felt hat in both hands, curling its floppy brim. His gaze slid to Courtney, though he didn't directly meet her eyes. Beau recognized the Mexican's humble confusion.

"*Dónde está* Señor Burgess?" Manuelo asked.

"He's dead," Beau replied in Spanish, giving him a brief account of Burgess' death. The man's weary expression changed to sorrow for the young widow.

"What did he say?" Courtney whispered to him while keeping an eye on the man. Manuelo's reply clearly startled her.

"I am sorry for your loss, *señora.*"

Holding back a grin, Beau asked, "Is Carlita with you?"

Manuelo failed to hide his curiosity, undoubtedly wondering why Beau wore only a towel in the woman's presence. "She is at the adobe with Marcos and Eduardo."

"It's good you're back. This little lady here needs guidance. It seems she's partial to the *sweet sheep.*" He winked at her and chuckled softly when her jaw swung open and shut in absolute astonishment. "I'd best be getting' back to work before the boss lady has my hide for neglecting my duties."

Courtney reeled with disbelief as he walked casually through the back door, leaving her in awkward silence with Manuelo. What must the Mexican think, finding a lady alone in the presence of a near-naked man? One glance at him and a full blush swept over her cheeks.

Disapproval filled his chocolate brown eyes.

"My name is Courtney."

"*Sí, señora.*" He gripped his hat tighter. "We returned from Taos late last night. My sons and I will get to work immediately." He hesitated. "That is, if you will keep us on."

"Keep you on? Of course, I will. I don't know the first thing about sheep. Mr. Hamilton assured me you are quite knowledgeable."

"*Sí, señora.* I learned from my father, and he from his father. This ranch gives me great pride. The sheep here are among the finest."

"Well, thank the Lord for bringing you back, Manuelo. I hope you'll teach me about sheep ranching."

"Do you mean that, *señora*?" At her nod, he sighed with relief. "Then you will not sell the ranch?"

"No, Manuelo, I couldn't. It's all I have left of Stanley."

"Of course, *señora.* I will tell my wife, Carlita. She saw to the house for Señor Burgess. Thank you, *señora*," he said as he backed away. "Thank you for making Rancho Ortega your home."

Rancho Ortega? Stanley named his ranch Ortega?

She closed the door, pondering the Mexican. Beneath his heavy accent was a well-educated man. What didn't make sense, though, was his poor manner of dress. The fabric of his trousers was worn thin and patched, and he'd bound his shoes with sack cloth, most likely to keep them together. Hadn't Stanley paid the man enough to buy decent clothes? Regret for his treatment of his ranch hand coursed through her. The first order of business with Manuelo would be to discuss wages for his family.

As Courtney removed a batch of sugar cookies from the oven, a shrill scream pierced the thick adobe walls. She dropped the pan to the stove, flung the door wide open and rushed outside. At the edge of the garden she skidded to a stop. A distraught middle-aged Mexican woman perused the manicured plants and mumbled rapidly in Spanish. Courtney noticed Beau moving surreptitiously around the corner of the house. His gun drawn, his features hard, he was summing up the situation. Then he stepped out in plain sight and sighed visibly with relief. He reholstered his gun and strode over to the garden. She didn't trust the glint in his eyes.

"*Buenos días*, Carlita," he said with a broad grin.

He was awfully cheerful, Courtney thought, unable—or perhaps unwilling—to comprehend his humor. "Do you know why she screamed?"

He shifted his shameless grin to her. "Ask her yourself."

The heavyset woman continued walking among the neat rows of plants, still mumbling under her breath. Every now and then a sob shook her matronly shoulders. She looked up with rueful brown eyes. Courtney stepped back, fearful the woman might raise a hand to her.

"What did you do here?" Carlita asked.

Beau was no help. He still wore that lousy grin on his face. Indignant, she raised her chin. "I pulled the weeds."

"*Dios!* Those were not weeds." Carlita lifted her hands to her cheeks. "They were herbs."

"Medicinal herbs," Beau added, his tone cocky.

Courtney was speechless. How was she supposed to know she'd pulled herbs instead of weeds? She couldn't tell the difference.

Carlita walked out of the garden and paused to give her a disparaging frown. "I must go to the Villanueva house. If I do not replenish the herbs..." She fell silent and wandered away, shaking her head.

Courtney couldn't see past her pricked ire to the twinkle in Beaus' eyes or the soft lines around his mouth. "Why is she so distraught?"

"Carlita is a *curandera*. She heals by using the *weeds* you pulled for medicine."

"If you knew that, why didn't you speak up when you saw me digging in the garden?"

He shrugged. "It wasn't any of my business."

"Going through my cupboards was your business and this wasn't?" She forcibly held back from giving him a good, old-fashioned slap to remove that infernal grin. Doing the only thing she could to save her from an unpleasant confrontation, she stormed back into the kitchen. About to slam the door, something solid got in the way.

Beau shoved her into the room and kicked the door shut. The wild shine in his eyes warned her of a brewing storm. Her wary retreat ended at the table.

"You have a way of trying to make me feel guilty whenever something doesn't go your way. I'm fed up with it."

Courtney rooted herself to the floor. "It's not intentional."

"Like hell it isn't. I won't feel guilty for any of your troubles. They began the moment you said I do to that pathetic low-life Burgess."

"Leave Stanley out of this. He's dead."

"And you're better off because of it."

Her hand flew up before she realized its intent. She'd swear on her mother's bible it had a mind of its own. Her palm cracked across his stubbled cheek, compounding her consternation. Too bad it didn't lessen her fury.

"Dammit, woman." He clenched his teeth and the muscles along his jaw danced erratically. He clamped an iron-strong hand around her wrist and pulled her behind him as he stalked angrily into the main room.

She made a desperate attempt to unclasp his fingers, but she lacked the strength to pry them loose. Digging her boot heels into the earthen floor was a mistake. Beau merely grunted from the feeble resistance and jerked on her arm. Shards of pain speared through her shoulder.

"Ow!" she cried. "Beau, stop!"

He halted abruptly. She didn't and slammed into his rock solid form. When he released his hold, she tumbled hard to the floor.

Beau thought his chest would explode. He was breathing heavily, kicking himself for treating her brashly. What the hell was he doing anyway? Where did he think he was taking her? God help him, but he wanted to ring that pretty neck of hers, then make love to her until there was nothing left of himself to give.

Dammit, what was she doing to him? He'd never desired to bed a woman more than once. Not until Courtney came along and he discovered he couldn't get enough of her sweet kisses. Last night merely whetted his appetite.

She remained on the floor, her brows furrowed. Beau balled his fingers into tight fists to alleviate his gripping tension. He had to do something before he forgot every vow he'd ever made and hauled Courtney off to the bedroom and lost himself in her soft flower-scented body. Aw, hell. *You've lost your mind, Hamilton.*

"I'm glad to see you were able to dry out your guns."

His features froze with disbelief. He was angrier than sin, and she had the nerve to bait him with the guns she almost ruined.

She rose and dusted off the seat of her Levis, then brushed her hands loose of dirt. Although his tension hadn't yet improved, her anger had obviously dissipated. She was changing right before his eyes, losing her obstinacy and turning sweeter by half. He grew leery.

"I baked a batch of sugar cookies. Would you–"

"Son-of-a...!" Beau hurried to the front door. There he paused. "I don't want your damn cookies. I want you to stay the hell away from me. I quit!"

The instant he exited the adobe, a shot rang out, forcing him back into the house. He slammed the door and crouched beneath a window, at the same time drawing his gun and ordering Courtney to get down. Looking cautiously out the window, Beau searched the yard. He saw no one. On the hill, however, he glimpsed a rider galloping away.

He unfolded and reholstered his gun. "Nice neighbors you got. Lucky for me the gunman couldn't hit a moving target."

Her face drained of color. "Do you think Mr. Stover shot at you?"

"It was one of his hired guns. And he wasn't shooting at me."

Her eyes grew as wide as the bottom of a whiskey bottle. "Why would he shoot at me?"

"Your property forces Stover to go out of his way when he drives cattle up from Texas. The fence prevents him from running cattle over the land. And when sections of fence are down, the sheep get onto his property, eating his cattle's prime grazing grass. You also have more river running through your land. To put it simply, Mrs. Burgess, you have everything Stover wants."

She remained quiet for a spell and lowered her gaze, giving Beau the perfect opportunity to study her. Her hair was braided into a thick, blonde column resting over her shoulder. Her blue flannel shirt was tucked into the waist of her Levis, clearly defining her feminine curves. Quicker than he could spit, he was as hard as an iron pipe. Damning his body's swift reaction, he shifted his stance.

"What would it take for Mr. Stover to leave me alone?"

He felt a twinge of sadness for the rude lesson she'd just learned. "Leave the ranch and go back to New York."

Her eyes narrowed, and anything he felt a moment ago was gone. Her dander was up again, and he braced himself for what was to come. "I've had enough of you telling me to turn tail and run, Mr. Hamilton. This is my home, my land, my sheep."

"You'd die for those stinking animals?"

"It's not only the sheep. It's about what is rightfully mine. And it's a matter of pride. So if Stover wants to play dirty, then so will I."

The tilt of her obstinate jaw turned his stomach into knots. She had no idea of the danger she was in. Stover would shoot his own mother to get what he wanted. "Stover has twenty men working his ranch. And another five are hired guns—men he pays to kill for him. I know these men."

"I suppose you would know your own kind."

"*My kind*," Beau stated harshly, "kill or be killed. It's a rule you best live by if you want to survive sheep ranching." He turned sharply to leave.

"Mr. Hamilton?"

"What?"

"Maybe I was a bit hasty in my demands when I hired you. You're not my servant, I know that. If you're still interested, I'd like you to reconsider your resignation."

Beau closed his eyes. *Say no, Hamilton. You don't need her kind of trouble.*

"I made the right decision when I hired you."

The knots in his stomach tightened like wet rope.

"I can only assume you have an aversion to working for a woman."

The little vixen was doing it again, trying to make him feel guilty and at the same time baiting the hook, thinking he would bite. Maybe he should, just to show her who really wore the pants in their working relationship. Taking his time, he faced her again.

"Am I to understand you want me to work for you even though I violated your first rule?" He arched a brow, expecting her to respond. All she did was stammer. He sauntered over to her. "What is it you really want, Mrs. Burgess?"

Despite his valiant attempts to leave her alone, he engaged her in a kiss that took the air out of his wind. It made him momentarily forget what he'd asked, made him believe she desired *his kind*. Reality sank in and he straightened away. She was warm and flushed, like a virgin bride. He gently ran his hand over her silky hair. The longing in her eyes confused him all the more. He wasn't accustomed to wearing his heart on his sleeve. A heart many said he didn't have. At the moment, he would disagree.

CHAPTER TWELVE

Courtney rested in the rocking chair on the front porch. On the far side of the barn, Manuelo and his two sons were heading home for the noon meal and a *siesta*. Naps were a fact of life in Santa Fe, she learned quickly, a necessity when the temperature rose so high even criminals lay low. Unfortunately, she never took naps, even as a child. She'd always been too curious with life to sleep during the day.

She followed Manuelo with her eyes. What would she have done without him? He and eighteen-year-old Marcos and Eduardo, who recently turned sixteen, tended the sheep and saw to the workings of the ranch. Carlita eventually came around. After their awful first encounter, she and the *curandera* relished a closeness two women developed in a business consisting mostly of men. In a sense, Carlita was the mother Courtney missed.

She closed her eyes and leaned her head back on the rocker. The warm breeze brushed softly across her face. The offensive smell of sheep didn't bother her any longer. In fact, ranch life had begun to grow on her. More so since it quieted down. There were no more gunshots, no dead sheep, no threats from Stover...no Beau. He'd been gone from the ranch for two weeks, since the day he quit. She'd offered him the job back, but he left before giving her an answer. Maybe he was gone for good.

Frowning at the thought, she opened her eyes and gasped softly at the sight of Beau approaching the adobe on horseback. Her heart skipped a beat. He was more handsome and appealing than ever in his buckskins. Judging by his posture, he seemed a little cautious.

He dismounted at the porch steps and dropped the reins, ground tethering the horse. He climbed them and leaned back against a post. "You're not thinking about slapping me again, are you?"

"Are you disappointed?"

"Don't rightly know. Maybe I need a good reason to get worked up enough to kiss you again."

A quick intake of breath lodged in her throat as heat soared through her body. How quickly she forgot about everything except that suggested kiss. Shaking free from the sudden constraints of desire, Courtney cleared her throat. "I didn't think you needed a reason to do anything."

He pushed away from the post and walked directly past her. "I don't."

When he entered the adobe, Courtney balled her fists on the arms of the chair, frustration returning. His nonchalant attitude inevitably rubbed her wrong. Bounding to her feet, she marched in after him.

Beau listened to her heavy footfalls as he crossed the main room. She was hopping mad. It certainly didn't take long for him to get under her skin. He barely smiled as he looked back. She was a sight in Levis, heavy boots and a chambray shirt. Her cheeks flushed a dusty shade of pink, and her single braid trailed over her shoulder, resting alongside her breast. His heart raced, his pulse pumped erratically.

He stopped near the kitchen door. She pretended to be subdued. Yet deep down she was mad as hell with him for staying away two weeks without telling her he was leaving. If he hadn't quit, she'd no doubt threaten not to pay him. All he'd have to do was quit again. Then she'd beg him to stay–in her own way, of course. And in a manner all his own, he'd begrudgingly relent. It wasn't much of a relationship, but then, he'd never asked for one.

"Stover must be making big plans for you."

"Why do you say that?"

"He's been quiet since I left."

"How would you know? And why would you care? You quit, remember?"

"I have my ways." He answered her first question but ignored the last two.

She splayed her slender fingers over her hips and planted her feet apart. Her fury was building, but he wasn't about to get into a heated confrontation so soon. He entered the kitchen.

"Where have you been the last two weeks?" came her suspicious inquiry.

"You sound like a nagging, jealous wife. Besides, I don't work for you, so it's none of your business."

"Fine." She looked as belligerent as a trapped possum.

"I'm starved. Got anything to eat?" He washed in a basin of water, then scrounged around for food. He fixed himself a plate of leftover chicken and tortillas. "Got any coffee?"

A smile briefly cut across his mouth as she poured a cup and slammed it down on the table. Coffee splashed over the rim in her recklessness. She was a sight to behold when she was irritated.

"I rode up north, Wyoming way, to talk to one of the sheep ranchers I told you about. The Bar H is interested in a thousand head of your sheep. The foreman rode back with me and took a room at the Exchange. I told him he could come out tomorrow to see what you've got here."

"You did what?" she bristled. "Without consulting me first?"

His good mood began to unravel. Dammit, he hadn't come here to argue with the stubborn twit. "You're in no position to throw a tantrum, Mrs. Burgess. By the end of the month a shearing crew will arrive. This is a good time to sell off what you don't need. The money will pay your debts to Seligman's, the cantina and the bank."

"How did... Who told..."

"Just shut up and listen," Beau said ungraciously. "After you pay your debts, you owe Manuelo back wages, then the rest of the money will pay the shearers. After you sell your wool, you'll have enough money left over to get you through winter and into next spring."

"Mr. Hamilton—"

"You can sustain the ranch on the sale of sheep wool without slaughtering sheep. It's what you wanted, lady."

He couldn't decide if she was angry, fed up or shocked. It was several minutes before she spoke again.

"How in God's name do you know so much about *stinking sheep*?"

Beau responded tightly. "I asked Manuelo."

"Why would he talk business with you and not me?"

"Because he doesn't know you well enough."

"That's hogwash and you know it."

His patience hung by a thread now. When she reached for his plate and cup, he grabbed her wrist. The uncertainty in her eyes pinched his heart. Still, he refused to let up. "Heed Manuelo's knowledge of sheep ranching. You'd be a fool not to."

The instant he released her, she busied herself with the dirty dishes. Beau walked over to the cupboard for another cup and poured the last of the coffee from the pot. It was strong enough to stand a knife in. Exactly the way he liked it. He reclaimed his seat at the table.

"By the way, I decided to stay on here."

The plate she was washing dropped into the basin, the water preventing it from breaking. She whirled on him, her eyes glowing like a branding iron. "Maybe I don't want you working for me."

"Lady, you need me."

"Like I need a toothache."

Beau grinned and balanced his chair back on the two rear legs. "I'm not that bad."

"You're insufferable, arrogant, presumptuous, rude and... insubordinate!"

"The exact qualities needed in a man hired to protect your welfare."

Her hands flew upward in stilted frustration. "I give up." Then she pinned him with a determined look. "I'll rehire you on one condition. You report to me and only me. Not to Manuelo. I'm your boss, and you must abide by my rules."

Beau eased the chair forward. He didn't take his eyes off her as he rose and walked around the table. "Rules don't apply to hired guns."

"But I didn't hire you for that reason."

"How do you think I'm going to protect you, Mrs. Burgess? By inviting Stover's men in for tea and a dance?" He leaned in close, inhaling that honeysuckle scent he'd missed while he'd been gone. "Well, am I rehired or not?"

He heard her swallow, heard her shallow breaths, heard her heart beating. He placed his hands on the counter, trapping her between his arms. Battling his conscience over whether he should kiss her or simply walk away, it seemed his will was stronger than his good sense. He kissed her as if his lips were touching fine porcelain. God she tasted good— sweet, just like he remembered. If only he could linger, but he couldn't allow himself too much pleasure or he wouldn't be able to stop himself from carrying her off to the bedroom. For now, his long-standing vow remained intact.

Beau stepped back, forcing himself to turn away from the sensual glow on her beautiful face. Gruffly he said, "I'll be back tomorrow morning with the Bar H foreman. Until then, decide if you want me working for you again."

He swiped his hat from the table and left the adobe the same way he came in.

"You have the best here, Mrs. Burgess," the foreman from the Bar H Ranch complimented. "Rancho Ortega always did breed the finest merinos."

From atop the bay gelding, Courtney shifted her attention from the sea of woolly animals to the foreman. His last comment piqued her curiosity. In the year Stanley owned the ranch, how did he build such a good reputation?

"My husband never settled for anything less than the best." She shot Beau a warning glance. This wasn't the time for him to air his deprecating opinions of Stanley.

"My bosses authorized me to pay two dollars a head. I'm sure the animals are disease free?"

"Of course they are," she replied quickly, assuming it was true. Manuelo never said otherwise. "Two dollars a head is—"

"Bird crap," Beau cut in. "Don't hornswoggle the lady, Braden. Hell, in '59 merinos were fetchin' four dollars a head."

Courtney twisted her lips with suppressed anger. "I'm sure Mr. Braden wasn't—"

"Give the lady a fair offer or don't waste her time."

Braden smiled, and his sun-darkened features wrinkled. "You drive a hard bargain, Mr. Hamilton. Three dollars a head then."

"Seven," Beau countered.

"That's a fair price for a few head," Braden admitted. "But I'm fixin' to take a thousand off her hands. My bosses won't go for it."

"I'll take five dollars. No less," she said, eyeing Braden, "and no more," she added, her eyes issuing a stern warning to Beau.

"You got yourself a deal," Braden said. "I'll meet you at the bank to sign the papers. My men are waiting in town. I'll inform them to prepare to move out within the hour." He shifted his likeable blue eyes to Beau then back to her. "I do get my pick, don't I?"

"Whatever you want, Mr. Braden." She didn't have the heart to say no to a man with five-thousand dollars ready to deposit into her account.

"Good. My men will take equal flocks of ewes and wethers. I expect two prime rams to be included."

"Why, certainly." When Beau opened his mouth to object, Courtney maneuvered her horse between his and Braden's. "I'll meet you in town then." As the foreman rode off, Courtney hung back. "What's a wether?"

A wry grin wrestled with Beau's lips. "A castrated male."

Courtney felt her face brim with color.

"A ewe is a female. A lamb is a young sheep, and a ram..." Devilment filled his eyes. "A ram is akin to a stud. He ain't got nothin' better to do than service the females."

"Oh! You'd certainly know all about that, wouldn't you, Mr. Hamilton?"

CHAPTER THIRTEEN

After meeting Braden at the First National Bank, Courtney paid her debts to the bank and Seligman's. Once the cantina was paid, she'd have fifteen hundred dollars left to pay Manuelo's back wages and to prepare for the shearing crew. Not bad for a city girl.

She entered the cantina, relieved to find very few patrons inside. She quickly tracked down José and handed over his money. As she headed for the double swinging doors, she caught sight of Beau sitting at the back of the cantina, coddling a beer. Why wasn't he at the ranch helping Manuelo get the sheep ready to head out with Braden and his crew? She wasn't about to cause a scene with Beau roosting in his territory. She'd give him an earful for his unprofessional behavior later at the ranch.

A flash of red stopped Courtney in her tracks. She narrowed her eyes on Celina sashaying toward Beau. The whore's provocative walk made Courtney blush. The consequences of confronting Beau in public was no longer an issue. Furious, she marched right to the table. Celina now sat cozily in his lap, blocking his view. Courtney watched in disgust while she eavesdropped on the pair, trying with all her will not to toss Celina from Beau's lap.

"Why do you not come to the cantina more?" Celina asked, her voice pouty.

"Maybe I'm bored with the company here," Courtney heard Beau say. When he said something harshly in Spanish, Celina sprang from his lap. Courtney glimpsed Beau's jaw, the muscle there jumping wildly, clearly using great restraint to curb his fury.

Celina spun away and pulled up instantly when she saw Courtney. The surprise in her eyes dissipated into malevolence. "Do not think to work the cantina, *señora*. This is *my* territory." She spat at Courtney's feet then turned back to Beau. "You will tire of this scrawny *gringa*. When you are ready to have a real woman in your bed, you know where to find me."

Courtney's face heated with humiliation, and she didn't dare search the many eyes fixed in her direction. What made Celina believe she was a whore? Worse, everyone in the cantina probably thought the two of them were fighting over Beau's attention.

"You can stand there all day, Mrs. Burgess, or you can join me."

She cast a quick glance at Celina before accepting Beau's invitation.

"Celina's afraid you'll take customers away from her. Your kind of woman would be a welcomed change here. You'd do well for yourself...if you like that sort of work."

"A scrawny *gringa* must be hard to come by in this part of the country."

Beau chuckled. "Glad to see Celina didn't pluck your feathers."

"She didn't. But you, Mr. Hamilton, are plucking me bare." At his salacious grin, she sought to correct her poorly chosen words. "What I meant was—"

"No need to explain, lady."

"Then what are you doing in the cantina when you're supposed to be at the ranch?"

"Manuelo will help Braden with the sheep he chooses."

Courtney eyed him bitterly. She should have hired a real ranch hand instead of a man of questionable character. But then, a ranch hand might be lousy at protecting her investments. "You don't take orders very well, do you, Mr. Hamilton? I know you don't like being told what to do, but as your boss—"

"As your *protector*, I do what I think is necessary for your continued good health. The cantina is the best place to hear what's going on."

"With a beer in one hand and a whore in the other?"

Beau's devastating grin turned Courtney inside out.

"Neither gets in the way of listening," he pointed out. Sitting forward, he set his elbows on the table and fit one hand in the other. "Was there anything else you need to say?"

Even though he had a way of setting her off quickly, he also had a way of disarming her, making her forget how infuriating he could be. It caused her heart an extra beat every time he looked at her with those gray eyes that, lately, seemed to be losing their steely edge.

"I never thanked you for bringing Mr. Braden down. I didn't want you to think I was ungrateful."

"Didn't think you were."

She could get used to this quiet side of Beau. It was charming, a huge change from his I-don't-give-a-damn attitude.

His warm breath fanned across her mouth, drawing Courtney from her private thoughts. She hadn't noticed him leaning closer. His head was slightly tilted, his lips precious seconds away from touching hers. But then his breathing slowed considerably, and she feared he wasn't breathing at all.

Sensing they weren't alone, Courtney half turned her head to see a stocky man beside their table. Another man slipped around to Beau's side, while a third positioned himself behind Beau's chair.

"Don't it smell *baaaad* in here?" the stocky man asked his friends.

"Yeah, kinda like the stink them sheep give off," the man at Beau's side replied. Leaning toward her, he sniffed the air. "Think she sleeps with 'em? After all, we all know how lonely widows get."

"Leave her alone, Jack," Beau warned as he leaned back. He set his steely-eyes on the reprobate. "Has Stover stooped so low, he's sending his men out to taunt women?"

Jack's hand went to his gun. "Stay out of this, Hamilton. It ain't your business."

Beau's gaze slid from Jack to Steve, the man beside him. Both were hired guns with nasty reputations. The man at his back was undoubtedly Lonie. Beau would bet his life on it. Lonie usually snuck up on a person and attacked from behind.

In the sudden quiet, the scraping of chair legs over the wood floor echoed ominously. Beau remained seated, but pinned Jack with an intrepid look. "Well, now, you're wrong there, Jack. Mrs. Burgess hired me to see after her well being."

From across the room, José pleaded, "No fighting in the cantina. Go outside."

"There's nothing to worry about, José," Beau assured the jittery Mexican. "These gentleman stopped by for a friendly chat. Isn't that right, Jack?"

"Yeah, that's right," Jack mumbled. He jerked his head toward the door, ordering Steve and Lonie out of the cantina.

The tightness in Beau's gut felt worse than the staggering pain from the bullets he'd taken in the ambush. He'd been afraid one of the men would touch Courtney. He would defend her, even if it meant killing Stover's men and suffering the consequences later. He'd never be able to live with himself if he failed to protect her.

"Who were those men?"

Her pale face troubled him. She sat rigidly in her chair, obviously spooked by Stover's henchmen. A pinch of compassion squeezed his heart. "Three of Stover's guns, same as those other two men who'd ridden out to your ranch with Stover." He drained the glass and replaced his hat. "I'm taking you back to the ranch."

His tone brooked no argument and, thankfully, Courtney rose and headed across the room.

Reaching the doors, he stopped and gently pushed her behind him. The instant Beau stepped onto the boardwalk, his right arm shot out to shield the blow he rightly anticipated. With his left, he jabbed a fist into Jack's underbelly and hooked his boot toe behind the man's knees, taking him down easily.

Steve lunged at him, the force knocking Beau to the ground. He rolled away from the lanky man and sprang to his feet, swiping the knife from the sheath at his calf in time to slice Jack's forearm when he charged. With his back unprotected, Beau could do nothing against Lonie's tackle. They fell hard to the ground, grunting. Beau was getting awfully mad. He didn't favor the three against one odds, and someone was going to pay for the lopsided fight.

He heaved Lonie off his back at the same instant he caught sight of Courtney yanking a rifle away from the man beside her. She lifted the heavy weapon and swung full circle, body and all. Everyone cowered to the boardwalk.

Beau scowled. "Put that damn thing down before you kill someone!"

He grunted when Lonie's fist clipped his cheek.

"Someone's got to help you," she shouted back, glaring at the witnesses lying belly down around her.

Beau swore when she raised the rifle and steadied it against her shoulder. The rifle exploded in a gray cloud of smoke, the force throwing Courtney to her backside. Beau crouched to the ground, leaving Lonie clutching at his rear and writhing in agony.

"She shot me! The bitch shot me in the ass!" Lonie hollered. He carried on as if he'd been hit with a full load of bullets.

From the corner of his eye, Beau noticed Steve drawing his gun against Courtney. He was about to warn her when she got to her feet and arced the rifle once again to her shoulder. Beau ducked.

"Crazy woman!" Steve squawked. "Women ain't got no business holdin' a gun."

"Then don't mess with me," Courtney warned, lowering the long barrel to Steve's vitals, "or I may find a better target on *you*."

"Damn crazy bitch." Steve helped Jack collect their injured friend. "We ain't through with you, sheep lady." He glared at Beau, a silent warning that they weren't finished with him, either.

Breathing unevenly, Beau calmly spoke to Courtney. "Easy, girl. Set the rifle down nice and gentle."

"Don't you dare talk to me like I've lost my wits. I'm not crazy," she huffed. "I take that back. Maybe I am insane for saving your ornery hide." She lowered the rifle as everyone began to rise. The butt hit the boards hard, and her finger accidentally brushed the touchy trigger. Another loud report sent everyone scrambling for cover again.

"Shit." Beau belly crawled to Courtney who sat semi-dazed on the boardwalk. He grabbed the barrel and yanked the rifle out of her hand, then shoved it at its rightful owner as he stood. Jerking her to her feet, he saw no other recourse but to treat her like a disobedient adolescent. "Don't you know any better than to play with guns?"

Her glowing eyes rounded on him. "I was helping you, you miserable wretch. Do us both a favor and quit again."

"Not a chance, lady," Beau said. "You really do need protection now. Stover's men won't give up. They'll go off and lick their wounds while they restore their pride. But the war has begun."

Rebel Heart

CHAPTER FOURTEEN

The moment Manuelo and Carlita bid Courtney good night, she piled her hair atop her head and donned a cool summer shift. From the threshold of the kitchen door, she watched the hot, sultry night close over Santa Fe. Rubbing her perspiring neck, she leaned back against the door jamb and studied the lacy crests of mountains sweeping from the lush grasslands. Incredibly, several peaks were still covered with snow. That intrigued her, wondering why the snow hadn't melted from the sweltering western heat. Often over the past weeks she'd gazed out the back window at the fiery sunset, marveling at the red glow of the mountains. The sight was as breathtaking as a brilliant painting.

A coyote howled in the distance. Its lonely sound chilled her to the bone despite the high temperature. Closer to home, crickets chirped in the shrubs against the adobe. Listening to the peaceful symphony orchestrated by Mother Nature, Courtney wished life could always be this serene.

"A beautiful sight, isn't it?"

Courtney jolted with fright, and her hand pressed against the enormous pounding of her heart. She inhaled repeatedly to settle her startled nerves.

"I didn't mean to frighten you," Beau apologized. "I saw the light."

He stepped out of the shadows, scanning her from head to bare feet. Courtney glanced down at herself. The low firelight from a candle on the table cast her in silhouette. Chagrined to discover he could see her naked outline through the thin cotton garment, she crossed her arms over her chest, but did little to shield the rest of her body from his perusal. She was grateful when he turned to view the mountains she'd been admiring.

"Those are the Sangre de Cristo Mountains. The name means Blood of Christ. The locals call them the Sangres."

"How appropriate." Unnerved that he remained there as if she were clothed decently, she wished he would respect her privacy and leave. However, it wasn't Beau's style, so she focused on the mountains and prayed he'd be on his way soon.

"The color is reflected from the setting sun," he went on. "I remember the first time I saw the Sangres at night." He gathered a clump of dirt and ground it between his fingers, letting the powdery matter float away on a mild breeze. After wiping his hand against his buckskin, he peered into her eyes. "I decided I should teach you how to shoot."

"Why? I handled myself fine today."

"Look, Courtney–" Beau nearly lost his self-control. If he allowed himself familiarity with her name, he wouldn't stop there. He rectified his blunder. "Mrs. Burgess, those men were playing with you today. You can't stand up to hired guns without knowing how to protect yourself."

"Isn't that the reason I hired you?"

He dragged in a long breath and held it awhile before releasing it with a resigned sigh. "Stover's got five guns. I'm only one man. As much as I'd like to believe I'm infallible, I'm not God. Don't you understand? Your life is on the line here. If you were their mother, they'd kill you. Their kind don't have a conscience."

"But you're their kind. Would you kill me?"

"Don't ask me that, Court—Mrs. Burgess. Although God knows sometimes I want to–" He swallowed his words. Dammit. She was turning him soft, forcing him to feel emotions he thought he'd buried all those years ago.

"Sometimes you want to strangle some sense into me, is that it? Well, you're not the only one. My father threatened me with that for years. I suppose when a woman has a mind of her own, the only way a man thinks he can control her is by a heavy hand." Her mouth tightened at the corners. "Is there a reason you're here, Mr. Hamilton?"

"Just making sure you had no more trouble."

"I haven't."

They turned in unison to the distant mountains. He should leave, but he didn't want to ride back into town just yet. More to the point, he didn't want to be alone. It never bothered him before. He was a loner by nature, always had been. Lately, however, he found himself wishing he could be near Courtney all day long. Then there were the nights, when loneliness crept over him, swaddling him in its cold blanket. God he hated the nights.

He tried to stop his gaze from wandering back to her, but he failed. One more look and his restraint broke. He selfishly drank in her beautiful feminine form, though he did so without giving in to the pleasure his body craved.

"You could have given this ranch up right after your husband was killed. Why didn't you?"

She seemed at odds with forming a plausible answer. Then her shoulders dropped and her voice lowered. "My father would have given me the I-told-you-so lecture the minute I walked into his house."

"Was that the only reason keeping you from going home?"

"That and..." She smiled coyly. "I started liking it here. More so now that Stanley's debts are paid."

Beau moved in closer, but she turned into the kitchen. Near the table, she stopped. He was afraid she'd bite into him for overstaying his welcome.

"I'm tired, Mr. Hamilton," she said quietly.

"Before you turn in, I need to know one thing." He crossed the room and without reservation, gathered her into his arms. In a whisper that could have passed for a plea, he said, "Kiss me, Courtney."

The instant she came to him, Beau realized the fear that had been riding him. Against his solemn vow, he would make love to her again.

Lost in the moment, his rationality fled. Her feminine scent and warmth were a drugging combination. He craved her touch, even if later he might regret it. She boldly pressed against him, the proof of her passion nearly his undoing. Her soft moaning sounds tickled his lips as she wrapped her tongue around his, pushing back into his mouth. The tentative action reminded him she wasn't worldly in the ways of men. She hadn't been married long enough to know how to please a man, or to feel the pleasure of a real man's seduction. Suddenly, he wanted her to know him like no other woman had dared.

Her breasts burned his flesh through their garments. He felt her shudder, knew she had experienced the same spear of desire, the same longing that had ambushed his own body. Before long, a fine sheen of perspiration broke across his forehead and blanketed his back where her hand wandered down the groove of his spine.

97

Beau snuck a hand under her shift and caressed her thigh, cherishing her soft flesh and shapely muscles. His palm turned damp, as if he suffered from a bad case of nerves. But the second he lifted her leg and circled it around his hip, he forgot about his fear of needing a woman so badly.

Molding his hand over one side of her nicely rounded buttocks, he eased her closer. Heat radiated from her core, exciting him, easily making him forget who he was fondling. He loathed losing his self-discipline to a woman, yet he desperately wanted Courtney in spite of his lifelong vow. Still, he couldn't let her rob his fortitude to turn his back on any female, no matter who she was.

Regretfully, he reached behind him, unwrapping first her luscious leg, then her arms. She protested with a soulful cry, but he refused to fall to that dolorous sound. "We can't do this, Courtney," he rasped. "I'm not the man you want or need."

"You should have thought about that before you took me the first time."

"I was wrong to come to you when I did. I was drunk." The crushed expression on her beautiful face strangely cut through his heart. "I promise it won't happen again."

She raised her chin, her pride winning out above the emotions she held inside. She walked calmly from the room, leaving him feeling empty and incomplete.

"You're a damn fool," Beau told himself with regret.

Astride her gray mare, Courtney observed Manuelo and his sons attending to the sheep lying on the ground. She noticed Manuelo's grave concern. Marcos fixed his black as night eyes on her. It was as if he blamed her for the sheep's misfortune.

"Is it injured?" she asked.

"*Sí, señora,*" Manuelo answered. "The ewe has a broken leg and internal injuries. She must have wandered through the broken fence onto Stover's land. I think she was trampled by cattle or a horse and thrown back."

"Isn't that the same stretch of fence where those other sheep wandered through a few weeks back?"

"*Sí, señora*"

"Why hasn't it been mended yet?"

"Without money, I cannot buy the wire to fix the fence."

Courtney noticed Beau riding toward them at a loping gait. It was about time he showed up. After throwing herself at him two nights ago, she was afraid she'd scared him away. She still couldn't believe she'd behaved as brazen as the whores in the cantina.

"Trouble here?" Beau asked Manuelo.

Courtney listened as Manuelo repeated his suspicions. All the while she couldn't pull her eyes away from Beau. Even though she'd seen him in his Levis and blue-striped pullover often before, he looked especially handsome today. She particularly liked the way his hair curled around the neckband of his shirt, caressing it like a baby's tiny grasp. At his chest, all four buttons were fastened, but wayward hairs eased over the top edge, teasing her senses. She knew only too well what lay hidden behind the shirt. When she followed the line of his muscular arm to his gloved hand loosely gripping the reins, she realized it had gone silent. All four men were staring at her.

Unduly peeved with herself for giving in to her misguided desire, she intentionally snapped at Beau. "Where have you been? You didn't come around once yesterday. It seems every time you decide to take a long *siesta*, something happens."

If the thick nerve along his jaw twitched any faster, it might have worked clean through the stubbles there. She barely noticed that he wasn't clean-shaven. All her tunneled vision saw was that flittering nerve.

"Yesterday was Sunday. My day of rest."

He was calm. Too calm. That disturbed Courtney. All the other times she'd spoken abrasively to him, he'd flown into a tirade. She should have realized there was always a calm before the storm.

"I suppose it's also a day of rest for evil men like Stover's hired bunch?"

"I'm not working seven days a week, lady." His calm began to unravel.

"Your job is to protect me and my sheep. That means day and night. So you might as well move your gear out of the Exchange Hotel. Manuelo will fix you a corner of the barn."

"Now hold on one damn minute. No one, and that includes you, bosses me around. I do what I want, when I want, and no pampered little twit in britches is gonna dictate my life. And I don't sleep in barns."

She heard his teeth gnashing. She noted the tautness of his lips, but it was that damned nerve along his jaw that kept drawing her attention. "Maybe sleeping in a barn when you're sober might change your mind."

A long silence ensued. The heavy beating of her heart throbbed faster with each passing second. Suddenly, Beau's features changed. He smiled, and his tense posture relaxed. She became leery, distrusting.

"I get it now," he said, arrogance quieting his voice. "You've got a needle stuck in your craw because I turned you down the other night."

Disbelief widened her eyes. How dare he mention that moment of indiscretion in front of Manuelo and his sons? She hated him for purposely humiliating her. She was certain he'd meant to, if only to repair his fleeting control over her. She'd fire him if she didn't need him so badly. Her horrified expression turned to spite.

"I suppose when you're used to whores, you wouldn't know how to treat a lady. So don't pride yourself, Mr. Hamilton. You're not worth this lady's time."

CHAPTER FIFTEEN

Courtney marched around the side of the adobe, fury riding her like a cumbersome saddle on a pony. She had never been so humiliated in her life. And she hadn't ever wanted to slap a man as badly as she did Beau. The man had no manners, no idea of the meaning of decorum. She wasn't stupid. She knew men in the West weren't known for their social graces but what Beau had said was inexcusable.

She spotted Carlita planting new herbs in the garden and marched to the edge of the cultivated dirt. The Mexican woman glanced up with concern.

"Is there something wrong, *señora?*"

"That man!" Courtney blurted.

Carlita winced as she stood. "Who, *señora?*"

"Beau Hamilton." Courtney paced to the corner of the garden. She swiftly retraced her steps, then abruptly stopped. "How well do you know him?"

"Not as well as you do," Beau said from the corner of the adobe. "I guarantee that, *mi amor.*"

Burning hot flames spread rapidly across Courtney's cheeks. Embarrassed and unreasonably angry, she stormed through the kitchen door, stomping loose dirt over the newly swept floor. Barely across the room, she was roughly yanked off her feet by the strangling grip of Beau's hand around her upper arm. She jerked her startled gaze up, meeting the storm in his eyes.

"I don't like women who order me around, who chastise and make an ass of me in front of my friends."

"I wasn't aware you had friends."

"Yes, Mrs. Burgess, even uncompromising bastards like me have friends."

"Still and all, it was unfair of you to say what you did. I *am* your boss, and you spoke to me with disrespect and insubordination." She rotated her shoulder, but his grip remained solid, numbing.

"You haven't learned how to be a boss yet. You haven't even learned how to run your own ranch. So what the hell gives you the right to issue orders to me or Manuelo?"

"I own this ranch. That's what gives me the right." She fought back.

Beau grew steadily intolerant. She was so damned mule-headed. And naïve, too. Too bad Burgess hadn't been man enough to tell her the entire truth about Rancho Ortega. That two-bit snake in the grass probably glorified his holdings and social standing in Santa Fe. Someone ought to tell Courtney all about the ranch. It sure as hell wouldn't be him.

"I suggest you start behaving like a sheep rancher." He tugged her over to the table, kicked out a chair and shoved her down. When her bottom hit the hard wood, she grunted.

"I won't let you bully me."

"Forget the you're-the-boss, I'm-the-subordinate crap. If you want to keep this ranch going, you'll listen to me. Personally I'd like nothing more than to see you turn tail and run home to your father. But I understand your reason for wanting to make a go of this place. I'm willing to help you, provided you stop pretending to be someone's boss and work like the owner of one of the best sheep ranches south of Cheyenne."

"You don't need to shout at me. I'm not hard of hearing."

"Maybe not, but you're damned hardheaded." Beau walked to the back door, leaned out and spoke in Spanish. Manuelo appeared, his floppy hat in hand.

"*Señora,*" he acknowledged, ever the gentleman.

Beau set his hat on a low cabinet. Using his forearm, he wiped away the sweat beading across his forehead, and pinned Courtney with a look that dared her to question what he was about to say. She was complacent for the moment, and he didn't like that. Something was brewing in that hot head of hers.

"Manuelo is going to explain what sheep ranching entails and what you have to do to help out. Ask questions, if you'd like, but don't argue anything he tells you. Comprende, *señora?*" At her leery nod, Beau glanced at Manuelo. The Mexican pulled out a chair to make himself comfortable. All the while, Beau kept a wary eye on Courtney. God help her, she had better behave.

102

The crew arrived a week later, as Manuelo said they would. Courtney was grateful the man had prepared her for the shearing. She'd never realized it was such hot, tedious work. She pushed back another sweat soaked clump of hair from her temple and hooked it behind her ear. Smoke from the pit dug into the ground rose upward as she turned the meat over the large grill. Fat dripped onto the flames, sizzling and crackling, spattering her hand with hot grease.

"Damn," she muttered, jerking her hand back to her lips. As she ran her tongue over the burns, she looked across the pit to Beau. He was ravishing, unfairly desirable. His work shirt parted down the front, revealing his glistening chest and stomach. The flickering flames reflected enticingly on his damp skin, accentuating the hard ridges she found utterly breathtaking. The garment molded to his shoulders and the muscles in his arms, revealing the power she knew existed in them.

She dragged her wayward gaze to his unshaven face. Dark blond stubbles caressed the granite line of his jaw, and his stubbornness showed in the angles marking his face. He had called her hardheaded. In that sense, they were alike.

He removed his hat and wiped his perspiring forehead with the bandana he kept in his back pocket. He came around the rock-edged pit and nodded at her hand. "You should set your hand in cold water." He lifted her hand to inspect the raised welts. "I think Carlita should have a look at the burns."

Courtney held her breath. It was the first time they'd been this close since he'd chased her into the kitchen about a week ago.

He brought her hand to his lips and gently kissed the burned area.

"Is that supposed to make it feel better?"

"My mother used to tell me it did whenever I scraped a knee."

Uncomfortable with the smoldering look in his eyes, she slipped her hand out of his. "I didn't mean the kiss."

"The cold water eases the pain. And Carlita will have salve to ward off infection."

Courtney gave him a tight smile before turning her attention to the Mexican men beyond the pit. They'd arrived yesterday afternoon and already sheared half her flock. The crew consisted of Manuelo's cousin Juan and six others who were amazingly efficient at their job. Tonight was reserved for rest and visiting with Manuelo and his family. Large cans were filled with wood and fire to keep the yard from total darkness. Carlita had prepared bowls of rice and beans, stacks of freshly made tortillas, and had bought enough beef and chicken to feed all of Santa Fe. For once, the air smelled delicious, relieving the strong odor of sheep.

One of the men strummed an old, beat up guitar. The tune sounded clear and soul bearing. Another of the men began to sing.

"They're characters," Beau commented.

"Yes, they are. Juan certainly is different from Manuelo. I can't say I've ever seen a man wear so many bright colors. He reminds me of a bowl of fruits." She angled her head to look at Beau. "Why are you laughing?"

"It's refreshing to see excitement in your eyes."

Beau brushed his fingers along her cheek. She was mesmerized instantly by his smile, and her heart flip-flopped in her chest as he bent to kiss her. The warmth and tenderness of his kiss was heavenly. It wasn't rough, neither did it promise that more would follow. Even so, when it ended and Beau straightened away, a wave of disappointment washed over Courtney. She returned to the man singing.

"*Ángel de amor, tu pasión no la comprendo.*" His intonation was lamenting, long suffering. "*Yo no siento el que me hayas querido. Yo no siento el que me haya amarlo.*"

"What is he saying?" she asked, hoping to fill the sudden void in her heart.

"The song speaks of one man lamenting over the love of his woman. He is trying to understand why she gave him up for another man. *Ángel de amor*–Angel of love."

"It's a lonely sound," she commented in earnest. The longing she saw in Beau's eyes charged shivers of excitement through her stomach.

"Shepherds are lonely men," he replied. "Many of the New Mexican folk songs came from shepherds. They spend months in the wilderness with no companionship other than their sheep, two dogs and one human partner. So they make up songs."

A gratifying smile graced her lips and reached to light her eyes. Beau couldn't begin to know where it came from. In his narrowed vision, he saw only her lips, their curvy shape beckoning him to take his pleasure from their warmth and softness. He studied her angelic features. She was forever drawing him deeper into her spider's web. His eyelids fluttered downward as he imagined himself alone with her at some magical place he knew couldn't possibly exist. As he leaned down to kiss her again, someone called to him, breaking the dream.

Juan strode up, exuberant as ever and spoke in Spanish. Beau quirked a brow, then turned his amused smile on Courtney. "Juan says you're beautiful. Your hair reminds him of a sunrise on a summer morning."

A blush crept over her already flushed face. She brushed a hand over the mass of hair she'd braided that morning. Silky strands had fallen free, sticking to her neck from the hot evening and the steam of the pit.

"Thank you," she mumbled.

When Juan spoke again, Beau chuckled with amusement. "Juan would be honored if you'd allow him to teach you how to shear," he related.

She excitedly jumped at the opportunity. "Yes, I'd love to!"

Juan glanced over his shoulder to his crew and nodded. Loud cheers erupted into the night. Before Courtney fully comprehended what she had accepted, her hand was lost in Juan's calloused paw, and he pulled her behind his hurried steps. He brought her to one of the corrals where the next batch of sheep had been singled out for shearing.

"Juan wants you to capture a sheep," Beau told her.

Courtney's dubious expression rounded on Beau's smiling face before she turned to regard the sheep.

"Follow Juan's lead," Beau prompted.

"Easy for you to say," she returned tenuously.

Beau's chuckle rang in her ears as she imitated Manuelo's cousin. Courtney quickly discovered that gaining a solid hold on the animal was harder than it appeared. After a few unsuccessful attempts, all she had to show was a mouth full of dust and sore palms from breaking her fall each time the sheep darted out of her grasp. Juan came to her rescue just in time. She was about to chastise Beau for laughing uproariously.

"What?" she asked of Juan's foreign rambling and cast a skeptical eye on Beau.

"He said he'll hold the ewe while you shear. But first you need to cut off the dung locks."

"The what?" She stared at him, aghast.

"You heard right."

She glared at Beau as he climbed to the top slat of the corral fence. Clearly trying to keep his amusement in check, he bit the inside of his cheek.

Clamping her jaw tightly, she faced the sheep. The poor animal had to be uncomfortable. Juan had wrapped its forelegs over its hind legs and held them from behind so it couldn't kick out and injure her.

"Pick up the cutters, Mrs. Burgess. If you don't do something soon, the sheep will get restless."

Hesitantly, Courtney grasped the cutters and pinched a gob of matted hair between two fingers. She snipped as close to the sheep's skin as possible without cutting the animal. "This is disgusting!" she cried, dropping the stained wool to the ground.

"You missed a few," Beau pointed out.

"You'll pay for this, Beau Hamilton," she promised.

After cutting off the remaining pieces of matted wool, Courtney stepped back. Juan turned the ewe and settled it down, using his hands and legs as restraints. He grinned while giving her further instructions.

"Juan said you should begin at the head and clip as close to the body as possible. Make sure you work your way back to the tail. Oh, and you need to keep the fleece in one piece."

"Should I spin it into yarn while I'm at it?" she said, her voice heavy with sarcasm.

"Just try to avoid second cuts or you'll reduce the value of the wool."

"Thank you, Mr. I-want-nothing-to-do-with-stinking-sheep."

Deep in concentration, Courtney had no idea how enticing she looked. Bent over, her Levis stretched across her sweet little bottom and the muscles in her legs shifted gracefully. The sight made Beau's breath stick in his throat. Sweat saturated most of her shirt, molding it alluringly to the curves of her waist and the gentle rise of her arm muscles. When her braid fell over her shoulder, she nearly sheared the end along with the sheep's hair. Beau's grin returned.

Aware of the cumbersome and hot work of shearing, Beau admired her tenacity. He didn't think she'd accept Juan's invitation. He had to admit, she surprised him once again. Now and then she glanced at Juan, and Beau saw the consternation tightening her features. It probably was due to the Mexican's never-ending grin.

At last, she straightened and stepped back, announcing proudly, "I did it."

A roar of laughter thundered around the yard. Beau grabbed the fence slat to keep from falling off. He hadn't laughed so hard since... He honestly couldn't remember the last time he'd gotten a stitch in his side from laughing.

"*La mofeta!*" Juan howled.

When Courtney heatedly spun around, Beau slipped off the fence and leaned against it for support. She was positively livid, yet he couldn't stop laughing.

"What did he say?" she demanded.

Beau dragged in a breath just so he could speak. Through a gulp of air, he managed to reply. "Skunk!"

Rebel Heart

CHAPTER SIXTEEN

Courtney vaulted to the top rail of the fence as if she wore springs beneath her boots. Frantically scanning the yard for the dreaded animal, all she saw were the men doubled over, laughing so hard one nearly choked. Next to her, Beau was having fits of his own. His shoulders shook with laughter. Courtney was beside herself.

"Lady...no one's gonna...forget this year's shearing," he managed to say as he fought to compose his laughter.

"What the hell is so funny about a skunk?"

He shook his head, snorting now and then. When he didn't answer – couldn't answer through his amusement–she smacked the hat off his head.

Still chuckling, Beau bent to retrieve his Stetson. He hung it on a fence post and climbed up to sit. "Take a look at the ewe you sheared."

She slid her wary gaze to the sheep. Apparently, she had missed a strip of wool down the animal's back. It did indeed resemble a skunk, although a mighty odd one. "All right, I'll be the first to admit shearing is one job I should leave to the experts." In spite of the ribbing from Beau and the others, and the soreness she already felt in her arms, Courtney grinned.

Juan turned the ewe over to two other men who forced the sheep into a long, narrow vat filled with a brew of sulfur and herbs to kill parasites and other skin ailments. The animal bleated through the entire process and long after it came out and was sent into another corral where it would be branded tomorrow.

"*Gringo!*" Juan shouted to Beau.

Courtney observed Beau closely as the Mexican spoke to him. A mischievous grin stretched clear across his face.

"Juan's challenging me. He seems to think he can shear faster than I can."

"My money is on Juan," she said with confidence.

"Really? What say we make a bet?"

"Name it."

"A night swim in the river. You and me... alone."

Courtney thought he'd lost his senses. "You're on. But only because I know where you stand on sheep. Oh, I saw you help out these past two days. You really should stick to being a gunfighter."

"I'll remember that, *querida*." He hopped down from the fence. "Make sure you remind me of my vocation after Juan embarrasses the hell out of me and bruises my ego."

The twinkle in his eyes was unsettling. He seemed awfully happy for a man who hated sheep. She shook off the butterflies in her stomach and watched Beau and Juan with keen interest. When the sheep kept darting out of Beau's grasp, Courtney felt more at ease.

Until the men took up the shears. Beau matched Juan's cuts inch for inch, like he'd done it for years. Before her eyes, she saw her bet with the rogue fall in his favor. When the contest ended, Courtney gawked in astonishment.

Beau took everything in stride. He accepted the congratulatory slaps on his back as if his due. Pressing her lips together, she swung her legs over the fence and jumped.

"I'll meet you at the river in an hour," Beau shouted. The amusement in his tone raised her hackles.

The pretty Spanish song drifted into the kitchen. Courtney sat at the table, listening while the silly bet she made with Beau loomed like a hairy monster. The crew had quit for the night and were enjoying their whiskey and beer. They'd be turning in soon. She prayed Beau would do the same. An hour crawled by, then two. A smidgen of hope lifted her spirits. Perhaps Beau made that bet in jest. Of course, he did. He'd simply been teasing her.

The back door swung open. Courtney jumped with fright. With Beau looming there, his hair slicked with sweat, the sickening taste of dread stuck in her throat.

"Didn't mean to keep you waiting." He braced his hands on the door's top frame.

"Are you...drunk?" she stammered.

"Not this time, lady. I can hold my beer. I made sure to stay clear of the rotgut." He stepped into the kitchen. "Let's go."

Courtney shrunk away.

"I'm hot and tired, Mrs. Burgess. You made a bet with me and lost. So get out of that chair or I'll carry you to the river."

"The contest was rigged." She tried in a desperate and feeble attempt to wriggle out of going with him. She wasn't about to give in to Beau again, or make him think she desired him. He'd said he wasn't the right man for her. He wasn't. Absolutely and most assuredly not the man for her.

"I never told Juan about the bet."

"But his sheep was bigger than yours."

"Nice try, but it doesn't wash. Both ewes were within a few pounds of each other. Now quit stalling." When he reached for her hand, she hid it behind her back.

"Wait. I-I think you're lying."

Beau inhaled deeply. "All right, Mrs. Burgess. I'll give you two choices. You walk or I carry you there."

She snatched a towel from beneath the cabinet and grabbed a bar of honeysuckle soap. Despite his weariness, Beau grinned as she marched past. He followed several paces behind, hoping she'd run out of steam before reaching the river. But when she threw her towel and soap to the grassy bank, he knew he would have to be somewhat sagacious in dealing with her fury.

He lowered to the ground with a grimace. All his muscles felt shredded. Holding back a groan, he pulled off his boots then got to his feet and stripped the sweaty clothes from his sticky body. To his annoyance, Courtney stood stone still, eyes downcast. He almost believed she was ashamed, until he recalled how badly she'd wanted him to make love to her just over a week ago. He hadn't imagined that, had he? Had he misread the signs, only seeing what he wanted to see?

"Do I have to undress you?" The thought pulsed excitement through his veins.

She shifted her stance. "Turn around, please." She acted like a shy little girl asking her father to look the other way.

"Modest, Mrs. Burgess?" Feeling cranky now, Beau didn't wait for an answer and treaded into the river. Without so much as flinching from the chilly water, he crouched on the river's bottom and instantly felt the tension of the day dissipate. A few minutes passed before Courtney stepped into the river. He was glad she didn't attempt to shield her body from his view. The moonlight softened her feminine figure, giving her an ethereal appearance. Beau was afraid she might fade into the night, only a vision in his distracted mind.

As he stood, his eyes remained on her features. He saw she was caught in indecision. Back in the kitchen she'd asked if he was drunk. Did she remember the night he'd come to her intoxicated? Many times he'd wanted to tell her how sorry he was—not for making love to her, but for frightening her with his insufferable condition. Beau frowned. She'd been right about him bedding mostly whores. Worse, she hit the target dead center, telling him he didn't know the first thing about a lady.

He waded toward her, the water rippling outward to where she stood. "Do you know why I made the bet?"

She shook her head. Her eyes locked with his in an obvious attempt to avoid perusing his nude body.

"I wanted you all to myself. Does that surprise you?"

Her nod was wary at best.

Beau chuckled softly. "It surprised the hell out of me, too." He lifted her hand to his lips and kissed her cool fingertips. They smelled like sheep and smoke from the pit. "I vowed never to make love to the same woman twice. You're making it hard for me to keep that vow."

He grasped her by the shoulders and dragged her alongside his body. Her breasts smashed against his chest, her taut nipples pressing into his flesh. Desire and need converged on him like never before. It wasn't enough to merely hold her. He meant to have all of her, to possess her and make her desperate to have him, too. He stole her lips as if the kiss were their last. He gave no thought to his strong grip biting into her shoulders or to the stubbles around his mouth chafing her tender skin.

She wriggled loose from his callous hold and placed her palms on his heavily pounding chest. Beau straightened, relieving his grip, but he couldn't let her go.

"Must you always behave like a brute?"

"I've never had to haggle a *lady* over a kiss before," he confessed, perplexed.

"Maybe if you'd ask instead of take," she suggested rather sharply. "And another thing. What was that comment about your vow?"

"Nothing," Beau snapped.

Courtney wondered what had dampened his desirous mood. After all, she'd spoken the truth. He didn't exactly act the gentleman. Or was it his vow she'd mentioned? Maybe he was sore because she didn't fall at his feet with lust in her veins. She almost had once, but never again would she open herself to the humiliation of his rejection.

As he retrieved her soap, she turned her head aside, not ready to study his male form in all its splendor. It was enough she'd seen him wearing only a towel. She preferred leaving the rest to her imagination.

He returned and stepped behind her. She glanced at him over her shoulder, but he busily lathered the soap. When he ran his hands and the soap over her back, she shivered. He was thorough, washing her from her neck to her waist. Courtney's breath hitched when he glided the scented bar over her buttocks. His touch never drew away. Instead, it slid up and down, one side to the other, until she caught herself moving with the same rhythm he'd composed. How did she tell him never to stop what he was doing without sounding wanton?

A moan brushed over her lips. With each stroke she fell deeper and deeper into a trance of euphoric delight. His arms circled her, and he pressed the small bar into her hand. When his lathered hands covered her breasts she thought she would jump out of her skin. She rested her head back to settle her shock and inhaled deeply, her expanding breasts filling his hands. As her eyelids fluttered downward, she heard him groan, felt it vibrate at her back. She glanced back, enthralled by the sight of his closed eyes and his mouth tightly drawn. If he felt half the bliss as she, Courtney knew his was a look of pure pleasure.

He turned her and commanded in a raspy voice, "Wash me."

Courtney wondered if it was wise to touch him. She feared it might cast her over the edge of propriety, if such a thing existed when a man and woman stood naked together. There could be no shame in what she was about to do, she decided. Not when both she and Beau desired the same end to their play.

She worked the soap into his chest hair. His muscles rippled like a flag in the wind beneath her fingers. Slowly moving downward, she sensed his stomach contract like a nervous fist. She ventured lower yet, and a sudden wave of desire overshadowed all her fears. At the base of him she lingered, wondering how to hold his hard staff. Was there a right way to grasp a man? She didn't know.

"Courtney," he pleaded, "don't tease me."

He thrust her fingers around his male shaft. They gasped in unison before Beau captured her lips. His hungry kiss shivered down her spine. She hadn't noticed he lifted her into his arms until the river swallowed most of her body. But the cold water didn't squelch their ardor. The soap dropped from her grasp when she wrapped her arms around his wide shoulders and molded to him, aching for the moment he eased the dire need gripping her body.

Beau's masterful lips laved over her ear and down her jaw, leaving a trail of heated gooseflesh. Courtney arched back, exposing her neck to his quest, and shivered when his tongue struck like a bolt of lightning. Her fingers plunged through his hair, guiding his head down toward her breasts. A long, satisfying groan floated away on a breeze the instant his warm lips closed over her stiff nipple.

"Oooooh, that feels wonderful." The breathy sound of her voice lingered in her ears.

Suddenly, Beau tensed. His lips stilled, and his ragged breathing sounded eerie in the night. He pulled her upright. "I can't," he said abrasively. "I won't!" He waded to the bank where he faced her with a ferocious glare. "Lady, what the hell are you doing to me?"

Courtney remained in the water as he dressed. Confused, she wondered if she'd been wrong in touching him as intimately as she had. She'd been so sure he enjoyed her caresses.

"Wash up. I'll walk you back to the adobe."

"But–"

"Dammit, wash up and don't say another word."

CHAPTER SEVENTEEN

Everything in the garden flourished again. It was amazing how Carlita's experienced hands nurtured the plants and herbs. Courtney still wasn't sure how Carlita used the greens, but she knew for certain that she was grateful the woman had forgiven her horrible mistake.

"Your garden is growing like wildflowers," she said to Carlita, who stooped over some plants.

"*Sí, señora.*" Carlita grimaced as she lifted her bulk. But her pain was forgotten the instant her eyes rested on Courtney. Concern traversed her face. "What is troubling you, *señora?*"

Courtney shrugged.

"You have not smiled in a week. You should be celebrating. The shearing went well and will be more profitable than last year."

"I'm happy for that, Carlita. It's only that..." She leaned against the adobe. "Mr. Hamilton has not been around since the shearing crew left. Do you know where he's gone?"

"No, *señora.*"

"I hope he knows I'm not paying him while he's away. He certainly hasn't earned the right to any wages."

"Do not be quick to judge Señor Hamilton."

"Why, Carlita? Where is he? *What* is he?"

"I do not understand, *señora.*"

"Never mind." Courtney pressed her fingers to her temples to clear her mind. "I'm going into town to buy the tools Manuelo needs for castrating the lambs."

"It is not safe, *señora.* Stover's men–"

"Don't worry about me, Carlita. I can take care of myself. I'm carrying Stanley's gun."

"A lot of good that will do when you do not know how to use it. Señor Hamilton said–"

"I don't care what he told you. After what happened at the cantina, maybe Stover's men will think twice before tangling with me."

"*Sí, señora. Vaya con Dios*, then."

Courtney looped the bay's reins over the post in front of the bank. As she stepped up to the boardwalk, the crisp sound of cracking whips and blaring horns captured her attention. Coming off the Santa Fe Trail, a caravan of wagons rolled down the hill and into town amidst huge balls of dust clouds. Shouts of *los Americanos* and *los carros* spread across the Plaza. Before long, everyone ran to join the throng of newcomers.

A smile remained on her lips as she entered the First National Bank. As usual, her presence garnered curious looks, but they didn't bother her anymore. She headed straight to Mr. Garcia's office.

"Señora Burgess, a pleasure to see you again."

Of course it was. She'd paid off her debt and was accruing a sizeable account. "Manuelo says the sheared wool will be ready for market this week. On Wednesday, a man representing a firm back East will be arriving to inspect our pile."

"That is good news, *señora*. Thanks to you, Rancho Ortega is restored once again to its prosperous days."

"Is it, Mr. Garcia? Perhaps you will enlighten me about those days. I've heard others refer to the ranch's past, but no one seems to be able to tell me much."

He smiled regrettably. "I am afraid I cannot be of help to you either."

"I didn't think so. People in this town know everything and nothing."

"*Sí*, Señora Burgess."

The banker whetted her curiosity more than ever now. There must be someone in town who could tell her the truth. She left the bank and headed across the Plaza to the cantina to buy a lemonade before riding back to the ranch. It was only mid-morning and already a steady stream of customers were coming and going from the place. Travelers from the newly arrived caravan descended on the cantina as if it were the only place in town to get food and a drink.

Inside, people were packed shoulder to shoulder. She squeezed through the crowd, wrinkling her nose from the awful odors clinging to the men. Maybe a lemonade wasn't worth the trouble after all. A heavyset farmer passed by, his overhanging belly pressing her into another man. She bumped into one body and another until she'd been pushed to the back of the room. Ignored like the runt in a large litter of puppies. Tired of the shoving, Courtney shoved back and yelped when she lost her balance. She fell helplessly into a man's lap, the beer in his hand spilling down the back of her shirt.

"Goddammit," the man cursed, slamming the mug down. "Why the hell don't you watch where you're going?"

Courtney's heart thumped faster at the familiar voice. She turned, her wide-eyed expression meeting his cold gray eyes straight on.

"Aw, hell," Beau swore again.

Dumbstruck, Courtney sat on his lap, paralyzed with shock.

He scowled. "Are you gonna sit there all day?"

Recuperating quickly, Courtney gathered her senses and sprang to her feet. She didn't know why her cheeks burned hotly, because she wasn't embarrassed in the least. Neither could she fathom why Beau would be so hopping mad. His nostrils flared like an angry bull's.

She was about to apologize for the impromptu meeting, but he spoke first.

"What are you doing in here?"

The apology fell by the wayside. "It's a public place, isn't it?"

Celina sauntered to Beau just then and made herself cozy and comfortable on his lap. The whore draped both arms around his neck. Courtney moved her scorching glare to the smug Mexican, purposely narrowing her eyes before tearing them away to splay piercing disapproval on Beau.

"So, you don't bed the same woman twice. Or is it only whores you sleep with more than once?"

"*Puta!*" Celina spat.

Whatever Celina said, Courtney figured it wasn't a word a lady would utter. "You two deserve each other, Mr. Hamilton," she sneered. "And don't bother coming back to the ranch. You're fired."

She fought her way to the front of the cantina. When someone grabbed her hand, she thought it was Beau and attempted to yank herself free. The man's voice beside her ear froze the breath in her lungs.

"Don't go fightin' me, girlie," Lonie gritted, trying in earnest to subdue her.

"Let go of me!" Courtney leaped for the swinging doors but was forced to halt her hurried flight or she would have flown headlong into two more of Stover's men blocking the entrance to the cantina. She spun around, alarmed to find Lonie advancing on her. With Steve and Jack at her back, she was trapped.

"You're a real pain in the ass," Lonie told her, chuckling. "A pain in the ass. Get it?" He laughed harder. All of a sudden, his features turned vicious and his lip curled like a snarling dog's. "Do you know how it feels to take a bullet in the—"

"It was your fault," Courtney charged.

His hand came up to strike her and she cringed. A tall figure loomed behind Lonie.

Thank God, Courtney thought with relief as Beau seized Lonie's wrist in a tight grip. The savage glint in Beau's eyes was startling, and she prayed he wouldn't kill Stover's man.

"Didn't your mother ever teach you it's not polite to hit a woman?"

"Stay out of this, Hamilton," Lonie warned.

Beau released the man's wrist with a flick. "You have a short memory," he said with a half-smile. The gesture construed anything but amusement. "You shouldn't anger this little lady or she might take a shot at your other side. You know, turn the other cheek."

Lonie's lips twisted maliciously. "I've had it with you, Hamilton. Why don't you step outside where we can fight it out, you and me? You win, I leave her be. I win, you stay out of her business."

Beau held a hand out toward the doors in open invitation. "After you," he said calmly.

"No!" Courtney grabbed Beau's arm with both hands. "Don't do this. Please."

Beau shook her off as if she were an annoying pest and kept on walking. She clutched at the fear knotted inside her stomach and fought desperately to quell the unpleasant tightening. If anything happened to Beau, she'd never forgive herself.

Rushing out of the cantina, Courtney stopped at one of the supporting posts under the portal. Anxiety stabbed her breast as she watched the two men face each other with malice in their eyes and their stance.

"What's your choice?" Beau asked, quickly noting the gunman wasn't as calm as he tried to show. He took stock of the man, from the erratic twitch in his jaw to his fingers crawling nervously over the butt of his gun.

"Indian style."

Beau nodded curtly with approval. Long ago he had argued with Paco over learning that particular style of fight. He hadn't seen much use for it. He was grateful now that Paco had insisted he learn.

He removed his dual six-guns and handed them to Courtney. Her eyes locked pleadingly with his, but Beau had already closed his heart to emotion.

"You stay out of this fight. Promise me."

"But—"

"Promise me!"

"I...promise," she replied, her voice trembling.

"Swear it, Courtney."

"Please, Beau. He did nothing–"

"Swear it!"

Her bottom lip quivered when she whispered, "I swear."

Beau turned his back to her before he did some fool thing like consoling her. She appeared vulnerable, frightened. And as much as he'd distanced himself, preparing his mind and body for the fight, his heart wasn't completely devoid of feeling. He wished she wasn't standing there watching.

Lonie untied his neckerchief and placed one end between his teeth. Beau did likewise with the other end.

"To the death," Lonie announced around the cloth.

Beau covered his astonishment. "What for?"

"Afraid to die, Hamilton?"

"No. I just hate killing a man for no good reason." Cold finality edged his words.

Lonie visibly tensed, and his hand trembled when he pulled a knife out of the sheath at his back.

"Say your prayers, Hamilton."

"Don't know any. Why don't you say them for me?"

Beau smoothly removed the Bowie knife from the leather scabbard strapped to his calf. He turned it in his hand, and the blade glistened under the reflecting sun. He kept his senses attuned to his surroundings. The fight wasn't merely between him and Lonie. Before it was over, Beau knew he'd be fending off Jack and Steve—and anyone else from Stover's unsavory bunch.

Sweat dripped down Beau's forehead, falling into his eyes and blurring his vision. His teeth ached from clenching them tightly on the kerchief. Determination kept him going.

Lonie wasn't spared either. Hampered by the same, he began stabbing erratically at the air. His distress made him careless. More than once he gave slack to the cloth separating them. Once again Beau saw his chance and lunged, nicking Lonie's upper arm. The man howled like a wounded dog, and the end of the kerchief fell from his mouth. He covered the gash with his hand, but that didn't stop the blood from oozing through his fingers.

Beau spit the kerchief out of his mouth. Breathing raggedly, he asked, "Had enough?"

Lonie glowered at him. "You stinkin' sheep lovin' bastard!"

"The fight's over, Lonie. We've had our fun. It's time to go home." Taking a grave risk, Beau turned his back to the man.

"Beau, look out!" Courtney shouted.

His reflexes like quicksilver, Beau spun around with his knife poised upward. Lonie launched himself, knocking Beau backward to the dirt. He twisted his upper body, narrowly missing the blade in Lonie's grasp. Grabbing a fistful of Lonie's shirt, Beau propelled him overhead and immediately scrambled to his feet. He realized he'd lost his knife. He didn't panic. Instead, he held onto his wits and sharp edge. Planting his feet firmly in the dirt, he bent his knees and anticipated Lonie's next move.

At the step of the planked walkway, Celina grabbed Lonie's arm. The gunman shook her off and lunged for Beau again, but tripped over his own feet.

Beau watched in stunned silence as the man fell onto his own knife.

Dead silence rippled through the Plaza. The crowd that had gathered watched in shock while Lonie's life's blood spread out from under him and bubbled over the dirt. He was gurgling now, a sure indication his last breath wasn't far away.

Paralyzed with horror, Courtney focused on Beau. He seemed unaffected, emotionless, like he'd been when he killed those two men who had abducted her. She shivered from his frigid expression and understood now—it was his gunman's façade she was seeing.

Beau's knife lay at her feet. When she bent to pick it up, she noticed the sheriff push through the crowd with Jared Stover on his heels.

The sheriff hastily surveyed the scene. "What happened here, Hamilton?"

"Isn't it obvious, Sheriff?" Stover interjected, then accused, "He killed one of my employees."

"Beau?" the sheriff questioned.

"Self defense," Beau replied.

"Like hell it was," Jack disagreed. "Me and Steve saw the whole thing. Hamilton challenged Lonie. Didn't give him no chance. Came at him like a mad man."

When Courtney stepped forward to speak up, Celina caught her arm. "Do not interfere."

"But it's a lie."

"Look around you, *señora*."

Reluctantly, Courtney did. The crowd was already dispersing, acting as if they'd watched a sideshow in a circus. There wasn't one person willing to challenge Stover or his men. But these people had seen what really happened, same as she had. Beau was innocent. What was wrong with everyone in this town?

"*El gringo* Stover is an evil man. Do not say a word or you will suffer the consequences," Celina warned.

Courtney stood by helplessly as the sheriff cuffed Beau's wrists behind his back and escorted him to the jail.

"Dear God," she whispered desolately.

"Not even He can help Señor Hamilton now," Celina said quietly.

Rebel Heart

CHAPTER EIGHTEEN

"I'm pressing charges," Stover said irately.

Sheriff Jeff Taylor shook his head sagely. "I wouldn't advise it. Lonie was your hired gun. No judge will take his death seriously. Besides, Lonie had badgered the Burgess woman once before. Hamilton merely protected her."

Stover shoved his face close to Jeff's. "Who are *you* protecting? An ex-gunfighter? Why, Jeff? Hamilton will never amount to anything, not like you could." He stepped back, gaining his composure. "Need I remind you who helped you become a respectable lawman?"

Jeff gnashed his back teeth with self-disgust. "No, dammit. But I can't lock up an innocent man."

"You know, Jeff, the governor won't be happy if he learns his sheriff used to ride with the same unsavory bunch as Hamilton once did. Do you think you'll get the same respect when Santa Feans hear their sheriff, the very man who was hired to protect them, is a hired gun?"

"*Was*," Jeff corrected tightly.

"Once a hired gun..." Stover's conniving smile sickened Jeff. "Will you be holding Hamilton on murder charges?"

"I'll hold him a few days until things die down."

Stover scowled. "Open the cell door."

Jeff hesitated. When Stover shot him a threatening look, Jeff compressed his lips into a grim line and snatched up the keys from his desk. Beau sat on a cot, his back propped against the adobe wall and his foot braced on the wood frame. Jeff threw him an apologetic look before he swung the iron door open and admitted Stover's men.

Stover yanked the keys out of his hand and locked Steve and Jack in with Beau. "Go about your business, Jeff."

Jeff wished he could defy the man. Instead, he left his office, regret hanging heavy in his chest. Outside he saw the Burgess woman coming toward him. The determined set of her mouth and her hurried footfalls pressed more guilt into

123

his heart. He closed the door and met her at the bottom of the steps.

"Sheriff, may I see him?"

She held Beau's weapons to her chest. Jeff glanced capriciously at them. "Mr. Hamilton isn't allowed to have visitors."

A loud grunt came from inside the jail. Then another. And one more. The thick adobe walls failed to muffle what Jeff knew was going on in the cell.

The woman's fearful gaze met his, and Jeff forced his guilt into hiding. "Please, Mrs. Burgess. Not now." He placed a hand at her elbow and steered her away from the building. "Beau won't hang. But you can't interfere. For his sake, stay away from town for a few days."

The door behind them opened. Jack stepped out first, releasing and tightening his fist. Steve walked out next, rubbing his knuckles. At last, Jared Stover emerged lighting a cigar, self-assured and pleased with himself.

"What have they done to him?"

"For God's sake, Mrs. Burgess. Go back to Rancho Ortega and forget what you saw here today."

"Sheriff!" Stover called. "I expect your full cooperation in the ruthless murder of Lonie Smith."

Jeff tensed. He loathed the man, but his hands were tied. He was as much a prisoner to Stover as Beau was now. Jeff gave the Burgess woman a contrite glance before heading back into his office.

Courtney would have chased after the sheriff if it hadn't been for Stover's men guarding the jailhouse door. Jared Stover approached. The man made her stomach crawl with disgust, yet she refused to cower before him like the meek women he undoubtedly preferred.

"Have you given thought to selling your ranch, Mrs. Burgess?"

"No," she answered tersely.

"You should. I might consider dropping the charges against Hamilton."

"You'll ask the sheriff to free him if I sell to you?"

Stover gave a slight nod.

Courtney stiffened her spine as she fought desperately not to pull one of Beau's Colts from its tooled holster and shoot the despicable man clean through his black heart. "Blackmail is a crime, Mr. Stover."

His features glazed over with disbelief. After a moment, he tossed the cigar to the dirt, his eyes meeting hers with as much warmth as an icicle. "You won't be so smug when your lover's neck is stretched by a hangman's noose."

"Don't threaten me, Mr. Stover. If I have to, I'll hire the best lawyer in the country to defend Beau."

A cold, empty laugh rumbled up his chest and settled like gunmetal in his eyes. "You couldn't afford to."

"Don't underestimate what I am capable of doing." God help her, she'd crawl back to her father on hands and knees if she had to.

Jeff set the breakfast tray on the cot and looked down at Beau's prone form. "Hope you're hungry. There's enough here to feed a small army."

Beau winced and held his breath as he struggled to sit. Leaning back against the cool wall, he gingerly held his stomach and ribs.

"Sure you don't want me to fetch the doc?" Jeff asked for the tenth time since Stover's men left the day before. "You could have broken bones."

Beau shook his head. "I've had enough broken bones in the past to know there aren't any broken now. Stover went easy on me. It was a warning." He grimaced. Breathing hurt like hell.

"He's pressing murder charges."

"Let him. Lonie fell on his own knife. There were too many witnesses."

"None will come forward, you know that."

"Maybe not now. Give it time to cool. Most folks in town hate Stover. Someone with a grudge will eventually speak up." Beau rested his head back and closed his eyes. "It was set up."

Jeff moved the tray aside and joined Beau on the cot. "How do you know?"

"Stover's men knew I'd take the bait if they bothered the Burgess woman. I didn't realize it at the time, but Celina had something to do with Lonie taking the fall. She tried to help him up after I threw him. I can't figure out why, but she tripped him."

"If that's what you believe, I'll question her."

"You gotta do something for me, Jeff. Wire Drake. The message should read, 'Tell Mother I'm sorry.'"

Jeff furrowed his brow as if Beau had lost his mind. "But your mother—"

"Do it, Jeff. And make sure Stover's men don't get wind of it." A sharp, cutting pain ripped through Beau's gut, trapping his breath in his throat.

Jeff rose with a sigh. At the door to the cell, he paused. "By the way, the widow Burgess came to see you after I brought you in. I told her to stay away for a few days. It's none of my business, Beau, but what does this woman mean to you?"

"Not a damn thing."

Courtney huffed in frustration. The sheriff closed the door behind him and practically pushed her down the steps to the jailhouse. He combed back his light brown hair and replaced his hat, fussing with its position and tugging at the brim. He was stalling, and Courtney was growing terribly impatient.

"Why can't I see him?" she asked again. "I've stayed away for three days."

Three long, miserable, agonizing days. She pressed Beau's weapons to her breasts, as if it might bring her spiritually closer to him. For now, it was all she had.

"I can't allow anyone in to see him."

She eyed the sheriff suspiciously. "He's still in there, isn't he?"

"Yes, ma'am."

It was her right to visit Beau. No one, not even Sheriff Taylor, would keep her away. She attempted to walk around him, but he agilely stepped in front of her to block her path. Furious, Courtney demanded, "Since when can't a prisoner have visitors?"

The jailhouse door opened then, and Courtney looked around the sheriff's arm. Jack and Steve exited the building, clenching and unclenching their fists, as they'd done three days ago.

"We'll be back, Sheriff," Jack said, smiling like a man who had won top prize in a boxing contest. The men sauntered off toward the cantina.

Courtney snapped her attention to the sheriff, but he was glaring at Stover's men. She didn't know what was going on, but she wouldn't leave until she got some answers. "I want to see Beau now, Sheriff."

"Please, Mrs. Burgess. Stay out of this. Let me handle it and I'll have Beau out by the end of the week."

Courtney stubbornly stood her ground.

After several uncomfortable minutes passed, he relented. "All right, but I have to warn you. Beau's had a bit of trouble."

Not liking the sound of his warning, Courtney prepared for the worse. With her nerves flittering wildly, she entered the sheriff's office. Halfway to the jail cell, she halted in shock.

Beau lay on his back, one knee bent and his right arm slung across his stomach. He moaned intermittently, breathing as if it were a chore. Blood trickled down his jaw from a nasty crack on his bottom lip. His cheek was red and swollen. When he turned his head, Courtney couldn't stop herself from gasping aloud.

Horrified by the sight of his swollen eyelids, she choked back a sob and whirled on the sheriff. "I demand to know what is going on here." All he gave her was an apologetic frown. "Answer me!"

Before he could, Beau's gruff words reached out through the cell bars. "Go away," he pronounced slowly, carefully. "I...don't...want...you...here." He grimaced, and his features paled frightfully.

"I want to help you, Beau."

"I don't need...your help."

Clearly he was in excruciating pain. Helpless, she could do nothing for him. How she wanted to comfort him in her arms. Her heart was hurting as strongly as Beau was suffering physically. "But I can—"

"Stay the hell out...of my life." He turned his face back to the wall.

Courtney persisted. "If for no other reason, let me help you because you're my employee."

Without looking at her he said, "You fired me."

Aghast, Courtney recalled how she'd fired him. "I was angry at the time. I didn't mean what I said."

"I'm through with...your stinking sheep ranch. Give my...severance pay to Jeff."

She choked back the tears perched on the rim of her eyes. He didn't mean that. He couldn't.

"Ma'am?" she heard the sheriff say.

Moving like the wooden figures on the old German clock in her father's study, Courtney handed Beau's weapons to Sheriff Taylor and left the office in stunned silence.

Beau eased his head around. Jeff set his gun belt and knife on the desk and faced him, clearly annoyed.

"A little rough on the woman, weren't you?"

He'd been more than rough, and it bit painfully into his heart to treat Courtney with so much enmity. She didn't deserve his rudeness, but she didn't deserve the alternative either.

"When are you going to give in to Stover?" Jeff asked.

"Do you know what he's asking me to do?"

Jeff nodded grimly.

"I won't sweet talk or..." He swallowed the dryness in his mouth and wiped away the blood congealing on his lips. "I won't coerce Courtney into selling to him."

"Because of the woman, or because of Manuelo's family?"

"Because of my conscience."

Beau sat ever so carefully, his stomach on fire. The only thing that probably saved him from serious internal injury from the vicious punches was his hard muscles. Despite all the bullet and knife wounds he'd suffered over the years, his physical condition was superb.

"How much more are you going to take? I've never known you to be a martyr."

"Stover won't kill me in jail. It would raise too many suspicions." Beau couldn't even grit his teeth to stave off the pain. Speaking with minimal movement to his facial muscles, he continued. "He'll drop the charges eventually. Any judge will question Stover's integrity. He's using me to persuade Courtney to give up the ranch."

"Dammit, Beau." Jeff rubbed the back of his neck, a nervous habit he'd had for as long as Beau had known him. "It's not right what Stover is doing to you. It's damn hard to stand by and watch you take this needless abuse. I'm getting you outta here. The governor's in today. I'm going over to talk to him."

"At what cost, *amigo*?"

"My badge, if it has to be."

"No, don't. Prove my innocence with lack of evidence. Find someone who will back up my story." Beau held his breath for a moment until the jabbing between his ribs decreased. "Stover won't carry through his threat to expose your past. He needs you right where you are."

CHAPTER NINETEEN

Bleary-eyed and listless from another sleepless night, Courtney moved like the figures on a mechanical bank as she pitched the hay in the barn. She hadn't been able to close her eyes without the image of Beau's battered face haunting the darkness. His bruised and cracked flesh clearly had been painful. He was suffering because of her, and that above all else had kept the tears flowing throughout the long night.

If he hadn't come to her rescue... If she hadn't left Stanley's gun in the saddlebags... The 'ifs' didn't count anymore, didn't seem to matter now that Beau wanted nothing more to do with her.

She stuck the pitchfork into the ground and leaned on the top of the handle. Resting her cheek on her hand, she forced back the threat of new tears. Every time she recalled the way Beau had told her to stay out of his life, the slit in her heart spread a little wider. All through the night she tried to figure out how she could hurt so badly for a man with whom she had nothing in common. A man who could be as rude as a drunk at a tea social. A man who didn't seem to know the meaning of compassion.

A man who had stolen her heart in spite of his shortcomings.

Against her proper upbringing, she had fallen in love with a man whose life represented everything she was raised to believe was wrong. Yet she loved Beau Hamilton. Nothing and no one would ever take that away from her heart.

Not even Beau himself. Evidently he was incapable of loving her back. And now that he had severed their short, turbulent relationship, she didn't know what to do or how to fill the void he'd left in her soul.

The creaking of door hinges snapped Courtney out of her unhappy reverie. She scanned the barn, but saw no one. "Manuelo, is that you?"

She leaned the pitchfork against the wall and stepped out of the stall. Halfway to the barn door someone snagged her from behind and threw her to the ground. There was no warning, no chance to scream. Rising above her like a bad dream, Marcos glared down. Courtney dragged in deep breaths in a valiant attempt to calm the erratic beating of her heart. She frowned at Manuelo's son, annoyed yet apprehensive about being alone with him. When she moved to stand, he placed a heavy work boot to her chest, driving her back brutally. Terror courted her nerves. Marcos hedged six feet, his still growing body lanky, but strong. Courtney feared he would rip her apart with his unjustified anger.

"Anglo whore," he spat, startling her. "You are not so brave now that your bastard lover is in jail."

He raised his arm to strike her. Out of some innate reaction, Courtney cringed. A spider web of fear prickled across her shoulders, and she cringed again when he laughed with spite and venom.

"Ah, so you are afraid. That is good. I can snap your whore neck with one hand. I can hurt you real bad."

"I have no doubt you could, Marcos. But I don't understand why you would want to." There was a slight tremble in her voice. He might smell instant victory if she showed fear and left her vulnerability exposed. So she tamped down the anxiety shackling her body and endeavored to reason calmly. "I've treated your family fair. They've had no complaints."

"You have no knowledge of what has been done to my family," he sneered.

"Marcos, I'm sorry your family has suffered. Surely you can't blame me—"

"*Cállate!*" He reached under her head, twisting her braid around his fist and yanked her to her feet.

Indignant, Courtney cried out, "Marcos, let me go at once!"

"No, *señora*. You are a whore, and I will treat you no better than a whore deserves." He tore her shirt open, popping buttons and scattering them to the hay. Tightening his grip on her braid, he jerked her head back viciously.

"Marcos, no!" Courtney howled. The sting on her scalp brought instant tears to her eyes. She grabbed a solid hold of his wrist with both her hands to prevent him from ripping her hair out of her head. Fighting with all her strength, she prayed he would come to his senses. All of a sudden, she fell backward. For whatever reason, he released her. She scrambled away. Breathing raggedly, she dared not move from the prickly hay and gawked at the gleaming knife blade pressed against Marcos' throat. She had never been more relieved to see Beau.

"Manuelo won't be pleased with your shameful behavior," Beau said in Spanish while he held his knife steady at the fool boy's neck. Marcos was a hothead, and there was no telling if the kid would pull the knife he kept hidden in his boot.

Beau glanced at Courtney, regretting doing so the moment he saw the state of her dress and the fettered fear in her eyes. She held the edges of her shirt together. Her cheeks were flushed bright red, and her hair was in disarray. His gut constricted sickeningly. Two minutes more and he would have been too late. He didn't dare think about what he would have done if Marcos had succeeded in raping her.

"Apologize," he told Marcos, his voice gritty and uncompromising.

"I will not apologize to the bitch. She deserves everything bad. It is because of her that my family continues to suffer in disgrace."

"It's because of *you*," Beau corrected harshly. "No one has disgraced your family more than you. I would have disowned you if you were my son. Manuelo was too soft-hearted and forgave you. And this is how you show your gratitude?"

"She is a whore!"

Beau twisted the boy's neck, pressing the blade's edge deeper into his dark skin. Just one swallow and the sharp Bowie would slice easily through his flesh. "Dammit, Marcos, apologize. Don't force me to hurt you."

With caution, Beau loosened his hold on the boy. He removed the knife, but held onto the back of Marcos' neck, forcing him to face Courtney. Beau reverted to English.

"Marcos has something to say to you. Isn't that right, Marcos?" He squeezed the boy's neck.

"*Sí*," Marcos bit off. "I am sorry."

Beau dug his fingers in cruelly. "Say it like you mean it."

Begrudgingly, Marcos complied. "I am sorry, Señora Burgess."

Beau released him, but maintained a solid grip on the knife for insurance. "Your father needs help in the north range. Get out there or I swear I'll whip the crap out of you for your stupidity."

Marcos hurried out of the barn without giving Courtney the scathing look Beau was certain he wanted to. With a gasp, Beau clutched his ribs and doubled over. His gnarled curse died on his lips as he worked to take deep, but gentle breaths.

Courtney rushed to his side and helped him lower to the bale of hay. God he wished she hadn't touched him. As much pain as he was in, his body reacted like a flash fire. She must have sensed it, for she suddenly put a few feet between them.

"My God, you should be in bed."

"Is that an offer?" he quipped with great effort.

She almost smiled. "You don't give up, do you?"

"I've been incarcerated. Have a heart."

She glanced away for a brief moment. "How did you get out?"

"Lack of evidence."

"You should have gone straight to the doctor."

Without thinking, Beau reached for her hand and pulled her down to kneel between his spread knees. Confusion ruffled her features. He saw she was unsure of his action. Hell, he wasn't sure himself. But there was one thing he knew for certain.

"I had to see you first."

Her mouth opened in surprise. She undoubtedly thought he had changed his mind and had come back to work. He hated to disappoint her.

"I'm leaving Santa Fe."

Her crestfallen features were too much to bear. He smoothed back the stray hairs and hooked them behind her ear. Unexpectedly, she leaned her soft, warm cheek into his palm and rested her hands on his thighs. Beau groaned inwardly, damning himself for returning to the ranch. Why didn't he ride out of Santa Fe straight from the jail?

"I don't know how long I'll be away. Don't worry about Stover bothering you any time soon. When Jeff let me out, I made sure plenty of the citizens in town saw me. They know Jeff wouldn't have done this. Stover won't risk making a wrong move now."

"Will you be back?"

"I've got a lot of thinking to do." Tears welled in her eyes, and he prayed she wouldn't cry. "I've spoken with Manuelo. You did good with your sale of wool. You'll have enough money to get you through a long winter and well into next summer. Listen to Manuelo. He cares for this ranch like it was his own."

She raised her hand to his face, but hesitation kept it poised in mid-air when he tensed and sucked in his breath. When she gently skimmed the distended scar on his right cheek with a fingertip, he released his breath with a soft sigh. Her touch comforted more than it hurt. Despite his rejection back at the jailhouse, she seemed pleased to see him. He was grateful she didn't turn her back on him, although she had every right to.

She rose higher on her knees and brushed her lips across his, careful not to disturb his healing mouth. "Your job will be waiting here for you," she whispered.

Beau tried to figure out which caused him to ache more—the physical injuries from the beatings or the heavy throbbing of his heart against his sore ribs. Part of him was disappointed. He'd hoped she would beg him to stay. It was ridiculous, of course. He wouldn't have given in. Yet a small part of him yearned to hear her say she didn't want him to leave, that she needed him here with her. That there was a slim chance she cared for him.

You're getting too damn soft, Hamilton. Jeff might believe he was still the hardened outlaw, but only Beau knew to what extent his heart had mellowed. It was all this woman's doing. Until she'd come into his life, he hadn't ever allowed his heart the freedom to care for a woman. But he cared for Courtney, cared more than he should.

Holding her slender hand in his, he rubbed his thumb over her knuckles. "I best get on my way. I want to cover a lot of ground before nightfall."

"Can't you postpone your plans until you're healed?"

"No, I have to leave now." He adjusted the Stetson on his head and slowly got to his feet. "Stay out of trouble. And for God's sake, let Manuelo and his boys handle the firearms if there should be trouble."

Three weeks. Three incredibly long, lonely weeks since Beau rode away from Rancho Ortega. Courtney kept busy, but there wasn't anything she could do to stop her mind from dwelling on him. He'd burrowed into her heart for good, and missing him had thrown her into a melancholy mood.

She pushed up in bed, fluffing the pillows behind her, and settled back into them. It was happening again, as it had every morning for the past two weeks. Her stomach churned, but it usually passed within a half hour. Until she walked into the kitchen and smelled the coffee Carlita left heating on the stove. For some reason, the smell of it made her feel like retching.

Laying her palm on her flat stomach, Courtney sighed with bittersweet sadness.

She didn't have to seek out a fortuneteller to predict what was in her future. If her calculations were correct, come February, very near her father's birthday, she was going to have a baby.

Of all the rotten luck. Only one time with a man, and she managed to conceive. Marriage and a family had been her dream once. But she was a widow now and in love with a man who had lived by the gun and no other man's rules most of his life. This was hardly the future she'd envisioned. The only consolation was there'd be no reason for anyone to believe it wasn't Stanley's baby.

She thought about the tiny life growing inside of her and smiled. Beau's baby. Even though he had no idea he was going to be a father, she was glad the baby was his. She might never see him again, but she'd preserve his memory with this baby.

"And then there's my father." Leif Danning wouldn't be overjoyed to hear he would be a grandfather. Believing the baby was Stanley's, he'd be furious. One thing was for certain. He'd be livid if he discovered the identity of the real father. She should write to him, but there was one problem. She hadn't yet informed him about Stanley's untimely death. Where did she begin to explain what had happened in her life since then?

Courtney swung her legs over the edge of the bed and got up slowly. The nausea subsided by the time she dressed in a pair of Levis and her chambray shirt. After braiding her hair, she plucked her hat from a nail on the wall and left the adobe.

The sky was unbelievably blue. Thankfully, the slight breeze kept the heat at bay. She entered the barn as Manuelo rode in from the opposite door. He dismounted, and his glum expression caused a flitter of apprehension in her stomach. Had he received word from Beau? Maybe Beau was in danger. Or...dead.

"*Señora*, we have lost two more sheep," Manuelo reported.

Thank God it wasn't Beau. She breathed a sigh of relief and fixed dear, sweet Manuelo with a look of understanding. They both knew Stover was warming up for battle. The cattle rancher had been quiet after Beau's release from jail, just as Beau had predicted. But Courtney knew it would be a matter of time before the man turned restless and elected to kill her sheep again.

"Please take care of them. I'm riding into town to talk to Sheriff Taylor."

Alarm for her safety flared in his eyes. "No, *señora*. You must not go."

"Don't worry about me, Manuelo." Stover was a cold-hearted man, but even he wouldn't be brazen enough to harm her in broad daylight. At least she hoped he wouldn't.

"*Por favor*, take Marcos with you."

"No!" Biting down on her bottom lip for speaking rashly, Courtney fought to calm the queasiness troubling her stomach once again. She had stayed clear of Marcos since the day he'd attacked her. She had also taken to locking her doors when she was alone in the adobe. "I don't need an escort, Manuelo. Really, I'll be fine."

CHAPTER TWENTY

"Sheriff, you can't turn your back on this." What would it take to make the man listen to reason, Courtney wondered? "I know Jared Stover is behind killing my sheep. He says they strayed onto his land. But Manuelo told me that sheep stay together. It takes a good amount of coaxing to get them to move, especially without the aid of dogs."

"Without solid evidence I can't do a damn thing."

"Can't? Or won't? Just like you didn't stop Stover's men from hurting Beau."

His shoulders sagged. After a moment, he relented. "All right, I'll investigate. If what you say is true, will you be pressing charges?"

"Damn right I will, Sheriff." She had worked up full steam long before she stepped into the sheriff's office. And now she was so hot, she was afraid she might explode into a tirade. Thankfully, with the sheriff's promise to check out her claim, she cooled down a bit. At the door she said firmly, "Keep me informed."

Outside, Courtney paused to gain her unraveled composure. The secrecy in this town was baffling. How could an entire town be afraid to speak out against one man's wrongdoings? What happened to Beau never would have happened in New York.

Across the street, Celina moved quickly toward the cantina. That damn whore knew something about Stover. About Beau, too. Courtney was sure of it. She hurried across the large Plaza with long, determined strides. When she entered the cantina, she encountered rude stares and hushed whispers. Carlita had told her about the rumors buzzing about town. Speculation about her relationship with Beau had spread like a bad disease. Apparently malicious words advanced faster than a military front line during wartime. Courtney refused to allow the ignorance of gossipers to undermine her right as a citizen. To hell with what these people believed.

Celina was easy to locate in her blood red skirt and off the shoulder sunflower yellow peasant blouse. Making her way to the bar, Courtney set her sight on the Mexican. Celina regarded her suspiciously.

"I'd like a few words with you." She spoke with confidence.

Celina's dark eyes glittered brightly. "Beau left town if that's what you came to ask."

"No, it isn't." Courtney cast a furtive glance about the room. "Is there another place where we can speak privately?"

Celina balked.

"Please," Courtney implored. She understood the woman's hesitation. They hadn't been friendly toward each other from the moment they'd met. Celina undoubtedly felt threatened that Courtney might lure Beau away from her. Admittedly, Courtney felt the same, maybe even jealous, even though Beau wasn't hers to defend. Compared to her, Celina was petite, with beautiful olive skin and shiny black hair. It was easy to see how she could attract a man like Beau.

At last, Celina nodded. Courtney followed her through buffalo hide curtains into the cantina's liquor storeroom. The only light available seeped in from the cantina's many lamps.

"I need to know why Sheriff Taylor doesn't do anything about Jared Stover's harmful shenanigans?"

Celina's brow lifted in surprise. "Why ask me?"

"I believe you know a great deal about what goes on in this town. You're in the perfect position to..."—how did she say this without affronting the woman?—"...to obtain information."

Celina smiled. "You came to me for this information yet you turn your nose up at me because I pleasure men with my body?"

"Our lives are very different, Celina. Perhaps I shouldn't have been quick to judge, but at this moment I am asking for your help – one woman to another."

"All right, *señora*. I will help if I can. I do not know why the sheriff does not stop Señor Stover. Is that all you need?"

"There's more. I may be forced into fighting for my ranch. But there is something about Rancho Ortega that isn't right. I can't find anyone who will tell me the truth."

"I cannot either, *señora*."

Courtney scrutinized Celina's shadowed features for a clue. "Who can then?"

"Señor Hamilton is the only person who can help you."

Courtney leaned back against the frame of the open door to the kitchen. It seemed ages ago that she'd been in the same position, wearing the same shift and gazing at the beautiful Sangres beneath the glowing red, setting sun. She recalled how Beau had appeared out of the darkness, almost frightening her to death. God how she missed him. Loved him.

In the distance, lightning streaked the sky and thunder rolled. Summer storms in Santa Fe were awe-inspiring, exquisite light shows in an otherwise dark sky. She wouldn't have dreamed that beauty could be found in a storm. Really, she hadn't ever given it a moment's thought until she'd come to this unusual, but addictive town.

Turning back into the house, Courtney shook with a powerful gasp. Marcos stood in the middle of the room, his eyes as black as midnight. Dear God, this couldn't be happening again.

She was about to run out of the adobe when she noticed Carlita amble through the door from the main room. The woman set a glass jar and a pile of folded garments on the table. "Go on back to the house, *mijo.* I would like to speak to Señora Burgess alone."

Marcos slid his surly look away from Courtney. His expression softened when he spoke to his mother. "I will wait on the front porch."

Carlita smiled fondly as she watched her son leave. "He is a good boy."

A violent shudder passed through Courtney at the thought about what that 'good boy' had almost done to her. Turning the conversation away from Marcos, she gestured to the things on the table. "What have you brought?"

Carlita's smile turned motherly. "I do not wish to offend you, *señora,* but I have noticed a change in you. Please do not think I am meddling. I am simply concerned."

"About what?"

"Your health."

"I'm fine, really. You needn't worry about me. But what about those?" Courtney nodded at the jar and clothing.

Carlita set her hand on the pile. "I wore these when I carried my sons."

Everything in Courtney's body froze.

"They will need to be altered, of course, but I will help you with that." Carlita's smile faded. "Have I upset you?"

Courtney shook her head. She wasn't upset, just amazed that Carlita figured out she was pregnant.

"It is important now that you take care of yourself." The woman rested her arm around Courtney's shoulders. "Are you happy?"

"For the new life inside of me? Yes, I am."

"But you wish the baby's father was here."

Courtney wished for Beau's return often enough, though it wouldn't matter if he did come back to Rancho Ortega. He never would share her joy over their baby. Marriage and family were two things a man like Beau Hamilton avoided.

"Do not fret, *señora*. The baby's father will return to you."

Astounded, Courtney narrowed her eyes at the woman.

"You cannot hide what is written in your eyes."

"Carlita," Courtney said with a nervous laugh. "This baby's father cannot return. He's dead."

"If you wish," the woman said in a placating tone.

"I don't wish. I mean..." She compressed her lips to stop their quivering. Incredibly, tears welled like huge ocean swells. "Stanley is dead."

"You may keep the truth from everyone else, but do not deny it to yourself."

She didn't deny it. Beau was the father, but dwelling on it only set her up for a life of misery. Holding her worries in wouldn't do either. Maybe it was time she spoke with someone about her situation. "I don't know what to do, Carlita. Beau is gone, and I may never see him again. If he does come back, I'm not sure he would be a good candidate to become a father."

Carlita chuckled. "He is not running for political office. Tell me what man stands on a soapbox and boasts of his qualifications for becoming a father."

Courtney grinned. Carlita was right, of course. "I must ask you something about Beau's past." That same wary look Courtney had seen in Celina's eyes slipped into Carlita's. She was afraid the woman wouldn't help relieve her curiosity either.

"I will try to answer."

"How was Beau cleared of murder? I mean, I know he was saved by an influential friend in Mexico."

"Sí, Paco. He hired the best lawyers money could buy." A twinkle shone in Carlita's brown eyes. "And the judge was Paco's brother."

"I suppose it's helpful to have friends in high places." It relieved Courtney to know Beau was no longer a wanted man. Explaining it to their child would have been difficult. "I spoke to Celina last week, but she refused to answer my questions about the ranch. She said only Beau can relieve my curiosity."

"That is correct."

"Then you will not tell me either?"

"*Lo siento, señora.*"

Carlita carried the clay jar to the cupboard. Courtney wouldn't pressure her into talking about the secret. For now, she would let the subject rest.

Carlita tapped the jar lid with her blunt, hard-worked fingers. "I have made a special mixture to help ease the morning sickness. Stir a spoonful into hot water and drink it down first thing upon waking in the morning."

"What concoction have you blended?"

"If I told you, you would not drink it."

Carlita couldn't stop her laughter at Courtney's wry expression.

The low flame flickered softly over the room, giving off enough light for Beau to see the angelic face and the halo of pale blonde hair spraying outward over the pillowcase. Courtney slept on her side, one arm draped over her hips and the other resting near her head. She was so damn beautiful.

He'd come in through the back door, surprised to find it unlocked and annoyed as hell that she'd been that careless. But one glance was all it took for his annoyance to abate. The urge to protect her, to envelop her in his arms and keep her safe from men like Stover and foolish boys like Marcos grew stronger.

As he gazed down at her from beside the bed, he was reminded of the loneliness that had engulfed him while he'd been away. At times it had been unbearable; twice he'd almost turned around and headed back to Santa Fe. Then he'd think about what he would do once he was back. That was when all his fears crashed around him and the main reason for the other vow he had made—to avoid commitment at all cost— brought him back to his senses.

Beau reached out to touch her hair. He had dreamed of doing so too many times, but he was afraid he'd awaken her. He couldn't, not now when his muscles hurt from a month in the saddle. Drawing his hand away, he smiled down at Courtney. No matter how badly he ached for her, he was fatigued and in desperate need of sleep. Besides, his head throbbed from all the indecision rambling around inside. It was either Courtney or avoid commitment. If he thought on it any longer, he'd drive himself insane.

Lifting the crisscrossing bandoleers over his head, he quietly placed them on the floor in the corner of the room. His gun belt followed, then the Bowie knife and his moccasins. He paused beside the bed again, drinking in the breathtaking sight of the woman who haunted his soul. If he wasn't careful, Courtney might be the only woman to make him break his vow.

Mindful of his movements, Beau slipped into bed and carefully scooted behind her. He wondered briefly if lying this close wouldn't tempt his passion into forgetting how tired he felt. He rested his arm around the curve of her waist anyway. She moaned in her sleep. He held his breath, praying she wouldn't open her eyes. Instead, she wiggled her bottom into his contour. Heat flared like wildfire racing across the desert. He nearly lost the will to leave her be.

Practicing his long-standing control, he started to count. At thirty he finally began to relax.

At fifty he buried his face into the clean, honeysuckle scent of her hair.

At sixty he closed his eyes. In less than a heartbeat, he was asleep.

CHAPTER TWENTY-ONE

Courtney strode toward the barn in unusually high spirits. She attributed it to the first night of restful sleep she'd had in months. Her body felt invigorated and tingled in a strange way. It was peculiar, really. The feeling lingered and put a much needed smile on her face. Today, she wasn't going to let anything trample her good mood.

As she approached the barn doors, she ran over a list in her head of all the chores she hoped to accomplish before the heat sapped her energy. First she would bathe the horses. It hadn't been done since she'd arrived at Rancho Ortega. Second, she'd clean out the storage shed in the barn to make room for the new supplies Manuelo said were needed for repairs around the ranch. After that she'd...

Courtney grounded to a halt when she heard a deep grunting sound coming from inside the barn. It was an exerted grunt followed by a thud, like something heavy was dropped. A chill embraced her in its icy cape and raised the hackles on her neck. She feared it was Marcos stacking the bales of hay Manuelo brought back from town yesterday. Courtney backed up and was about to return to the adobe when a disgruntled curse caused her heart to race. That wasn't Marcos. She knew that inhospitable tone, had heard it too often not to recognize it.

Apprehension wrapped her in its uncertain hold, and suddenly she couldn't seem to place one foot in front of the other without her knees trembling. Somehow she made it to the half opened doors and hesitated a second before stepping quietly into the barn. Pulsing blood pounded heavily in her ears. Her palms dampened, and her heart thudded against her ribs. Then she heard it again, a grunt that lifted her hope and spirits higher. Only one man belonged to that sound.

Beau tossed another bale, maneuvering it to stack evenly with the others. He removed his hat, wiped his sweaty forehead with his shirt sleeve, and straightened for a moment, giving in to his mind's wandering.

It had been damned hard to walk away from Courtney this morning. She'd looked too inviting, like an angel, innocent, loving. Damned tempting. They'd remained in the same position all night, her curvy behind molded into him, his arm around her waist. He couldn't recall the last time he'd had such a restful night's sleep. He replaced his hat and grinned. Hell, he'd softened, all right. Maybe it wasn't only his heart that was mellowing. Maybe his past had finally released its stronghold.

He grabbed another bale, turned and...froze. His stricken gaze locked on Courtney, studying, searching, lapping up every beautiful inch. In her Levis and blue shirt, she appeared a ray of sunshine. He couldn't stop staring. Her expression baffled him though. He couldn't tell if she was happy to see him, or if she stewed over his long absence. The building ache in his arms reminded him about the hay he held, and he pitched it onto the others.

"When did you return?"

Beau noticed a lilt in her voice he'd never heard before. "Last night."

"Did you get all your thinking done?"

He grinned. "My brain hurts from it all."

Her smile blossomed. "What have you decided?"

"That I need to do more thinking."

It was good to see her smile. "Your face is healing nicely."

They fell silent and regarded each other like long lost friends. Beau removed his hat again and tossed it onto the bale of hay beside his leg.

"Any trouble while I was gone?" He pulled at the fingers of his gloves and dropped them to the same bale of hay next to the hat.

Courtney shook her head. Awed by the roguish sight of him, she couldn't speak. She tried not to stare; it wasn't polite. But her desire for Beau was far stronger than her will for propriety, and she drank in what she'd missed these past weeks. His unbuttoned work shirt exposed his chest and stomach. His flesh glistened with sweat. When he raised his arm to swipe his sleeve across his forehead, she gawked at the way the fabric caressed his corded muscles.

Moaning to herself, Courtney prayed she didn't appear as lustful as she felt. She was afraid she might throw herself at him, hug him and welcome him back with a long, passionate kiss. Then he did the unthinkable and removed his shirt. Every nerve inside her broke free, reigning chaos over her senses. Her heart pounded with fury, drumming in her ears and head. She was spellbound by the hard, sculptured shape of his body and the beauty of his muscles gliding beneath his damp flesh.

Clearing the dryness from her throat, Courtney tore her tremulous gaze away and fixed it on his eyes. Those eyes. There was a sparkle in them she'd never noticed before. Their gray seemed grayer, yet their clarity gave her a brief insight to his soul. What she saw confused her more than the abrupt, abrasive Beau she remembered.

"A week ago." She floundered helplessly over what she should say. She inhaled to revive her scattered senses. "Manuelo found two more sheep. They were shot."

"Stover's lettin' you know he hasn't forgotten."

"I don't understand." *Please put your shirt on*, she begged in silence. She simply couldn't think with him half naked in her presence.

"I don't understand, either," Beau admitted. "I expected him to make a move already, especially with the skirmishes down south in Lincoln County. Stover has a Texas cattle baron's mind. He believes God's green earth was meant for cattle only, and sheep are a disease because they eat all the good grazing grasses. Like I said before, cattlemen hate sheep ranchers because they erect fences that prevent cattle from being driven across a wide open range."

"But there's abundant land and grass for both Stover's cattle and my sheep."

"Stover doesn't see it the same way. He's forgetting this territory was home to sheep long before cattle."

He ran his shirt roughly over his head, drying the shaggy mess. It had grown longer since she'd last seen him. She liked where it hung, close to his shoulders. The length softened his features some, lessened the granite edge that gave him that intimidating demeanor.

He draped the shirt over the back of his neck. "I know Stover's working up something we're not going to like. You ought to think about what to do if he should force your hand."

She knew Jared Stover would stop killing off her sheep sooner or later and resort to something more sinister. How ruthless would he become to gain her property? Would he go after her? Or would he hurt the people who meant the most to her to persuade her to sell? There was only one thing she could do if she planned to beat Stover's pressure, and that was rely on Beau. The thought of coddling him didn't sit well. True, she'd missed him terribly. And yes, she loved him. But his arrogance still reflected in his posture, and she hated stroking his aggravating ego. She didn't wish to admit it, but she needed him in more ways than solely her heart's desire.

Simultaneously they said, "The job offer still stands." and "Is the job still open?"

Beau's lopsided grin pulled a smile from Courtney. "Yes, the job is still open. But the sheep haven't changed. They still stink."

His dazzling grin deepened, and Courtney thought she would melt. He sauntered over to her, planting a twinge of panic deep inside. She wasn't ready for him to get too close, to touch her or – she gulped – kiss her. She inched her way backward, but he lifted his shirt over her head, wrapping it across her lower back, and pulled her toward him. He left her no room for denial.

"I'll put a clothespin on my nose."

"That's not funny." Feigning insult, she slapped his arm. She couldn't keep a straight face for long and wrinkled her nose. "I think the sheep are going to need the clothespins."

"That's cruel, Mrs. Burgess," he teased. "I've been working hard all morning."

"I know." She pinched her nose closed with flair.

"Heartless witch," he whispered, dropping the shirt and holding her against him. He smoothed her hair back and cupped her cheek in his hand. Beating back her soaring passion, Courtney pressed her face into his familiar warmth, believing she was in control. He touched his lips to hers, perhaps testing her acceptance, then kissed her tenderly.

He raised his head and his lips in a pleasant smile. "I'd best get back to work."

"Yes," she croaked.

Courtney whacked the carpet with vengeance. She wielded the rug beater like a whip, taking another swing and another. She didn't realize her teeth were clenched until a sharp pain blasted through her jaw.

Whack! God, her shoulders hurt, and she grimaced with the next swat. The dingy gold carpet danced over the clothes line. Very little dust floated off of it anymore, but she kept on swinging the cane as she concentrated with piercing hatred on her mission.

"You can't keep on beating a dead horse," Beau told her from the back corner of the adobe."

"Can't I?" She heaved another mighty swing.

"I just rode in from town."

"Good for you."

Beau frowned. "What's eatin' you?"

She didn't answer.

He hesitated before moving closer to her. No telling what a woman bent on destruction was capable of doing. He'd best go on about his business and say what he came to tell her before she turned that wheezing beater on him.

"I figured out what Stover's planning. I recognized some new faces in town, hired guns mostly."

She halted her next blow, the cane poised in mid-air. "Hired guns?"

Beau nodded grimly. "Stover's planning to run you off your land, and he's hired the worse lot of renegades to back him. They'd as easily rip your heart out as they would fight *mano a mano*."

That determined look she got when she set her mind to something glazed her eyes. "There aren't enough of us to fight him."

"Being prepared is the best defense." A hint of a smile crossed his face when his eyes landed on the cane. He realized now what had prodded her temper. She'd been thinking about Stover and his wrongdoings going unpunished. "You plan on using that against Stover?"

"What?" She glanced at the cane gripped fiercely in both hands. Her eyebrows arched and she set her lips askew.

"I think you're gonna need more than a cane to beat Stover at his own game." Beau whipped out his six-guns, concealing a grin when she jumped with fright. "I'm teaching you how to shoot."

Beau planted himself behind Courtney once again. His arms lined hers as she positioned one of his Colts between her hands, the barrel pointed at a can on the fence post.

"This time, keep your hands steady and your eyes open," he directed in a tight voice.

Courtney was hard pressed to keep from laughing. Aware that she was the direct cause of his waning patience, she decided she liked frustrating him. Perhaps it wasn't fair to toy with his genuine concern for her safety. But she had Beau all to herself for now, and if she continued to mess up, he'd have to stay awhile longer.

His breath on the back of her neck gave her a chill each time he moved behind her and bent his knees in order to see the target at her level. She wondered if he noticed the goosebumps on her exposed forearms.

"Now concentrate."

Grinning, Courtney squeezed the trigger. The gun barked, rocketing her hands skyward.

"Dammit!" Beau exploded. "I told you to keep your hands steady. Were your eyes open?"

Glancing back over her shoulder, she gave him a tentative smile. Meekly, she answered, "I don't know."

"Jesus! How the hell are you going to defend this ranch against Stover's bunch?" he blustered, then expelled a long breath of hard-fought patience. "All right," he said, his tone more subdued. "We've been at this for an hour. Let's get a rifle in your grip."

While he explained how to load the weapon, Courtney observed him closely. Frustration carved gullies on his handsome face. The discoloration was gone and only a few minor scars were left as a reminder of what Stover's men had done to him. She almost felt badly for Beau. He was trying his best to teach her, and she was making it more difficult than it actually was.

He bent his head forward, and his hair rested carelessly about his neck, caressing his shirt collar and catching on the stubbles at his jaw. Unconsciously, he pulled the strands away. Courtney smiled fondly. But the second he looked at her again, she quickly put on her sweetest face. She really shouldn't do this to him.

"Press the butt against your shoulder or you'll break it."

"The butt?" she asked innocently.

"Your shoulder!" he snapped.

"Don't get testy."

"Don't get..." he repeated, then clamped his teeth against the retort she knew clawed to get out.

Doing as he instructed, Courtney turned her back to him, grinning again. "Like this?"

He positioned the rifle against her shoulder. "Now, do you think you can squeeze back gently this time?"

"I'll try," she said sweetly.

The rifle exploded, forcing Courtney back into Beau. Taking him unaware, he lost his balance, and they toppled together to the dirt.

"Goddammit, woman!" Sitting, he pushed her to sit between his outstretched legs. "I said gently." Gripping her elbow, he helped her stand as he got to his feet. "You don't yank on the trigger like it was an udder."

Pretending to react to his harsh words, Courtney revealed her impertinent side. "I didn't yank on it. Maybe you don't know how to teach me to shoot. Ever think of that?"

"Damn me if I ever volunteer to teach anyone to do anything ever again," he mumbled.

Courtney snapped her shoulders back indignantly. "Well, damn you for being so short-tempered and impatient."

Beau shoved her shoulder to turn her attention back to the target. "Try it again. And this time—"

"I know. Squeeeeeze gently." She bit the inside of her lip to stop a grin as she gently applied pressure as if holding an egg between her fingers. "I did it! I hit the fence post," she said excitedly.

"It's about time." Beau scratched his head, obviously confounded by her clumsiness with a weapon. "Lady, I think you gave me a few white hairs."

Rebel Heart

CHAPTER TWENTY-TWO

The wagon rattled and clanked as Courtney pulled to a stop in front of the sheriff's office. She wrapped the leather lines around the floor peg, hopped off and straightened her vest and riding skirt before entering.

Sheriff Taylor stood behind his desk, talking to two men. One was a Mexican wearing a blood red sombrero, striped pants tucked into curved-top leather boots and a jacket cropped at the waist. He carried dual guns at his hips and two bands of bullets crisscrossed over his upper torso, same as Beau had worn.

The other man wore buckskin and a breechclout hanging down to the moccasins on his feet. A red cloth around his head kept his waist-length raven hair in place. The Indian was as tall as Beau, but he had the thickness and musculature of a bull.

The three studied her closely, the Mexican and Indian with sharp-edged eyes, the sheriff with loathing and something else that told Courtney he wasn't too pleased to see her in his office again. Nothing was going to take the steam out of her engine. Not the sheriff, and certainly not the two strangers with their chilling expressions. She was as fed up as a dog chasing its own tail, and she meant to rectify the problem of Jared Stover.

"Mrs. Burgess, what can I do for you?"

"I want to know what you're doing about Stover. He's planning something awful against my ranch."

"What makes you think—"

"Mr. Hamilton told me."

"Unless Beau works for Jared Stover, where would he get information on Stover's plans?"

"How should I know?" She snapped a reproachful look to the other two men, but neither flinched beneath her hostility. She returned her attention to the sheriff and frowned. He acted like a horse wandering around with his bridle off. His sudden restlessness puzzled Courtney.

"All right, Mrs. Burgess. Suppose Stover is scheming against you. What do you want me to do?"

"Make him stop. You *are* the law in Santa Fe."

"Without evidence of any wrongdoing, I can't bring him in. He hasn't done anything–"

"Hasn't done anything?" She balled her fists into her hips and changed her stance from stern to bellicose. "Who do you think has been killing my sheep?"

"Do you have proof?"

"No, but–"

"Then I can't help you," he told her flatly.

"If you won't put a stop to Jared Stover, then I'll have to fight him myself."

"Sometimes fighting for what you believe in isn't worth it, Mrs. Burgess."

Courtney glanced at the other men once more. They hadn't lifted their austere scrutiny from her since she'd walked into the sheriff's office. "I hope I won't be coming back to say I told you so, sheriff."

"No, Mrs. Burgess, I'm the one who hopes never to say those words to you."

Beau left the cantina in a foul mood. The information he hoped to gain wasn't worth the beer he drank. Either he was dead wrong about Stover, or his informant was holding back. He stepped beneath the portal and glanced across the Plaza. Courtney hurried out of the sheriff's office. The way she hurled herself into the wagon seat revealed she was none too happy. He wondered why she'd sought out Jeff. What the hell was she up to?

She grabbed hold of the lines and turned her head. From across the open square, Beau felt the glowing heat from her eyes. He realized the reason for it when a pair of slender arms snaked around his stomach.

Celina brushed invitingly against him as she moved to his side. "I will take no customers today if you come upstairs with me."

She ground her hips into him, but Beau's posture remained as stiff as the post supporting the awning. Celina followed the direction of his eyes, and hers instantly narrowed with hatred. She tugged on his arm then. Beau didn't budge, not even when she placed his hand on her breast. "Forget that *gringa*."

Courtney jerked away. Beau knew instinctively she'd hold Celina's indiscretion against him. He bit off a curse before it left his mouth and pulled his hand free. He glared down at the whore. "I told you, I don't take the same woman to bed a second time."

"You lie! How many times have you eased yourself between that *puta's* thighs?"

In his mind, more than he cared to admit. He stepped off the boardwalk and mounted his horse. "Forget about me, Celina. Seek out the new crop of bastards in town. Show them what a whore does best."

"*Bastardo!*" she shrieked.

Beau easily ignored Celina, his mind on the hot-headed woman heading up San Francisco Street. At a steady lope, he caught up to her wagon.

Studying Courtney's profile, he recognized the fury in her stiff posture. Her back was straight, her head erect, her mouth pinched into a neat pucker. He hoped she didn't draw him into an argument. He wasn't in the mood for one.

"What did you see Jeff about?"

Her eyes remained on the road ahead. "What did you see Celina about?"

"Are you telling me it's none of my business?"

"That's exactly what I'm telling you."

He attempted to figure out why his seeing Celina would burrow under Courtney's skin. She behaved like a jealous woman, not that she had any reason to. Then out of nowhere, he did something he'd never done in his life–he explained himself to a woman.

"I didn't go to the cantina to see Celina."

She half-turned her head, raising a single pale brow into a dubious arch. "And I didn't go to the sheriff's office to see Sheriff Taylor."

Beau compressed his lips tightly and ground his back teeth to get the upper hand on his tottering patience. He tried, he really did, to practice self-control with Courtney. Damn if she didn't always find a way to undermine the long-standing composure he'd developed when his guns had been his life's blood.

With the town behind them, they made their way across the open road in silence. There was some relief from the heat today, though it was still early in the day. By afternoon, Beau knew it would be hot enough to roast a chicken in a pit without the aid of a fire.

To conserve his energy, he relaxed in the saddle and let Paco take the lead. About ten minutes later, he noticed three men on horseback in the distance. He found a few more to their left, another two to their right. He remained poised while his senses sharpened.

"Did you find what you needed at Seligman's?" he asked cordially, calmly.

Courtney eyes widened in surprise. She probably thought he was a feather shy of a full headdress. But if he didn't engage her in pleasant conversation, he was afraid she might panic. The group of ruffians weren't exactly the town's social committee.

She grunted in answer.

"I'll take that as a yes."

"Oh, my God!" she gasped.

Beau reined in his fears. The band of eight riders bore down on them. His nerves sizzled with anticipation, but he kept his fingers away from his guns. If he had to, he'd shoot every last one of the bastards. If it meant his life, he'd die protecting Courtney. It was what he'd been paid to do. More than that, it was what he wanted to do, to protect her and keep her safe. If harm came to her... He bit down, his grinding teeth working the muscle in his jaw like it was a dead man dangling at the end of a rope.

"Pull up," he ordered. "Let me do the talking." When he caught her veiled movement, he swore. "Leave the damn rifle alone. You pull it and we're as good as dead."

"But I can shoot."

"Yeah, and I can sew a quilt with my eyes closed," he sneered. "Do as I say, dammit."

She sat contrite, her wary gaze fixed on the ungodly bunch. Beau's gut constricted with renewed fear. He prayed she wasn't fool enough to lift the rifle against them. He'd learned first hand, she was unpredictable.

The men created a half-moon before him and Courtney. They were Stover's men, although he recognized only Jack and Steve. He scanned their faces, the other six of Mexican heritage. Something about them ruffled the hairs behind his neck.

Jack nudged his horse forward. He cast his mocking expression on Courtney. "Mr. Stover ain't been happy with you."

She desperately wanted to respond. Beau saw it in her eyes. God help her if she disobeyed him and they made it out of this alive. He'd give her a hard lesson in knowing when to keep her mouth shut. For once, however, she did as she was told.

"Doesn't Stover have anything better to do than send his men out to threaten women?" Beau asked, testing Jack's mood.

"Stay out of this fight, Hamilton. Ain't you already learned? Don't go messin' with Jared Stover," he warned smugly.

Jack was feeling his oats because of the beatings he'd given him without getting pummeled in return. Was the man too stupid to realize revenge had its place and time?

Beau searched the faces of the Mexicans and spoke in Spanish. The six men whispered among themselves, repeating one of the words Beau had spoken—*Padrino*.

Jack twisted in his saddle, swearing maliciously when the Mexicans widened their circle to give Beau and Courtney room to pass. He jerked himself around, the rabid hatred in his eyes directed at Beau.

"What did you say to them?" Jack demanded.

"I can't rightly recall," Beau lied. Without backup, Jack didn't dare instigate a gunfight. Beau's reputation with a gun was widely known. Jack knew he wouldn't stand a chance in hell against his lightning-quick draw.

"This ain't over, Hamilton," Jack promised.

"No, I expect not. You might want to pass along a message to Stover. Rancho Ortega isn't for sale at any price. Mrs. Burgess is considering a partnership with the Bar H in Cheyenne. Your boss can easily figure out what an operation like that can do if it joins with Rancho Ortega. The Bar H has thirty thousand sheep. The owners might run about ten thousand head down to this territory."

Jack glared at Courtney as if the message had come directly from her mouth. He bared his yellowed teeth in a sneer, then ordered the men to move on.

Courtney cast her displeasure at Beau. "Why did you tell him that? Now Stover will attack my ranch for certain. You've backed him into a corner and have probably succeeded in single-handedly losing Rancho Ortega to that slimy toad." She slapped the lines with a heavy hand. The horses whinnied and stomped in protest. "And another thing, don't ever tell me not to arm myself again. I can shoot, I tell you. And I can very well protect myself."

Courtney brought the wagon to an abrupt halt at the back of the adobe. Her ire riding shotgun, she sprang from the seat and jumped to the ground. Convincing herself Beau had said what he did to save their hides did little to settle her agitation. No doubt she should thank him for his quick thinking, but she hated his overstepping her authority and making her appear like a feeble woman instead of the owner of a ranch. She was his boss, after all.

Stomping toward the adobe, Courtney almost collided with Carlita as the woman hurried out of the kitchen. Startled, Courtney clutched her stomach to stop the sudden nausea. If her body didn't stop trembling, she might very well lose what little she had eaten for breakfast.

Carlita's fright quickly passed, and she smiled unreservedly. "I prepared *arroz con pollo* and fresh *tortillas* for you."

Courtney gagged.

"*Señora?*"

She waved off the woman's concern. "I'm all right, Carlita. The ride home was a little bumpy."

Carlita nodded, clearly not convinced. "Two plates are sitting on the stove to keep warm. After lunch and a short *siesta*, I will return to help you stock the cabinets."

"Don't rush. I'll be taking a nap myself today." She gestured toward the wagon bed. "Half these groceries are for your family. Send Eduardo for the wagon later."

"*Gracias, señora.*"

Beau dismounted beside the wagon. One measly look at him and Courtney felt her agitation climb another plateau. She witnessed his secretive wink to Carlita as the woman passed by. When his amusement found her, Courtney grumbled with discontent.

She began to unload her half of the canned goods, cheeses, jugs of cider, coffee, salt, spices, and dried fruits. All the while, Beau leaned casually against the wagon and watched. He didn't even offer to help. She did her best to ignore him, but each time she went back for more, he'd give her a cursory grin.

Finally, her portion of the food was in the kitchen, except for the heavy flour and sugar sacks. She'd ask Eduardo to bring them in later. For now, she could stock some of the canned goods. The rest she'd leave for Carlita. Preoccupied, Courtney vaguely heard Beau enter the adobe.

"Where do you want these sacks?" He balanced one on each shoulder, stretching the limits of his shirt.

"Over...there." Her eyes seemed to have a will of their own and tracked him as he walked over to the corner she'd indicated. He leaned forward and nudged the sacks loose, then bent a little more to drop them to the floor. Courtney's eyes riveted to his small, tight backside. She couldn't stop ogling the sight of his denims pulled tautly across his buttocks or the way they accentuated the long, corded muscles at the back of his thighs.

Gasping for air, she clutched her throat, desperate for an easy breath. Good Lord! The lusty images in her mind made her lightheaded. Heat surged into her cheeks, and she touched her fingers to them, fearing they had truly caught fire.

How could you, she reprimanded herself, bewildered by her inappropriate conduct. *God will strike you blind for that.*

"What about the other sacks? Do you want them in?"

"Uh...yes. No!"

Beau tilted his head at her indecisiveness.

"Only the two at the front of the wagon." After he walked outside, Courtney released a tremulous sigh. She must get hold of herself, steady her nerves. Her cheeks still hadn't cooled, but at least they were only simmering hot now. Lord, how could she have leered at him as if she were a whore seducing a man? What if he'd caught her?

Beau came through the back door again and set the last two bags on one of the low cabinets.

"Thank you," she said while she fussed with the utensils and cloth napkins Carlita left on the table.

"The food smells good. I'm starved," Beau said as he threw his leg over the chair and plopped down.

Courtney gaped at him. Did he think he was the rooster in this coup? "You weren't invited for lunch."

"There are two place settings."

"Carlita arranged them."

He peered around her shoulder. "Two plates of food, too."

"Don't you understand?" she said, flustered. "You are not invited for lunch."

He stripped his gloves and slapped them down on the table top. "You're gonna waste the food?"

Of course he would mention a valid point. She should allow him to eat. She didn't have to stay. "All right," she conceded. "But don't even think about eating without washing your hands."

He crossed to the counter. Grumbling to himself, he rolled up his sleeves and plunged his hands into the bucket of water, scrubbing clear up to his elbows. After drying his hands, he pinned her with an unforgiving look.

"Can I eat now?" Without waiting for an answer, he reclaimed his chair.

Courtney set the water-filled glasses on the table. "Why must you behave rudely?"

"Lady, you haven't seen rude."

"Yes, I have. It goes by the name of Beau Hamilton."

"If I wasn't so damn hungry, I wouldn't stay and listen to your nagging. Give me my food and I'll be outta here."

"Give?" Her voice cracked as it elevated. Impulsively, she picked up one of the plates from the stove and hurled it across the table at him. It clipped his head, spilling rice and beans all over his shirt. She was mortified by what she'd done, and her feet bonded to the floor.

Beau rose with deliberate slowness. His unmerciful features drove fear deep into her soul, a fear that facing a pack of hungry wolves couldn't do. He stepped around the table, walking toward her with the predatory grace of a stalking animal. Having no desire to be his frightened prey, she willed her feet to move, to carry her away before he lunged. It took a scant second to dart across the room, but he was faster, his reflexes sharper. He caught her at the door and dragged her back by her wrist.

"I didn't mean to throw the plate," she said by way of an apology. "You get me so...so riled. I think you do it on purpose."

"Why the hell would I do that?"

"I-I don't know. But we always end up arguing when we're together."

"You have an argumentative nature," he pointed out.

"I do not!"

"Like hell you don't. Every time I say turn left, you go right. I say stand up, you sit down. You're deliberately defiant."

"Look who's lecturing me about defiance."

"Don't, Courtney," he warned.

"Fine. We'll only have another argument."

"No, we won't." With one sweeping motion of his arm, the contents from the table flew onto the floor. The glasses shattered noisily amid the settling silverware. He lifted her onto the table and jutted his hips between her legs. "Not this time, lady."

Rebel Heart

CHAPTER TWENTY-THREE

Beau cupped the back of her head with one hand, easing her face closer to his. He studied her wide-eyed expression, knowing he was responsible for the fear he saw there. While it wouldn't have fazed him some months ago, he realized now, he didn't want her to be afraid of him.

Their lips met, tentatively at first, but Beau's inflamed passion left no room to idle. He deepened the kiss, filling her mouth with his questing tongue. She tasted as he remembered–sweet like candy and fresh like summer fruit. A searing flame shot through his body, the intensity catching his breath. He tore his mouth away with a tortured groan.

Fumbling with the buttons down her vest, he couldn't believe how badly his hands trembled. Never had he come down with a case of jittery nerves with a woman. What was it about Courtney that made him feel as if he was an inexperienced youth? When he finally unbuttoned the last one, he encountered her shirt. He made quick work of those buttons as well and tossed both garments to the floor.

God, he couldn't get her undressed fast enough. He felt awkward as he removed her riding skirt and boots. Another obstacle stood between his eagerness and her nudity. He stared at her lacy underclothes in bewilderment. Damn woman wore too many clothes.

Swiftly stripping off her frilly undergarments, he lifted her to the table again and nudged her long, luscious legs apart with his hips. She shivered, and he figured she was cold. He wrapped his arms around her to share his warmth.

She opened her mouth, perhaps to speak, but the words never came forth. Instead, she shocked the hell out of him by moving toward him, her tongue poking out to trace the outline of his mouth.

Beau helped her remove his shirt while their lips remained locked in a fervent kiss that left him breathless and set his blood ablaze. He nestled intimately between her thighs, caressing her creamy smooth flesh up to the curve of her hips. She fit his hands comfortably, like she'd been created solely for him.

Beau kissed the corner of her mouth, laved his tongue along that willful jaw of hers, then pressed his moist lips to the elegant column of her neck. The faint smell of honeysuckle would be imbedded in his senses forever. He kissed a feverish path under her chin and back up again, reclaiming her mouth with an urgency that had him incredibly impatient to tear off the last of his clothes and plunge recklessly into her delectable body.

Slow down, Hamilton. Enjoy the woman. Take your time.

He circled her waist with his hands. Something felt different. The inward curve wasn't quite as deep as he recalled. His fingers ascended her ribcage and brushed her breasts. Her nipples stood erect, and he rubbed the pad of his thumbs over their tips, eliciting a breathy moan from Courtney. The sensual complacency on her features made his heart constrict almost painfully. With her eyes closed, her lips parted and the softness in her flushed cheeks, he ached so far down inside for the love of a woman he could never have. A woman who was about to make him break his lifelong vow.

He lowered his lips to her breasts. They were reminiscent of the classical beauty he had once seen in a painting. Savoring the moment, he touched his lips to one plump mound, like a kid taking his first lick of a candy stick. She was warm, lamb's wool soft, enticing his already heightened senses. He teased her, repeatedly flicking his tongue over her sensitive nipples, taking them carefully between his teeth. Her body jerked from a strong spasm, and he knew instinctively she was perched on the edge of ecstasy.

Blood pounded in his loins. If he didn't get out of his pants, the fabric might strangle the life out of his ardor. He hastily discarded his gun belt and unbuttoned his Levis and placed quick kisses over her belly as he eased the pants down his hips.

"Beau!" she gasped when his lips touched the inside of her thigh.

The plea in his spoken name lifted his need unbearably. He felt her desperation first hand, shared the anticipation of culminating the lust driving both of them. He straightened before her. Her jade eyes shone with raw desire, and he found

it hard to believe she wanted him that much. With a groan of pure delight, he captured her mouth again.

She wrapped her arms around his shoulders, holding him like a woman who entrusted him with her life. With little urging, she locked her legs about his hips, bringing him closer to the exuding heat of her womanhood. His patience came to an abrupt end, and he held his breath as he slowly entered her.

She tensed. Beau searched her features. Desire covered her cheeks with a warm hue, but in her eyes he saw uncertainty. He could have sworn she was desperate to have him. Easing into her a little more, he watched her closely, waiting for a denial, a change of heart.

Courtney leaned her head on his solid shoulder and buried her face into his neck. She hardly noticed the layer of sweat blanketing his body, or the manly scent of his skin. She was too aware of the feel of his manhood resting within her, keeping her moist and throbbing around him. She wanted him in the worst way, but she was afraid to make him aware of it. He had broken his vow, and she had trouble deciding what that meant. Maybe it was too late to have a conscience now. She was carrying his baby, and they were in the most intimate position a man and a woman could be in.

Lifting her head, she looked into his eyes, curious about the concern she saw in them. Gently, he stroked the area above her buttocks. Courtney moved her hips a little, gasping in the face of his sharply indrawn breath. Her eyes met his.

"Don't ask me to stop now," he beseeched, his voice gravelly, strained.

He spread one hand across her lower back, the other over her thigh. She lifted her buttocks, melding their bodies even closer. Using her palms for leverage, she tilted back and rotated her hips. Beau's breath hissed in between his teeth. The faster she moved, the more he seemed to react, holding his breath, closing his eyes. She crossed her ankles above his tight haunches. A staggering discharge inside Courtney coursed white hot blood through her veins. She threw her head back with a startled cry, the sound of her own pleasure unfamiliar.

Beau thrust into her with fury, his thighs slapping against hers from his quick, urgent movements. She fell into the rhythm, pushing when he did, pulling back as he readied for another plunge. Her breasts jerked back and forth, but

Courtney was beyond the scope of embarrassment. Their joining felt right, as if they had done it a hundred times before.

His lips twisted, his teeth bared and clenched. His head whipped back, and he thrust forward one more time, growling her name like an oath. His powerful eruption rocked her body, his pulsing within her teasing her already sensitive womanhood. Gaining control over her breathing, Courtney basked in the sensual glow in Beau's eyes. He settled his hips, his body still a part of her.

He rained kisses over her face, lingering at her lips. Her heart swelled with love. He hadn't walked away or turned his back on her. Instead, he kissed her with the selfless abandon of a lover. Enchanted, Courtney sighed when the kiss ended. After a minute, maybe two, he disengaged himself and stepped back to pull up his pants. She glanced at the back of his shoulder at a tattoo of a heart. A lightning bolt zigzagged through a hole in its center and three droplets of blood dripped from the tip. She couldn't imagine why she hadn't noticed it before now, not the day he had stood in her kitchen wearing only a towel, and not even at the river that night after he had won the shearing contest.

"What is that?" she asked, intrigued.

Beau glanced over his shoulder. "A tattoo."

"Yes, I know," she said quietly, turning crimson when his eyes raked over her. She crossed her arms over her chest, an inane gesture considering how often he'd seen her naked. Strange, but her nudity hadn't bothered her moments ago. "I've seen tattoos before, on men at the shipyard. They told me every picture has a tale. Does yours?"

He dipped his head, and when he raised it again he wore a sheepish grin. "It means I was passed out drunk and woke up with it." His grin turned into a gentle smile. "I got it in Mexico. I guess the woman I was with thought I needed a tattoo. Her cousin did it while I slept. She told me the lightning bolt is a symbol of my quick draw with a gun."

"And the hole in the heart?"

Unbelievably, he seemed shy. "She said it represents all the broken hearts I've left behind."

Courtney understood the significance of the injured heart. One day it might be *her* heart embedded in his shoulder.

She observed him in silence while he finished dressing. After he slipped the end of his gun belt into the loop, he picked up her shirt and draped it over her shoulders.

"I have work to do," he told her gruffly. He planted a chaste kiss on her cheek, then headed for the back door.

She sat there all alone, but not lonely. Passion lingered, and she enjoyed the enveloping feeling. He must have forgotten that he'd been famished. Glancing at the plate and scattered food over the floor, Courtney grinned. Maybe it had been one hell of a lunch after all.

Night descended early under the threat of a summer storm. The air smelled of rain, but not the fresh, welcomed rain that fell during spring. This rain brought the oppressive heat, the kind that made a person sweat while standing still.

Manuelo wiped his neck with his bare hand, dismounted and followed Señor Hamilton into the barn. While he and the *gringo* unsaddled and brushed down their horses for the night, Manuelo glanced up now and then, frowning. Something troubled the young man.

"What do you make of Señor Stover's silence?" he questioned.

"He's gathering a small army. I saw some of his men in town today. I crossed paths with a few of them years ago. They're cutthroats. There's a small group who won't trespass, though. I'll bet my Stetson that Stover is unaware he's hired several of Paco's men."

Manuelo's jaw dropped. "*Es verdad?*"

"*Sí*, it's true."

"Paco will not be happy," Manuelo said grimly.

"No, but it will be to our advantage for those men to remain in Stover's employ. They won't cross Paco, and I know a way to get a message to them."

"If they cherish their lives, no they will not cross him." Manuelo shook his head in disbelief. "There could very well be a war. If that is God's will, you do not owe this land your life, *amigo*."

"I owe Paco my life. For him I will stay on and help. Besides," the *señor* said with an amusing grin," someone has to look after *la gringa*. She is more harmful to herself than are Stover's men."

Manuelo chuckled. "She is a good woman."

The young man remained silent, brooding again.

"Does she suspect? About Señor Burgess and Rancho Ortega?" Manuelo asked.

"No." *El señor* rolled out a blanket near a row of hay bales, then removed his boots and set them nearby. "Those who know haven't said anything to her. Don't worry, *amigo*."

Nodding, Manuelo led his horse into its stall. He closed the gate and headed for the door. "Should I douse the lamp?"

"Not yet."

"*Buenos noches.*"

Beau unbuckled his gun belt, placing it within easy reach, and stretched out on the thin wool bed. He locked his fingers behind his head and stared at the domed ceiling.

Courtney.

She was fixed in his mind and buried in his heart. Whether working or resting, she was never out of his thoughts. He closed his eyes, mulling over what it was about her that made him burn with untamed desire. What did she have that other women didn't to make him crave her with every breath he took?

A noise across the barn sharpened his senses. He closed his fingers over the butt of his gun and moved it gradually to his side. Lying deathly still, he felt his heart pound heavily in his chest as he listened to the cautious footsteps of someone approaching. He was afraid one of Stover's men decided to seek revenge for today's meeting. Jack and Steve wouldn't attempt facing him alone. And the threat of Paco's wrath undoubtedly deterred the others. Who then?

Feigning sleep, he maintained steady, shallow breaths. He sensed the person at his side now. He could lie still and wait for a bullet to put another hole in his already marked body, or a knife blade to carve a new scar.

Or he could surprise the trespasser.

Like a startled rattler in a bed roll, Beau struck, closing his fingers around a booted ankle and taking the man's feet out from under him.

A shrill scream pierced the air.

Every nerve in Beau's body twanged like a plucked wire.

"Aw, shit!"

CHAPTER TWENTY-FOUR

Sprawled on her back, Courtney was certain the shock on Beau's face mirrored her own. She lifted to her elbows, waiting for her head to stop spinning so she could sit upright. Holding his gloves in her outstretched hand, she said, "You left these today. I was returning them."

He yanked the gloves out of her grasp and threw them onto the blanket. She frowned at his irrational mood. After all, she was the one who'd suffered from the fall. Rubbing the back of her head, she noticed a bump already forming. It was tender, and she winced.

"You shouldn't sneak up on a man at night," Beau grumbled. A deep frown etched grooves on his forehead. "Let me have a look at your head."

"It's only a small bump." Courtney brushed away his offer and attempted to stand. Lightheaded and dizzy, she swayed on her feet.

Beau curved his hands over her shoulders, forcing her to sit again. He moved behind her and parted her hair at the back. He didn't say anything for several minutes. Courtney grew impatient as he pressed his fingers lightly over her scalp. When he touched the bump, she jerked forward.

"Hold still," he groused.

"You don't have to be so grouchy. I'm the one who was knocked to the ground."

He ignored her and walked around on his knees to face her. "The skin's not broken."

"I could have told you that." Slowly rising, she made certain her footing was solid before standing fully.

"Don't go," he said, his voice subdued.

She measured the seriousness in his eyes. She didn't want to go, but she couldn't stay, either. There was no hope for them. Beau would take off for good eventually, and she refused to leave her heart unprotected to that kind of hurt.

"You can't put it off any longer. If you want to beat Stover, you need to hire more men."

Stover's impending move bothered Beau. Not her...not them. Why did she expect anything more? "I don't know if I can. A bloody war over sheep versus cattle–"

"Ignore Stover's warnings and you'll learn about war the hard way. Do you think you will be able to close your eyes at night when Stover sacrifices human lives to convince you to sell? Men like him don't give up."

"I don't want a war, and I don't want anyone to die because of a piece of land. There must be another way."

"There isn't."

After a moment, Courtney nodded. "I'll think it over."

"Think hard and fast, lady. Time's runnin' out."

Silence descended between them. Courtney looked down at the hay in thought, troubled and bitter over what Jared Stover was forcing her to do. He took advantage of her being a woman who knew nothing about ranching. Beau was right. She must make a decision soon.

Unfortunately, more than Stover troubled her. Fighting off the cattle rancher didn't seem as difficult as defending her heart against breaking if she lost Beau. He'd broken his vow with her. She tried not to read more into it than what it truly was–a man giving in to lust, and a woman giving in to inexperience and a curiosity that shouldn't have been.

"What is it, Courtney?"

The tender concern in his voice cut deeply. She avoided meeting his eyes. "This afternoon, at the house...I don't want it to happen again."

"What don't you want to happen?"

"The humiliating way you... The table..." She trailed off in private shame.

Beau reached for her hand and tugged her down to his lap, stilling her when she protested. He didn't manhandle her, and she quickly realized he wasn't going to try and make love to her again. Quiescent, she studied his eyes, unsure of the gentleness she saw in them.

"I've got a lot to learn about ladies, don't I?" He brushed his lips over hers in a thoughtful kiss. "Be patient with me, Courtney."

Beau entered the sheriff's office right on time. His meeting with Raul Rivera and Cloud had been set up by Jeff, and Beau knew the men would be punctual. He walked past the desk and cells and through a door leading to a patio. He waited a few minutes, glanced into the office to make certain he wasn't followed. He strode across the private courtyard to another building. Inside, he wound through a deserted corridor, passing through a door that opened to an alley behind another set of buildings. Scanning the nearby adobes, he slipped through one last door.

Cautiously entering the room at the very back of the millinery shop, Beau listened to the quiet. Not many knew the private room existed. The only access was the route he'd taken.

Jeff struck a match, setting it to a lantern wick. The room, not much bigger than a horse stall, glowed yellow and orange. It was then Beau noticed they weren't alone.

Raul Rivera detached himself from the shadows of a corner, his bandito style clothing making him a fearful sight. His heart of stone for those he didn't trust gained him a merciless reputation. Beau noticed a few fresh scars on the man's face, minor nicks compared to others he'd received over the years.

From another corner, Cloud emerged. His formidable appearance was intimidating, even to Beau's accustomed eyes. The men remained silent until Beau stepped farther into the room.

"You sorry son-of-a-bitch," he said, clasping Raul in a friendly bear hug.

The Mexican laughed heartily. "Do not be quick to judge, *amigo.*"

Beau nodded in acknowledgement to Cloud, then smiled at the huge Comanche warrior. They were the same age, but there was no mistaking the superior power behind Cloud.

"I am indebted to you and honored that you would leave your people to help mine," Beau told him with sincere appreciation.

"It is my people's wish to help their blood brother. You saved them from grief many times. We will do no less for you."

Beau nodded again, accepting Cloud's offer to fight beside him. "You don't have to be in on this, Jeff. The less you know–"

"I'm not turning my back again, Beau. I'm sick of Stover blackmailing me. It's time to break that bastard."

"In that case," Beau said, "we have plans to discuss."

Standing at the window of the main room, Courtney anxiously watched the barn. For the last four days, Beau seldom came near the adobe. She knew he'd been working the ranch; she'd seen him riding with Manuelo. She simply couldn't imagine why he was avoiding her.

Miserable, she wondered if he regretted breaking his vow. She didn't. She was glad he'd made love to her again. Sober, he was much more attentive. The next time—if there was one—she might suggest they use the bed. It was sure to be more comfortable than the floor and the table.

A heavy sigh fell short when she saw Beau riding toward the barn. He dismounted and disappeared into the building. Seconds later, he hurried out with a rope that he hooked over the saddlehorn. A movement pulled her attention to the hill. She glanced at Beau, then back to the hill.

"Oh, my God!" She grabbed the rifle beneath the window and threw the door open wide. Planting her feet to the porch, she positioned the rifle, burying the butt firmly into her shoulder.

Beau looked at her and scowled. Following the direction of her aim, he gritted his teeth and marched across the yard. "For Christ's sake," he growled as he bounded onto the porch and pressed the rifle barrel to the boards.

"What are you doing?" she asked, her anxious gaze darting back to the hill.

"Preventing you from making a stupid mistake."

"That man is one of Stover's," she argued.

"Is he?" Beau said harshly.

"But –"

"Besides,"—a teasing gleam replaced his anger—"you might have missed the man and clipped me instead."

Courtney yanked the rifle free and balanced it on her shoulder, the muzzle pointed somewhere behind her. "I'm a better marksman than you think."

"No, *querida*. I've seen you shoot."

She huffed and swung around to go back into the adobe. Beau ducked to avoid getting knocked in the head by the rifle barrel. He grinned broadly and looked out toward the hill. At this distance he couldn't see Raul Rivera's face clearly, but he knew the Mexican found the hot-tempered *gringa* amusing.

Courtney slammed a set of utensils on the table. She plodded over to the storage cabinet for the salt. Rummaging through the canned goods, she located the box and didn't bother fixing the cans she disturbed. Turning swiftly, she balked for the briefest moment. Surprise turned into annoyance when she saw Beau leaning casually against the table. She scolded him with her eyes, but it didn't affect him at all. He acted as if everything between them was as calm as a sleeping tiger.

"I know that man on the hill," he told her.

Courtney banged the salt box on the counter. "I didn't think you associated with Stover's scum."

"Raul Rivera is nobody's scum. He's a leader. Have you heard of the Comancheros?"

She had read they were traders, but the tales she'd heard from people who'd gone against a Comanchero had been horribly frightening. "Isn't he far from home? I thought they raided from Mexico through Texas."

"He recently came to New Mexico Territory. Remember those Mexicans who confronted us with Jack and Steve last week? They used to ride with Raul."

"Then he's working for Stover."

"Not necessarily."

Courtney rolled her eyes. "Either he is or he isn't."

"Don't worry about Raul. Just don't try to shoot him the next time you see him on that hill."

Intuition told her what little Beau revealed was the truth. For whatever reason, he was close-mouthed as a corpse and intent on remaining as enigmatic as ever. Frowning, she turned her back to him to prepare her lunch.

"That food smells mighty good," he remarked.

Still perturbed with him over the scene on the porch she slapped a tortilla on a plate. Did he think she was some twittering female without an ounce of sense? She was only trying to protect her home...and his ungrateful hide.

"It's gotta taste better than the jerky waiting for me in the barn."

"I'm sure Carlita's rice and beans are much tastier than eating leather."

"Why do I sense you're unhappy with me?"

She came around then, regarding him curiously. He was still leaning against the table, his hands gripping the edge and his ankles crossed. The arrogance in his stance extended to the smirk on his face. She arranged her features with the most becoming smile, the one she'd used on the eligible society bachelors in New York.

"Do you bargain, Mr. Hamilton?"

"What do you think?"

Courtney shrugged, as if to play down the significance of her question. "I thought perhaps I would invite you to join me for this delicious lunch in exchange for the truth. You have been lying to me from the first day I met you, and don't deny it."

The slightest flicker of muscle edged his strong jaw. He must have tightened his back teeth. "You're a distrusting person."

That wasn't the reply she expected to hear. "Only because you give me reason to be."

"Then let's clear up whatever it is you think I'm hiding."

They were dancing around each other without music. It was time to strike up the band. "All right. How well do you know Raul Rivera?"

"We crossed paths years ago." His first answer and already he was lying.

"Why is he here?"

"I don't know." Second lie. He hoped it didn't show in his eyes. When her brows lifted dubiously, he raised his, offering her to challenge his responses.

"Why didn't you inform me about the Bar H being interested in a partnership with Rancho Ortega?"

He brushed it off with a shrug. "I forgot."

"I don't believe you. You never forget anything."

She marched over to the sink and ladled water into a glass, spilling most of it back into the bucket. She set the glass down on the low cabinet and kept her straight, imposing back to him. She was as mad as a horse with his belly cinch too tight. He tried to figure out what in hell triggered her temper. *Good luck, Hamilton. You'd be better off making friends with a rattler than figuring out that woman.*

Dammit. She was making him walk the fence, and that was the last thing he'd do for any woman.

His stomach growled. He was as hungry as a half-starved wolf, but he'd be damned if he'd be reduced to begging for food. The jerky sounded much better now.

"When you've cooled your heels, you can find me in the barn taking a *siesta*."

CHAPTER TWENTY-FIVE

Beau spotted Courtney from the hill overlooking the ranch. She was kneeling in the dirt beneath the sun-filtered semi-shade of a piñon tree, doing something in the garden, hopefully nothing Carlita wouldn't approve of. He grinned, recalling the alarm on Courtney's face when she'd learned she'd mistaken the medicinal herbs for weeds. He probably should have mentioned it to her, but he'd figured it wasn't any of his business.

"Hamilton, sometimes you're an ornery bastard."

Chuckling, he guided Paco down the hill and headed toward the adobe, his eyes riveted to the woman who'd captured his heart and soul. It bothered him to admit Courtney had done what no other woman had been able to. She turned his head and made him desire only her. There wasn't anything he could do about it, either. He supposed he could leave town, never see her again. He'd thought about it often. But he'd be unhappy, probably a miserable wretch, without Courtney. Just looking at her awakened his emotions, and he discovered he didn't mind. He'd guarded his heart for so long, it felt good to give it free rein. Still, he'd practice caution around the woman. If he wasn't careful, she could drive him to marriage. And *that* he'd never do.

Beau dismounted near the stable and walked toward the garden. Courtney wore a dress today, a simple outfit, not as elegant as he might have expected. His sharp eyes closed in on her backside as she reached for an orange flower among the cactus. She wasn't wearing any petticoats. It was obvious by the way her dress draped her like a clinging tablecloth. Hot damn, she had a tempting little bottom.

Beau grinned like a fox in a hen house. Reliving the feel of her bare buttocks in his hands, he curled his fingers into fists to stop from throwing off his gloves and filling his palms with that delectable ass of hers. He slowed his steps, his moccasins as quiet as a whisper over the ground. She was unaware of his approaching. He hated to disturb her, especially with the appealing view she presented him. But she'd no doubt fly into a fit if she caught him ogling.

"That could be a dangerous offer to a man," he teased.

She popped up rather quickly. Damn him, he'd startled her again. His eyes widened in horror as she lost her balance. The flower in her hand dropped to the dirt when she tipped backwards.

"Courtney!" Beau dashed into the garden, but he was too late.

"Ow, ow, ow!" she cried, trying desperately to disengage her backside from the cactus.

Anguish knotted Beau's stomach. The sharp needles pinned her dress to her flesh. He lifted her into his arms, awkward in his fear that she might be terribly injured, and carried her into the house. "It'll be all right. Don't cry."

"It hurts," she lamented, moaning between tears.

He kicked open the door to the bedroom and gently laid her on her stomach on the bed. He pushed back the curtains. When he turned around, he felt the blood rush from his face. "I'll fetch Carlita. Don't move."

"Where the hell would I go?" she snapped.

Beau followed Carlita's instructions, making a poultice out of the juice of a cactus plant and the goat's oil she'd brought. He gathered fresh tree leaves at the river, all the while worried that Carlita might not be able to stop Courtney's wounds from becoming infected. It was all his fault. He shouldn't have come up on her so quietly, not with her leaning over the cactus.

He sat at the kitchen table, enduring Courtney's wails, one after the other. How many cactus needles were embedded? Covering his ears to drown out her cries, he rested his elbows on the table. His gut constricted and burned, feeling every ounce of her pain until he could take no more and jumped to his feet.

"*Por Dios,*" he mumbled.

He bounded into the main room, skidding to a halt at the closed door to the bedroom. When he raised his fist to knock, Carlita's consoling voice stopped him cold.

"Do not worry about the baby. The fall was not so bad."

Every muscle in Beau's body pulled taut. Baby?

"No, it wasn't," Courtney replied. "But I sure picked the wrong place to fall."

"You will be fine, *señora*. The discomfort will pass soon enough."

Silence. Beau dropped his hand and stared at the door in a daze. Baby?

"Have you told him?" Carlita asked.

"Told who what?"

"Señor Hamilton."

"No, he doesn't have to know."

"*Señora–*"

"I think it best he doesn't, Carlita."

"As you wish. I will make herb tea to help you sleep."

Preoccupied with what he'd overheard, Beau didn't realize Carlita was leaving. When the door suddenly opened, he startled.

"Señor Hamilton?"

He glanced at Courtney lying on her stomach, a sheet covering her body to her waist. Her nightdress covered the rest of her. He swallowed with uncertainty. "I came to check on...how is she?"

"You don't have to whisper," Courtney said, annoyance in her voice.

"She will be fine," Carlita assured him. To Courtney she said, "I will return with the tea."

Beau stood in awkward silence, unable to think what to say. Apologizing crossed his mind, but he'd never been good with apologies. He'd probably mess it up anyway and make her more irritated with him. So he kept quiet, wishing he didn't feel so rotten inside.

Courtney craned her neck to see him. His features and demeanor came across as pathetic and lost. She might have taken pity on him any other time. At the moment, she was in too much pain to sympathize with the helpless feeling she was certain claimed him.

"What do you want?" she asked bluntly. She wasn't in the mood to speak otherwise. He was looking at her strangely now. She couldn't begin to understand his wounded expression. Maybe he felt guilty for the painful mishap. He rightly should.

"Stanley Burgess was one lucky son-of-a-bitch."

"What?" She twisted a little more for a better view. "What do you mean by that?"

"I overheard...about the baby," he replied, oddly reserved.

175

Courtney closed her eyes briefly, not wanting to believe he'd learned about the baby. Thank God she and Carlita hadn't said anything more.

"The fool had a mighty powerful–" He inhaled and glanced away for a very short minute. "It's too bad he's not alive to share your joy. You are happy, aren't you?"

God, what do I say to him?

Appealing to God seemed inane. It was all her fault for giving in to temptation in the first place. Yes, she had tried to deter him. But in her heart she knew she hadn't tried hard enough. Worse, she shouldn't have fallen in love with Beau.

Clearing the clutter from her mind, she replied, "Yes, I am happy."

Silence descended like a quiet prairie night. Beau didn't say a word, didn't growl or bite. He didn't even turn around and stalk away, proving, in her mind, that he truly didn't care if she was carrying Stanley's baby.

"Well," he finally said. "I only came to see if you were doing all right. Carlita will take good care of you." His gaze lowered briefly. "I best get back to work. I promised Manuelo I'd ride the fence with him. The northern tip of the ranch has a dangerous gully where the sheep often wander." He moved forward to leave, but then whirled back to face her. The light in his eyes was both pained and angered. "Dammit, Courtney. Why didn't you tell me about the baby?"

"Because my baby does not concern you."

He seemed to be battling over whether to stay or go. He rocked back and forth on his feet while working his jaw into a multitude of muscle spasms. In a heartbeat, his eyes glazed over and coldness hardened his features. "You're right. It doesn't. It damn well doesn't."

Beau entered the adobe through the back door. He hadn't been back since Courtney's accident four days ago. She'd probably be angrier than spit with him for not showing his face sooner. He couldn't. He had too much thinking to do. Too many hurtful emotions to deal with.

Leaning back against the closed door, he stared off across the room, seeing nothing but the image of Courtney cradling a baby in her arms. Dammit! Why couldn't he let it go? She wasn't his woman, never would be. Why couldn't he get that through his thick head?

He moved toward the opposite door, but stopped short midway across the kitchen. What the hell was he doing? She didn't need him checking in on her. She might get to thinking he cared. He did. But he didn't want her to know that. He had no place in her life now, not with her carrying Burgess' baby.

He sank down onto a chair. Love was hell—pure, undiluted hell. Being in love with a temperamental, headstrong woman added to the torture.

Carlita came through the door from the main room, moving in her usual bustling way. As soon as their eyes met, she bunched her mouth and closed the door hard. She didn't slam it. She didn't have to. Beau understood. She was unhappy with him for staying away from the adobe.

"*La señora?*" he asked after Courtney's well-being.

"*Hrumph*," Carlita grunted. Shaking a finger beneath his nose, she scolded, "Why did you not come to see her before now?"

"Carlita, don't start in on me," Beau warned.

"*Aiyeee*, if I was your mother..."

Disappointment shifted her features. She pulled out a chair and eased down with a weary sigh. "You show respect for me and my Manuelo, but you do not give the *señora* the same. For this you are *loco*. You will be sorry when Señora Burgess becomes tired of waiting for you to stop behaving like an *hombre* too stubborn to admit he is in love with her."

"*Mierda*." Beau gnashed his back teeth together. "Do you see my heart on my sleeve?"

"No, but I see it in your eyes each time you look at her." Carlita inclined her head, sternness creeping into her voice. "Well? Are you going to admit it?"

"To her?" Beau shook his head. "It wouldn't do any good."

"You think not?"

"I know it wouldn't. She's having another man's baby." Beau sighed heavily as he removed his hat and set it on the table. He combed through his hair with both hands trembling. "I don't know if I can accept Burgess' baby, knowing the kind of man he was."

"You should accept the baby because it is a part of her." Carlita's features softened, and she placed a reassuring hand on Beau's where it rested on the table. "When you are in love, you must be blind to some matters."

"I can't."

"You are a fool then." She straightened her spine and swept gracefully out the back door.

Beau might be a fool, but it was better than playing second fiddle to another man's baby.

CHAPTER TWENTY-SIX

Ten minutes. He stood at the bedroom door that long before he finally worked up the courage to knock. His heart pounded like cannon blasts in his chest, in his ears and at his temples.

Courtney's sweet voice drifted through the door. "Come in."

Taking a deep breath, he pushed the door open slowly, wondering what to expect. She had every right to reproach him for staying away. Would she? Or would she be happy to see him again? Little knots tangled in his stomach, making him sick. He wasn't accustomed to apprehension rifling his nerves because of a woman.

He hadn't expected to see her sitting in bed, reading by lamplight. She looked like an angel with her flaxen hair spread over her shoulders. Her face was sweet, her eyes bright and her lips set in a sort of pout. He wasn't fit to be in her company. He hadn't shaven for two days, and although his facial hair was blond, it was thick and untidy. He hadn't cleaned up, either. After a long day of hard work, his Levis and shirt needed a good washing. Yet she didn't seem to mind. At least he didn't think so.

"I'm happy to see you're able to sit."

"Carlita's herbs worked their magic."

Beau shifted, an unaccustomed feeling of diffidence creeping in. "Things have been running smoothly. On the ranch, that is," he added in haste.

"Yes, I know. Carlita has kept me informed."

"Of course." God how he wished he held his hat to occupy his hands. He shoved them into his pockets, as clumsy as it was to do because of the dual guns around his hips.

"Any word on Stover's next move?"

"No one is talking, but a man would have to be blind not to notice the increase in manpower around Stover's ranch."

"If what you say is true, what is taking him so long to attack us?"

"My guess is he's waiting until he has enough men to overpower us."

"I suppose we have no choice but to prepare for the worse."

His knuckles scraped the coarse fabric when he attempted to make a fist. He removed his hands from the pockets and let them dangle at his sides. "You're not part of the 'we.' A pregnant woman has no business getting caught in a range war."

"Need I remind you that I own this ranch?"

"Why are you so damn stubborn? You have to think of your unborn child."

"I *am* thinking of my baby. This land, this ranch," she spread her arms outward, indicating the adobe and everything beyond, "will belong to my child one day."

"Not if you both die fighting for what doesn't..." He pressed his lips together.

"Doesn't what?" she demanded. Grit and determination settled in her eyes.

"Nothing." He plowed his fingers through his hair to tone down his agitation. Remembering one of the reasons he'd gone to see her, he tugged an envelope from inside his shirt. "This came for you. I picked it up in town today."

The tumult in his voice rubbed Courtney's nerves raw, and without intending to, she snatched the envelope from his fingers. She glanced at the writing. The Madison Park address jumped out boldly, unsettling her stomach. For a horrible moment she thought she was going to be sick. Her father never wrote letters.

She broke the seal on the envelope and pulled out the cream colored paper inside. Her hand trembled as she read the letter. She reread it, confused by what it meant. Taking another look at the envelope, she realized it had been addressed to Stanley, with the word 'confidential' at the very bottom. Her cheeks heated with shame and disbelief.

"What is it?" Beau's voice sounded tight with concern.

"I've been such a fool. A stupid, stupid fool," she said bitterly. "This letter was meant for Stanley. I knew Father disliked him, but I never realized how much until now." Her eyes warmed with tears. "To be honest, I never understood Father's aversion to Stanley. They'd only met on two occasions."

Courtney sighed sorrowfully. Her father had known the kind of dishonest man Stanley had been before she discovered it for herself here in Santa Fe. He'd tried to warn her, but she'd stubbornly refused to listen.

"It seems Father paid Stanley ten thousand dollars to leave New York."

Beau tensed. He prayed he'd be able to keep from reacting. It was damn hard not to, since he'd known all along about the pay off. Now he was caught in the middle of Leif Danning's deceit and Courtney's appalling discovery about her father's obsession with the man she'd married.

"Apparently Stanley took the money and left. Now I understand Father's insistence that I shouldn't go to Santa Fe. At least I think I do. Oh, God," she moaned miserably. "I'm so confused."

Careful, Hamilton. She's vulnerable right now. It would be too easy for you to comfort her in your arms.

Beau sat on the bed beside her legs. The tears sliding down her cheeks might as well have been his own. Seeing her downtrodden squeezed the tender side of his heart. "Don't be quick to judge until you've heard both sides," he advised sagely.

She sniffled. "What do you mean?"

He studied her features, debating on whether to reveal what he knew about her dead husband. The truth might devastate her even more. Then again, it might ease the distress the letter caused. Hell, how had he gotten caught in this emotional mess? *You've gotten too damn caring, that's how.*

"Courtney," he sighed, seeing the irony in it all. He never thought he'd be comforting her over her father's motives. "After Burgess gambled away every cent he had, he tried to bilk your father out of a substantial amount of money by luring him into a fraudulent investment scheme. But he couldn't hustle your father."

"No," she denied, shaking her head.

"Ask your father," he challenged without thinking about the consequences if Leif Danning found out who told his daughter about Burgess' duplicity. "Your father was about to have Burgess arrested, but the bastard purposely gained your trust and affection. You easily fell into his new scheme. He went to your father and demanded ten thousand dollars to leave you and New York behind."

"Why would my father pay him?"

"He knew Burgess was a lying, cheating bastard." His lip curled in a sneer. It happened every time he thought about what that man had done to her. "Not long after he arrived in Santa Fe, he got caught up in the diamond scandal farther west. That's where he lost all his money. So he tried to get your father to invest in a nonexistent mine in Denver."

She kept shaking her head, denying the words he spoke. "No matter what Stanley had done, he wouldn't have used me to blackmail my father. This ranch is proof that Stanley was turning his life around."

"Courtney, please. Don't force me to reveal the ugly truth. Can't you trust me just this once?"

She drew in a shaky breath. After a brief silence, hurt turned to suspicion. "How is it you know all this?"

"I told you, your husband and I drank together on occasion. He had a tendency to run off at the mouth when he was drunk." It wasn't a total lie, although most of what he knew about Burgess came from Leif Danning.

Courtney shivered and hugged her arms around her chest. "Stanley was never in love with me, was he?"

The desolation in her voice ripped at Beau's heart. He desperately wanted to hold her until every last vestige of pain flowed out of her body. Instead, he denigrated Burgess' memory further.

"Your husband lived for expensive liquor, women and a shady scheme or card game where he could cheat some unsuspecting fool out of his money."

Her bottom lip quivered uncontrollably. "Celina?"

"She was his constant companion," Beau said quietly.

A sob leaped to her throat. He realized how hard she was trying not to lose any more tears over her scoundrel husband. He forced his arms to remain close to his body, though he didn't know how much longer he'd be able to keep from wrapping her in their protective embrace.

"My father hired an investigator."

He tensed again. What would she do if she learned he was that investigator?

"I thought he was overreacting. I realize now he was only trying to protect me from a broken heart." She sniffled and dabbed the moisture pooling in her eyes. "Do Carlita and Manuelo know?"

Beau nodded in silence.

When she inhaled, her chest trembled. "Thank you," she said barely above a whisper.

"For what, *querida*?"

"Your honesty."

He felt about as low as a man who'd lost his family to a gang of outlaws. Nothing else could make him feel guiltier than he did at this moment. Not even the realization that he'd revealed Burgess' insidious character for selfish reasons. Compared to her dead husband, maybe his own past might not seem as unfavorable. Maybe she would see that, in spite of his gunman's reputation, he wasn't the weasel Burgess had been.

She looked at him as if he'd performed an admiral deed. If she only knew the lies he'd been weaving... He laughed scornfully to himself. He wanted her to believe he was a better man than her husband. *Nice try, Hamilton.*

As Beau moved to stand, she caught his hand. Her gentle touch shot bolts of shock through his veins, heating his blood with intense desire. He observed her, seeing her vulnerability much clearer now. She was reaching out for consolation in a moment of unguarded pain, and all he could think about was making love to her.

"Please don't leave me. I need...someone to hold me."

His heart slammed against his chest and pounded so hard he thought he'd stop breathing. "*Dios*, Courtney. Do you know what you're asking?"

"I'm asking for companionship. Nothing more." She tilted her head, her expectant features too damned hard to resist. "Please."

How the hell was he supposed to say no to that? He searched her features, noting the sincerity in her eyes. Did he trust himself to be what she wanted – a companion? Or did he turn his back on her, walk away without a care? He sighed with resignation and removed his gun belt, folding it neatly on the floor beside the bed within easy reach. Then he sat on the mattress and pulled off his boots.

Courtney scooted over to make room for him. As soon as he lay back, she came into his arms. Using his shoulder for a pillow, she snuggled as close as possible, wrapping her arm over his stomach. The muscles beneath her limb contracted, and his entire body tensed.

"Good night, Beau."

"Good night," came his tight-lipped response. He didn't dare move. She felt too soft, too tempting with her breasts pressed into the side of his chest. *God help me make it through the night.* It damn well was going to be a long one.

Beau started counting.

CHAPTER TWENTY-SEVEN

Pressing her head into the pillow, Courtney stretched her neck. The stiffness in her back slowly abated, and all the tension worked out happily from a good night's sleep. She must have been terribly exhausted last night. It was the only explanation for her sleeping so well. Oddly, her stomach didn't roil like it usually did in the mornings. Whatever the reason, she decided she'd use her renewed energy to get back to ranch business today.

Glancing to the ceiling, she inhaled deeply and smiled. Of a sudden she stilled, listening, wondering where the soft sound of breathing was coming from. Fearful, she turned her head and swallowed a sharp gasp at the sight of Beau lying beside her, sound asleep.

Memories of the night before flooded her head. She had asked him to stay with her because she didn't want to be alone. How could she have been so forward and...

And so desperate? She had pleaded with him not to leave. Oh, God, she remembered it all now and closed her eyes, shame burning her face.

Not a minute later, she rolled to her side and watched Beau. She had never awakened with a man in her bed and didn't know what to do.

"Oh, no," she barely whispered. Hesitantly lifting the covers, she peeked underneath. What she saw made her sigh with relief. She wore her nightdress; Beau still wore his clothes. Thank God they hadn't...

Or had they?

Shifting her attention back to Beau, Courtney studied him selfishly. In sleep he didn't seem so tough. It was hard to imagine him being abrupt and short-tempered when his features were relaxed and soft. Yes, soft. And quite young. He saw the under side of thirty, but he looked years younger, even through the stubbles. She would have brushed her fingers across his firm lips, ran a fingertip along the scar on his cheek and kissed the line of his strong jaw, but she was afraid to disturb him. It would be best if she tried to get out of bed without him knowing.

Moving as little as possible, she lifted the covers away and rolled to the other side. The mattress creaked, and she froze. She listened for movement behind her, any indication that Beau had awakened. It remained quiet, except for the even sound of his breathing, so she started to sit. Beau grasped her wrist, scaring the daylights out of her. She snapped her head around and met his glimmering eyes.

"Good morning."

"Good...morning," she stammered.

"Are you all right?"

All right? Why wouldn't she be?

"You're not going to be sick, are you?"

"Sick?"

"Yeah, you know, the morning and all. Don't pregnant women get sick in the morning?"

Courtney swallowed hard. He shouldn't have asked such a personal question. Men didn't inquire about a woman's state during pregnancy. That was one subject never spoken of in mixed company in New York. Then again, neither did an unmarried lady awaken with a man in her bed. Flames of shame licked up her neck to her cheeks.

"I think you should leave," she said, her voice quiet.

Beau's attitude changed right before her eyes. The corners of his mouth curved down and his eyes turned murky, cold. He probably couldn't fathom her reason, but there simply was no diplomatic way to ask him to get out of her bed.

"I guess in the light of day you don't need my companionship," he remarked sharply.

She lowered her eyes. "I shouldn't have asked you to stay last night. It was a mistake."

"No, Mrs. Burgess. I'm the one who made the mistake. A hired hand has no business comforting a woman like you, does he?" He sprang from the bed, shoved his feet into his boots and scooped up his gun belt. "It'll never happen again."

"You say that about as often as you quit."

He snapped to a halt, holding his gun belt at his hips. "Don't goad me," he warned.

She laughed derisively. "It doesn't take much to do that." It sounded like a challenge, though for the life of her she didn't know why she'd challenge his unpredictable disposition. "Go on, get out."

"That does it, woman. I've had enough of your orders." He let go of the gun belt, and it dropped heavily to the floor. Courtney hardly noticed. All she saw were the dark clouds building in Beau's impassioned eyes.

He closed his fingers over her wrist and yanked her to her knees. She was foolish enough to jut her chin in defiance, showing him he didn't frighten her. Inside, however, she trembled like the ground under a stampede. Not from fear, though. She realized the instant his mouth closed over hers that she had purposely instigated his surly nature.

Courtney folded her arms behind his neck, pressing him closer, absorbing the rapid pounding of his heart through their clothing. The intensity in his kiss matched the rhythm beat for beat. She pressed closer still, rubbing against him, growing feverish from the strong desire to have him naked in her arms. His virility excited her, made her impatient. Any modesty she might have retained vanished.

Her moans vibrated at their lips. Needing no encouragement, she pulled his shirttails out of his pants and unbuttoned his shirt. They parted briefly when she yanked the garment over his head. She toyed with his small, hard nipples until he groaned and deepened his kiss. With their lips seared together, Courtney brushed her hands down his ribcage, enjoying the feel of his warm flesh. When she unfastened the first button on his pants, his breath sucked in. She searched deep into his eyes, puzzled by what she saw. The storm abated, replaced by a light of longing. Blatant desire warmed his eyes, the kind of desire that began in the heart.

Nervous and uncertain, her hands trembled over the remaining buttons. Every time she brushed his hard ridge, his body jerked. He helped her, and in mere seconds his pants were laying on the floor with his shirt. Her nightdress quickly followed.

Courtney shivered. The ache between her legs grew stronger. She almost begged him to touch her there. But she wasn't ready to verbally tell him what she craved, at least not sexually. It was enough that she'd asked him to sleep with her. And now she goaded him, knowing he'd release his frustration by making love to her.

Threading her fingers through his hair, she brought his lips whispering close to hers. "Kiss me."

The urgency in his touch rippled through Courtney. Beau splayed one hand across the small of her back, his other supporting her head as he laid her down on the mattress. Courtney lost herself in his warmth, his hot kisses, his soothing caresses. Nothing and no one existed beyond her and Beau. If this was a dream, she never wanted to wake up.

Tucked in Beau's embrace, both lying naked in a tangle of sheets and blankets, Courtney felt a sense of peace from the even rise and fall of his chest. She never imagined lying with a man could be so exciting, so consuming. Beau was the perfect lover—kind and considerate, passionate, shockingly thorough. Still reeling from the inexplicable sensations when he'd kissed her and touched her intimately, Courtney blushed all over again. She stirred and pulled his arm around so she could intertwine her fingers with his. But first, she held his hand and studied his palm, noticing he hadn't a single callous. In fact, his skin was as smooth as saddle leather. Her brows angled down in thought. Even her father sported calluses.

"Why do you have a banker's hands?"

"I wear gloves when I work. It's a long-standing habit. Callused hands are a hazard to a gunfighter. The feel of a gun in his grip is important."

"But you're not a gunfighter anymore." She looked at him. "Are you?"

"You're awfully curious this morning, Mrs. Burgess. But I'm afraid I can't satisfy your curiosity. If I don't get my carcass out of bed, I won't be much good to Manuelo today."

"Why not?"

Taking her hand, he brought it down to his burgeoning male.

"Oh!" she gasped, her cheeks flaming once more. She didn't know a man could be ready so soon after.

"Oh, the hell with Manuelo today," he growled playfully and pressed her back into the mattress. "There are more important things in a man's life than"—he grinned mischievously—"stinking sheep."

Not long after the noon hour, Beau entered the adobe through the back door. He halted right inside the kitchen and grinned shamelessly at the sight of Courtney's bottom straining the material of her Levi's as she bent over the open oven door. His grin turned sheepish.

"A mouth watering sight if ever I saw one."

Courtney straightened and set the pan of cookies on the stove. For once his entrance didn't startle her. The creek of the door hinges gave his presence away.

Beau strode to the table and set his hat down before going to the sink to wash his hands. "What are you burning that smells so good?"

"They're sugar cookies, and they're not burnt. They're just a little well done."

"Exactly the way I like my sugar cookies." He shook the water from his hands and searched for a towel. When he didn't find one, he wiped his hands on the front of his shirt.

"What are you doing?"

Beau pulled out a chair and sat down before replying. "About to have lunch."

"I didn't invite you to have lunch with me."

"You didn't?" He gave her a wounded look, hoping it would temper whatever tick got under her skin. "Well now, I enjoyed breakfast so much, I couldn't resist coming back for lunch."

A bright red flush unfolded over her face. Beau chuckled at her chaste response. Sometimes he forgot she wasn't practiced in the ways of men. He reached for her hand and pulled her to his lap. She lost her steam, growing quiet, almost shy.

"Don't think I'm making light of this morning," he told her as his hand roamed up her spine to caress the back of her head. At first she resisted, but he didn't give her the chance to reason with the impropriety of fondling her in the middle of the day and in the kitchen where Carlita could walk through the door at any time.

Lowering his head, he kissed her breasts through her shirt. He released the top button and touched his lips to her soft skin, kissing and laving his tongue up her neck until he captured her mouth. He felt her tremble, felt her body grow. Felt her sudden need when she lost her fingers in his hair, guiding him back to her breasts.

Nerves throbbing, he beat back his own urgent need. "The bed, Courtney. Let me take you—"

She cut him off with a hungry kiss. Her hands framed his face, and she deftly maneuvered herself around to straddle his thighs. Passion surged through his body like a speeding bullet. To hell with the bed.

189

He lifted her as he stood, and she wrapped her legs around his back. Her arms locked behind his neck. He set her gently on the table, and this time there was only his hat to clear away.

"*Querida*," was all he seemed capable of saying. He couldn't believe how impatient he was. Hell, he couldn't believe how insatiable she made him feel.

She quickly undid the buttons of his shirt and pushed it eagerly halfway down his arms. But their ardor came to a crashing end when a man cleared his throat. Beau immediately shielded Courtney with his body. When he glanced over his shoulder toward the back door, a prankish grin cut across his face.

"I swear, Beau, women are gonna be the death of you," the man teased.

Beau shrugged back into his shirt and grinned at Courtney. She wasn't smiling. In fact, she was mortified. He'd have to make it up to her later. For now, he faced his half-brother. "Good to see you, Drake."

Courtney glanced around Beau's shoulder. The man's smile was dazzling. He was slightly taller than Beau, his eyes a blue-gray and his hair a lighter shade of blond.

"Where are your manners?" he asked Beau, but his eyes were locked on hers.

"He doesn't have any," she remarked impetuously. The stranger gave her a puzzled look and glanced at the table. Realizing how promiscuous her position must appear, Courtney hopped down.

Beau moved aside. "This is Courtney Burgess."

"Burgess?" Drake shot Beau a skeptical glance and stepped into the kitchen. "This is the pestering intransigent you—*humph*!" Drake grasped his side where Beau elbowed him.

"Don't mind Drake," Beau said. "He has a problem with his mouth. It tends to run like a river. Oh, by the way, this is my brother."

Courtney's mouth went slack. When she recovered, she sputtered, "B-b-brother? But..." Her tone turned to accusation. "I thought you didn't have any family?"

"Did I say that?" Beau retrieved his hat and tilted his head into the crown. "Drake is my one and only brother. However, I take no responsibility for his straight-laced manner."

Courtney couldn't stop watching Beau. All of a sudden, he was a changed man, lighthearted and easygoing. Suspicion crept in, even as Beau leaned to kiss her cheek. She thought that would be the end of their tryst, but he swept her up in a one-armed embrace and molded her intimately to his clearly unsated body. He spread kisses along her neck and jaw, moving smoothly to her mouth. His tongue invaded it thoroughly, possessively.

He freed her at last, and all Courtney could do was take in gulps of air. The rogue grinned devilishly, and she blushed right down to her toenails.

"I guess I'll be passing on lunch." He gave her a conspiratorial wink.

Courtney compressed her lips in exasperation.

"Well, brother, let's ride out to the cantina. I'll buy you a drink. Then I'll introduce you to some of the pretty *señoritas...*" His voice faded as he ushered his brother out of the adobe.

Courtney inhaled deeply. "Men!"

Rebel Heart

CHAPTER TWENTY-EIGHT

Courtney reined in the gray mare at the barn door, swung her leg over the animal's neck and jumped to the ground. She felt wonderfully invigorated. She hadn't ridden that briskly since she'd left New York. The hard run cleared her mind and helped bring a little perspective to her life. She was more focused on the delicate situation with Beau and the baby he didn't know was his. Although she hadn't come to any decisions about her future, she'd decided to be with Beau as much as she could, until he moved on.

She led the snorting mare by the reins into the barn and unbuckled the saddle girth. With a solid grasp on the saddle, she gritted her teeth and slid it from the horse's back. Her knees buckled under the weight, but she managed to stay on her feet. The blanket slipped to the ground, and she kicked it aside so she wouldn't trip.

A short while later, she slapped the horse's rump, sending it into its stall. As she brushed the horse, voices outside the barn slowed her movement. She hadn't thought Beau and Drake were at the ranch today. Ducking down, she held the brush against her heavily pounding heart and prayed the mare wouldn't give her away. Through the wood slats, she saw the brothers walking across the barn. Beau looked irritated.

"She has the right to know," Drake insisted.

"Manuelo made me promise to keep quiet. What am I supposed to do?"

"Beau, the girl is living a lie. I can't believe you won't do anything about it." Drake grasped his brother by the shirt sleeve. "If what you told me is true, then she must leave Santa Fe at once. If she won't, at least get her off this ranch."

"I've tried." Beau tugged his arm free. His hurried footsteps carried him swiftly to the storage closet where he stored his weapons. "There isn't one single person I know who can break through that woman's damn stubbornness."

"Then you'd better have a talk with Manuelo. He should tell her about Rancho Ortega. The man's put his life's blood into this ranch. The charade can't go on."

"It will as long as Manuelo wants it to."

"Dammit, Beau. This is Manuelo's ranch. *He* built it. *He* made it a successful sheep ranch. Until that swine Burgess came along."

Beau released a long, slow breath. "The fact still remains. Burgess conned Marcos into that card game then cheated. The kid was naïve and stupid. He didn't realize Burgess lured him into a trap. When Marcos put up Rancho Ortega and lost, Manuelo's pride forced him into honoring the bet. And you know Manuelo. He won't say anything."

"What about Stover?" Drake asked.

"Courtney or Manuelo, Stover doesn't care. He invaded the area with his cattle, and now he's trying to squeeze out the sheep ranchers. He's not about to get Rancho Ortega," Beau vowed as he loaded the rifle.

Courtney stepped hesitantly out of the stall. Time suspended. She saw the brothers through the haze of her shock. Their expression differed – Drake's with sorrow, Beau's with a cold distant void. He had lied to her, had kept the truth from her even though the ranch and her life were in danger. And now he was angry with her for learning the truth, probably angrier that it had come from his own mouth. Disappointment and hurt surfaced, leaving her numb. She couldn't even light a fire under her precarious temper. For once it was dead, buried beneath the emptiness in her heart.

"Why wouldn't anyone tell me about Stanley?" she asked, her voice thick from holding back her unstable emotions.

"It's not easy telling a woman that the man she married was a low-life reprobate."

"Beau," Drake cautioned.

"Stay out of this, Drake." Beau's cool gaze remained on Courtney.

"Marcos was too young. His lost bet never should have been honored," she reasoned.

Beau's anger intensified. "Manuelo's son learned his lesson the hard way and at the expense of his family's holdings. Only because Manuelo's pride was in this ranch did he stay on. And it turned out to be a wise decision. Your husband didn't know a damn thing about sheep."

Courtney digested the truth and realized how enormous her responsibility in the ranch had become now. She held another man's past and future in her hands. If only she'd known the truth up front. It seemed they were all victims of Stanley's dishonesty and deception.

"A few nights ago," she recalled aloud, "you were about to tell me Rancho Ortega isn't really mine, weren't you?"

"Unintentionally, yes. But I couldn't go against Manuelo's wishes."

She understood not wanting to break a promise. It was admirable of him to preserve Manuelo's trust. But she was glad the secret was finally out in the open. Things finally made sense—Carlita's garden, the comments about how prosperous Rancho Ortega had once been, Marcos' loathing of her.

"Courtney," Drake called gently, gaining her wayward attention and Beau's sharp glance. "I realize this has all been a terrible shock to you. But you've got to forget it for now and consider leaving the ranch."

She studied the concern written on Drake's face. He had some of his brother's qualities – the straight nose, the squared jaw. What he didn't have was Beau's hard edge, neither temperamental nor abrupt. On the contrary. Drake would have fit in with the gentlemen of New York's society.

She sighed. The past couldn't be changed, but she could do something about the future. Determination slipped into her demeanor. "I will not leave this ranch."

"Didn't I tell you she was stubborn?" Beau said to Drake. "Goddamn stubborn," he muttered, turning back to the storage shed.

Grinning in apology, Drake continued to reason. "It will be too dangerous for you to remain here."

"Ask her why she won't leave," Beau said.

"*She* won't leave," Courtney began, mimicking his irritated tone, "because she owes Manuelo. She feels obligated to make up to him and his family all the wrong her husband did."

Bemused, she watched Beau stuff boxes of cartridges in his shirt pockets and shove several rifles between his arm and body. He slammed the door, then pivoted curtly to face her.

"You owe Manuelo nothing." A vein in his neck protruded. He turned back to the shed, jerked open the door and laced filled cartridge belts over his head and across his chest. He was a one-man arsenal by the time he finished. When he faced her once again, his scowling expression invariably turned hers to haughty disdain.

"Manuelo would never ask you for anything, especially your pity. He reconciled with Marcos long ago. The boy carries the guilt for his foolishness. Don't complicate the issue by trying to make things right. You're not in your comfortable highbrow society in New York. It's the West, lady. Men here use cacti for pillows. And you damn well better remember that."

Courtney balled her hands at her sides. She would have taken a mighty swing at that arrogance of his if she knew it would do any good. But he'd still be arrogant, and she'd probably get hopping mad because she'd hurt her hand on his granite jaw. Her fists clenched tighter.

"I suppose men here spit bullets, too," she retorted. Huffing in frustration, she was about to turn away when another irritating thought tumbled into her head. "What I don't understand is why you've remained here for so long. You once told me you'd never lose your life over *stinking sheep*."

Expecting no comment, she marched to the barn door, missing Beau's glower and Drake's shock. She was so riled she'd forgotten what she'd been doing before the two brothers entered the barn. On her way back to the house, it came back to her and she abruptly turned around. She'd never neglected a horse like she was doing now. Damn Beau Hamilton, anyway. He was turning her inside-out.

She stomped back into the barn, ignoring Beau and Drake, and went directly to the gray mare to rub her down. Engrossed with Beau's revelation, she didn't realize she was taking out her fury and agitation on the animal.

"You fixin' to make horsemeat out of that animal's hide?" Beau questioned incitingly.

"I'm sure I know more about horses than you do. I'll thank you to mind your own business."

"Anything you say, Mrs. Burgess," Beau snapped. He hurried out of the barn as if his shirttail was on fire.

"Arrogant, insensitive lout," she muttered.

"You may be partially correct," Drake said. "But Beau's not the complete ass you may think he is."

"Could have fooled me."

Courtney stepped onto the front porch of the adobe and stretched her sore limbs. Her shoulders ached from the vigorous rubbing she'd given the mare. It was entirely her fault. She shouldn't have let Beau get under her skin. Her muscles were paying for it now.

Glancing at the hill, she noticed a man sitting astride a black horse. Lately, she'd seen one stranger or another standing guard there. From that point, all of Rancho Ortega was visible. If they were Stover's men trying to intimidate her into giving up the ranch, their ploy failed. Yet she had the distinct feeling they weren't part of Stover's nasty bunch. Beau never seemed alarmed by their presence. If he wasn't concerned, then those men were undoubtedly there because of him.

She leaned against the post and thought about the scene in the barn this afternoon. It was just like Beau to get angry at her because she discovered his well-kept secret. It still rankled. The more she thought about it, she realized any anger between those involved in Stanley's deception was misplaced. Without him here to admit to what he'd done, there was no one to vent their frustrations on except each other. Marcos, Beau, even Manuelo and Carlita. Their behavior was much easier to comprehend now.

A noise came from inside the adobe. It sounded like–Courtney listened more closely–exactly like the clacking and pinging of rifles against the ground. She swung open the door. After her eyes adjusted to the dim light inside, she gaped at the sight. Guns and rifles were everywhere! He'd turned the barren main room into a depository for weapons. Flinging the door behind her with a meaningful slam, she planted her hands on her hips. She was too stunned to do anything other than gawk. Beau stepped out of the kitchen then.

"What is all this?"

"Exactly what it appears to be."

"Ever since I came to Santa Fe, you've been assuming and bossy. I own this ranch, regardless of how it came into my possession. And as an employee, you must abide by my rules. Obviously, I can't seem to get that through your damn skull."

"I've had a belly full of you and your demands. I've worked my tail off trying to keep you out of trouble. I'm the one who's had it with *your* assuming and bossy tone."

Each heated word brought him a step closer. Courtney backed up to the closed door, pinned there by the icy sharp glare in his eyes.

"Instead of arguing, we should be getting this place shored up. Just a matter of time before Stover attacks."

"How do you know?"

"Take my word," was all he offered. "I've checked all the windows in this house. What the hell did you do with the shutters?"

"You mean those ugly wood things with holes in them?"

He closed his eyes briefly, shaking his head. "They were meant to be functional, not a fancy adornment."

Courtney disliked his sarcasm and cranky mood. "They're in the fireplace."

"Woman..." He raised his hands in frustration. "I should have said no," he mumbled to himself as he strode across the room. "I should have turned a deaf ear to him. I'm not a goddamned nursemaid."

"What are you going on about?"

Ignoring her, Beau grabbed the shutters then rocked back to his feet and stood. "Why don't you rustle us something to eat while I hammer these back on."

"I'm not your servant."

Beau whipped around, disbelief and thunder contorting his features. "Then *you* hammer these shutters in place, and *I'll* make supper."

He dropped the shutters, and as he stalked past her, Courtney grabbed a fistful of his shirt sleeve. Contrite, she muttered, "I'll make supper."

Courtney entered the kitchen as Beau finished eating. He refilled his cup with coffee and glanced at her. A frown ruffled his mouth.

While he had refit the shutters, she fried together most of the leftover food from lunch, a concoction of meat, rice and vegetables. With the tortillas Carlita had left, there'd been enough to feed Beau and Drake. Unfortunately, her appetite had gone missing.

She went over to the sink for a glass of water and felt Beau's eyes at her back. She drank down half the glass before she faced him. He lounged in the chair and seemed relaxed, except for his finger tapping nervously on the tabletop.

"How do you know Stover is ready to make his move?"

"Rumors I heard in town."

He was lying, but she wasn't up to challenging him and let it go.

"Don't worry," he went on. "This ol' house is secure enough. The adobe won't burn and the walls are thick. As hot as it is, we might have to light the fireplace to keep any of Stover's men from shimmying down the chimney."

"They would go that far?" She suddenly had misgivings about her decision to stay and fight.

Beau nodded solemnly. "But not if the fire's going, if they have any smarts. I got the shutters all secured. And the holes," he added with a wry grin, "are there for the barrel of a gun and for the shooter to see through."

Courtney stood straight and tall. "You didn't expect me to know that, did you?"

He wagged his head from side to side, amused–or perhaps confounded–by her lack of ranching know-how. "I hope you remember all I've taught you about shooting."

"Of course, I remember. Besides I already–"

Drake entered through the back door, making enough noise to disturb a hornet's nest. He glanced at the two of them, relief smoothing his mouth into a handsome smile.

"Glad to see the two of you having a normal conversation," he remarked, then chuckled. With a nod, he indicated the weapons cradled in his arms. "I've made sure these are fully loaded. Where do you want them?"

"In the bedroom," Beau instructed.

"I bought enough cartridges to arm a nation," Drake joked.

"Get the windows open while you're at it," Beau said. "But leave the shutters closed."

Courtney remained silent while Drake crossed the kitchen and disappeared into the main room. The weapons distributed throughout the adobe were more than she had ever seen in one place. She managed to keep fear from creeping into her bones, but she was helpless to stop her stomach from fluttering with apprehension.

"How are we going to fight off Stover's attack?"

"The way this house was built, there aren't any blind spots. The three of us will have the rooms covered. With all that ammunition, we should be able to last a week."

"A week!"

"Until reinforcements get here."

"Whose reinforcements?" she asked, alarmed.

"Ours, of course. All you have to do is follow my orders. Do you think you can do that?"

She nodded with uncertainty. Not because she wouldn't follow his orders, she had no choice. It was because she'd never dreamed she'd get caught in a gun battle.

Beau smiled softly. "I won't let anything happen to you. Or to your baby." Longing washed over his eyes. It lasted for a brief moment, then he pushed to his feet and stretched, yawning and grimacing when a bone in his back snapped. "You should get some sleep. Morning will come early. Drake and I will bed down in the house. Manuelo and Carlita and their sons are guarding the ranch from their adobe."

Courtney almost told him how grateful she was that he chose to help her fight for the ranch. That he'd put aside his aversion to sheep to see her through this dreadful situation. But she couldn't without throwing her arms around his neck and clinging to him for security. She was afraid – for her life and the life of their baby. And for Beau.

"Good night," she said.

"Courtney?"

"Yes?" She searched his eyes, he searched hers. Her heart hammered against her breast.

"Good night," he said and turned away.

CHAPTER TWENTY-NINE

The front door vibrated beneath the forceful pounding. Beau jolted awake from where he'd fallen asleep on the floor near the fireplace. The urgent sound brought Drake in from the kitchen, a lighted lamp in his hand. Beau exchanged an anxious glance with his brother. It wasn't quite dawn. Both knew what that meant.

"Beau, open up! It's Jeff!"

Throwing back the lock, Beau opened the door just enough to admit him. Jeff rushed in, gasping for breath, and leaned back against the cool adobe wall until he could talk comfortably. At the far side of the room, Courtney came out of the bedroom, tying off the belt of her robe. Jeff looked back to Beau, irresolution clouding his eyes.

"Have you heard something?" Beau asked.

Jeff's gaze shifted uncomfortably to Courtney again. "Raul got word. Stover's men gathered a few hours ago."

Beau knew what Jeff was thinking, that nothing he or Drake or Carlita said got through to Courtney. "How many?"

"Eighty, ninety. He's enlisted outriders from cattle spreads down Texas way. Word is he won't let up until he runs Mrs. Burgess and Manuelo off, along with the sheep."

Jeff glanced at Drake, then Courtney once again. Beau recognized the fear in Jeff's eyes and wondered what he wasn't saying. "What else?"

Jeff lowered his gaze briefly before meeting Beau's eyes. "He's ordered his men to kill you."

Courtney's gasp echoed across the room. "But Jared Stover's fight is against me and Manuelo. Why would he want to kill Beau?"

"Because I killed his father." Beau had guarded himself against revealing the painful memory. Jeff knew about it, but Beau had never mentioned the man's identity to Drake.

"Stover's father was the man you were defending your mother against?" Drake asked. "That was fifteen years ago. If

Stover's still carrying a grudge, why didn't he come after you sooner?"

Jeff cleared his throat, his demeanor sorrowful. "I'm sorry, Beau. Stover gave me no other choice. He knew you and I hooked up fifteen years ago in Amarillo. He put the simple facts together and forced me to fill in the holes." He raised his bandaged left hand. "If he hadn't broken my fingers—"

"Son-of-a-bitch!" Beau swung his hard-edged eyes to Courtney. "Get dressed. You're leaving Santa Fe."

"I told you, I'm going nowhere."

"This is no time to—"

Courtney returned to the bedroom, saying over her shoulder, "I'll get dressed and prepare breakfast. Then I'll take a post at one of the windows. You're going to need all the help you can get."

Jeff's hand on his arm stopped Beau from marching across the room and shaking some sense into that hard head of hers. Vexed, he shook free.

"It's best she stays here, Beau," Jeff said. "Stover's men are likely spreading out by now."

Beau watched the closed bedroom door. He should have never allowed her to stay. He should have physically removed her himself. God help him if anything happened to Courtney.

The morning evolved in deathly silence. Outside, an eerie quiet descended over the breaking day. No chirping birds. No bleating sheep. No neighing horses. Only silence.

Inside the adobe, the ominous quiet spread over Courtney as she sat beneath a window in the main room, anxious and tense, listening intently for the slightest indication of Stover's arrival. She glanced toward the kitchen, wondering how Drake fared. He hadn't been as calm as Beau. That came as no surprise. After all, Beau was the experienced gunman.

The sheriff waited with a load of weapons in the bedroom. She was afraid he wouldn't be able to handle a rifle with only one good hand. Aware of how badly his broken fingers were hurting, she regretted what Stover had done to him. Somehow, she felt responsible for their situation. She shouldn't. Stover would have waged his war whether or not she controlled Rancho Ortega. Yet there might have been something different she could have done. Or could have said.

Courtney slid her knees to her chest and hugged them. She focused on the soft light beam poking through the shutter above her head and cutting the room into portions. The last two hours seemed like an eternity. She prayed to God that Stover developed a conscience and decided not to attack the ranch. Deep down, though, she knew better than to hope Jared Stover had a conscience at all.

She was acutely aware of Beau at the other window. He sat back against the wall, his forearm resting on his raised knee. Now and then she'd glance at him, amazed at how relaxed he appeared. She wondered if this was how he prepared for a gunfight.

Another hour crept by. Courtney listened to Drake pacing in the kitchen and Jeff tapping his foot in agitation in the bedroom. The prolonged wait was making everyone edgy.

"What were Sheriff Taylor and Drake talking about? What happened fifteen years ago that forced you to kill Stover's father?"

Beau didn't immediately answer. He pondered her questions, his inner voice summing all the reasons he should tell her the truth, and most of the reasons why he shouldn't. The past was something he wasn't particularly fond of dredging up.

She moved, stretching her legs out before her. "Is it so horrible to talk about? Or are you thinking of more lies to hand me?"

Beau's lips tightened. She had every right to that last remark, yet it didn't sit well, knowing he hadn't had the guts to be honest with her. His first reaction was to slam the door in the face of her personal inquiries. But he wasn't about to run from his past anymore.

"I haven't talked about it in fifteen years," he said, his voice gruff.

"Maybe you should. It might knock that intimidating block off your shoulder."

Beau grinned at that. "And I thought you liked me arrogant and hard-nosed."

"Not funny," she remarked, smiling. "I suppose I could get used to you without the sarcasm."

"That'll never happen." He grew serious, contemplative. "I want to talk about it, but I..." He closed his eyes and rested his back to the wall. "I can't just yet."

The sudden desolation in his heart gave him a start. He thought he'd gotten over that part of his life. Strange, but it seemed as if it happened yesterday. The only difference, he wasn't that same young kid full of hostility and hatred.

"Answer one question for me," Courtney said.

Beau didn't know if he could speak at all. Even so, he nodded.

"Why hasn't the sheriff done anything to stop Jared Stover?"

Revealing the secret Jeff had guarded for so long could jeopardize his job if word spread. Worse, the truth might put Jeff's life in danger. Without question, Beau trusted Courtney enough to tell her. Maybe it was time to bury the ugliness of his past and Jeff's.

He sighed through pursed lips. "Stover's been blackmailing Jeff. In return for Jeff looking the other way when Stover is up to no good, Stover promised not to spread rumors about Jeff's past. He'd been a hired gun like me, but he was never cleared."

She sat straighter. "A sheriff who was a hired killer and is still a wanted man?"

"Exactly the reputation Jeff didn't need while trying to turn his life around. You have to understand, Jeff wasn't a cold-blooded killer. He shot a man in self-defense, but the marshal down near Abilene didn't see it that way. Jeff had no choice and took to the hills like I did."

"What about the governor here in Santa Fe? Couldn't he pardon Sheriff Taylor?"

Beau's chest jerked from his short, cynical laugh. "Stover has two elected officials in the governor's office on his payroll, and there's no way to prove it."

The crack of gunfire rang out. Beau jumped to his knees and cautiously rose to look through the shutter. He motioned Courtney to stay low, then barely turned his head to speak. "Drake, see anything?"

"No movement here," Drake called from the kitchen.

"Jeff?"

"Nothing here, Beau."

"Beau!" Courtney gasped. She had defied his silent command and watched through the shutter's hole.

"Got him." Beau's rifle barked once. The man sneaking near the barn fell to the ground. The loud noise frightened Jeff's horse, and it took off toward the stream. "Son-of-a-bitch," he snarled. "If we put up a long fight, Stover's gonna torch the barn."

"No, he can't! The horses..." Impulsively, Courtney bolted for the door. Beau was quick to take her down and pin her to the earthen floor.

"Listen to me. There's nothing we can do. If we step out that door, we're as good as dead. Do you understand?" His stomach twisted sickeningly at the thought of the horses perishing in a fire, but the possibility of losing Courtney was more unbearable. "Promise me. Give me your word you'll stay put if Stover stoops that low."

"He can't," she cried softly.

Beau drew her to him and held her against his heavily pounding heart. "God, Courtney. I don't want it to happen, either. But I won't risk losing you."

At that moment, all hell broke loose. An explosion of gunfire erupted around the adobe. Beau released her. He gave her one last look, his heart wrenching at the horror and pain riddling her face. Then he closed his features and his heart to emotion and turned his unequaled concentration on the line of riders forging down the hill.

Throughout the day, Stover's small army attacked and retreated like a teasing tide over sand. Dead bodies lay scattered across the front yard. None of those men were the gunmen Stover hired to win the war. They were only the diversion and the warning. Beau knew that. So did Jeff. Stover was saving the real hired guns—the ruthless but expert marksmen—for the end when he'd close in for the ultimate kill.

Beau took advantage of the momentary respite to reload the weapons and to check in on Drake and Jeff. When he returned to the main room, he found Courtney trembling in the corner. His heart sank with alarming speed. She hadn't been hit, he was certain, but he was afraid the gunfire had in some way physically affected her or the baby.

"You all right?" he asked from the middle of the room. He fought powerfully hard not to go to her, not to let his guard down. He couldn't risk tangled emotions now.

"Never been better," came her caustic reply. She wiped away the tears with the back of her hand.

Despite their situation, Beau grinned. She never let up on her spirited disposition. He moved to her and hunkered down, placing a crooked finger beneath her chin, and lifted her watery gaze.

"You're doing a good job. You killed the barn with your first shot."

She jerked away from his touch. "That's not funny. I killed men today. Took human lives." Her chin quivered.

Careful, Hamilton. Keep your wits about you. She may be aching inside, but you can't afford to give in.

His tone gentled. "You had to, Courtney." It was too damn difficult to remain detached from her feelings. He understood what she was going through. He'd gone through it every time he'd been forced to kill a man. He brushed away the new trickle of tears on her cheeks and pushed her braid over her shoulder. "Do you want to get some rest?"

"No," she sniffled. "I'll be fine."

"Maybe you should get something to eat then."

She smiled tremulously. "Is that concern I hear?"

Beau sat back on his heels, watching her. Yes, it was concern, but he didn't dare admit it outright. If only she understood that he'd been staying on at Rancho Ortega because he was in love with her, not because her father paid him to assure her well-being. He was fighting her battle because he wanted to protect her. He was dying inside because he knew she could never be his woman.

"I don't want you gettin' sick on me, that's all," he said. "I've got enough on my mind."

He helped her to her feet. "Yes, you're right. I suppose I could use a little food. Can I get you anything?"

"A beer." Beau got to his feet. "Since that's out of the question, coffee will do."

"You're going to wear a hole in your boots if you keep that up," Beau said after an hour of watching Courtney pace. He observed her building agitation and was afraid she'd do something irrational, like run out of the adobe to reason with Stover.

"It's strange, but I'd rather hear gunfire than the quiet," she admitted.

"So would I." He frowned as she continued to walk the same short path over and over. He prayed the lengthy reprieve meant Stover had given up. No such luck, though. Stover used an age-old ploy and tried to break them mentally. A ruse, Beau swore, that wouldn't work. "Save your energy.

Stover's going to attack by night. He's thinking we'll be too tired to fight back."

A minute later, she settled down beneath her window. She curled up, resting her arms on raised knees and nodded off almost immediately.

Beau trained his eyes on her, drinking in every detail of her huddled form. She gave his life meaning, gave him something that had been missing for most of it. She taught him how to love, to desire and want only one woman.

He rose, removed his vest and walked over to Courtney. Carefully laying her on her side, he set the vest under her head and kissed her forehead. Quietly, he went back to his position.

Rebel Heart

CHAPTER THIRTY

Silence dragged on. For Beau, the waiting was far worse than the actual gun battle. He stretched his legs out in front of him and glanced at Courtney's shadow in the dark. Maybe the night was a blessing. What he was about to say had been bottled inside him for too many years. He didn't know how he'd react to talking about his other life. Cautiously, he began.

"Drake and I had the same father, but different mothers. Drake's mother died when he was four. They lived in San Francisco, not far from where my mother had worked as a...a prostitute. Dad went to her for comfort after his wife's death. He fell in love with my mother and thought he could reform her. They got married, but it didn't work out."

Beau inhaled slowly, wondering if Courtney was listening. He released his breath, thinking he'd revealed enough. But the dam's wall suddenly crumbled, flooding him with the desire to flush out everything that had burdened him all his life.

"When I was three, my mother took me to Amarillo. She got a job there at a reputable whorehouse. The madam was good to us. She gave me my own room at the back of the building, but it didn't isolate me from the goings on there."

Inhaling again, his breath shuddered. He was taking a chance by exposing his past to Courtney. He wouldn't blame her for turning her back on him. What respectable woman got involved with a reformed outlaw and the son of a whore?

"Beau?" she called.

God, how her sweet voice warmed his heart.

"How long did you live with your mother?"

"Until I was fourteen. By then I despised every man she took to her room. She was my mother." His teeth clenched against the memory of that emotional pain. He swallowed hard, his now unseeing eyes focusing across the room into a dark corner.

"She had one customer in particular—Jared Stover's father. The man was a cattle baron and had wealth and power. He'd come to the cathouse once or twice a week to see my mother. He made her happy at first. Then he took to beating her. She made excuses for him even when he made a habit of using her for a punching bag."

A sickening taste rushed into Beau's throat and settled in his mouth. The hostility of his youth returned. He didn't realize he was grinding his back teeth until a sharp pain shot across his jaw. He opened his mouth to relax the tension. Then he continued, keeping tight control over his voice.

"I used to sit outside her room and listen to his fist crack against her flesh. She begged him to stop, but he'd laugh and called her a whore. I burst into her room one night. He'd pinned my mother to the bed and was sitting on top of her." He swallowed repeatedly, biting back the rising bile. "He was punching her face with both his fists. I tried to stop him." Beau laughed with contempt. "A scrawny fourteen-year old has no business picking a fight with a man like Stover. He was built like a bear. I found his gun belt and pulled his own gun on him. He knocked it from my hand, then grabbed me by my shirt and backhanded me across the face. His ring sliced open my cheek."

Courtney remained silent. Beau wanted desperately to know what she was thinking. Was she condemning him for his past? Did she pity him? God, he didn't want that from her. Pity was the one thing he refused to accept. But her opinion mattered more than outliving his haunted dreams.

"What happened next?"

She *was* listening. And there wasn't a trace of condescension in her voice.

"When my mother begged me to leave, Stover silenced her with a hard slap. I thought he killed her. I went crazy and lunged for the gun. Blood was pouring down my cheek. It hurt like hell, but I was incensed. He came at me, and I...I shot him."

"Dear God, Beau. Surely any judge would have found you innocent. You were protecting your mother and yourself from a cruel man."

"Whores don't count," he sneered.

She knelt beside him and rested her hand on his forearm in a tender, comforting gesture. A shiver crept along his arm, and he forced himself not to turn to her for solace.

"What did you do next?" she asked gently.

210

"I ran away. That's when I met Jeff. He was hiding out, too. We roamed the country eluding authorities and finally ended down Mexico way."

"Where you met Paco?"

Beau nodded. "Paco took us in, fed us, taught us how to survive, then offered a place to stay permanently. But Jeff and I thought we were too good for Paco, so we left. Trouble followed us wherever we rode. It all came to an end when I got caught in an ambush.

"When I didn't arrive at one of our meeting places, Jeff rode into the mountains searching for me. I was as close to death as any man could be. He took me to Paco. Nearly dying was enough to make me and Jeff decide to go straight. I don't know how, but Paco cleared my name. Jeff wanted to clear his on his own. I never saw him again until I came to Santa Fe."

Courtney cupped his face in her hands and rubbed her thumbs across the stubbles on his chin. She smiled tenderly. "Maybe that block on your shoulder isn't so awful after all."

"It kept me alive through those years." Beau placed his hands over hers, holding their softness to his cheeks. "When we get out of this mess, promise me you'll go back home."

She withdrew her hands and responded with a tired sigh. "I can't."

"I'm sure your father will understand." He doubted it, but he couldn't let her know that. She'd hate him if she learned about his connection to her father. He wished he hadn't taken on the job. Given the circumstances, he would have met Courtney eventually.

"You don't know my father. He'd never let me forget how right he'd been about Stanley. I'll be miserable if I go home. Anyway, he'll never forgive me for this baby."

Beau's brows slanted down with concern. "What's there to forgive? You were married first."

"So I was."

She didn't sound overjoyed, and he wondered if she regretted marrying Burgess. It was on his mind as she sat beside him.

"Beau, hold me...please."

He groaned to himself. "Any time, *querida*."

She came into his arms and rested her head on his chest. She felt comfortable there, like she belonged snuggled against his body. Deep down he exulted in the fact that she knew the awful truth about his past and hadn't turned away from him. It left a glimmer of hope in his heart.

Beau jerked awake. His body tensed, and his mind was attentive. Light flickered through the shutters, dancing eerily across the darkness of the room. He prayed it was a bad dream. But the crisp pop and crackle of flames and the high-pitched whinny of frightened horses made it horribly real. He closed his eyes in anguish and disbelief.

"The bastard," he gritted out, his jaw locked painfully tight.

Dropping his gaze to the woman resting peacefully against him, her flaxen hair shining brightly in the fractured light, he felt his heart chip and break away. He slid his hand over her head and whispered, "I'm sorry, *querida*."

Courtney stirred, the familiar scent beneath her nose a comfort. If she could, she'd stay in Beau's embrace for the rest of her life. She moved her limbs, moaning when her muscles stretched uncomfortably. Stiffness and pain seized places they had never before troubled.

She wrinkled her nose. Something wasn't right. Raising her head a little, a choking, acrid smell attacked her senses. She refused to open her eyes. It was a nightmare. It had to be. Lifting her eyelids tentatively, she choked back a sob when she saw the erratic streams of light awash over the room. She straightened and turned to Beau.

"The barn?"

He nodded grimly. They lifted to the window together, and Beau pulled open one side of the shutter.

"My God!" Courtney cried.

The barn was engulfed in flames. There was nothing either of them could do. Even if they could, it would be too late to save the animals. Tears of anguish coursed down Courtney's face. She wept softly, praying the horses would be spared a painful death.

One of the barn doors heaved, undoubtedly from the intense heat. Courtney hated feeling helpless. She was about to turn away when the door heaved again. Fire didn't pound on doors.

She tugged on Beau's shirt sleeve. "Look."

The wood gave, and a thunderous roar followed by a loud crack as strong as a bolt of lightning split the night. The doors splintered into a thousand pieces, showering the yard with wood. Beau's horse reared, posing in fury as he clawed at the smoke-thickened air. Paco broke free into the yard and stopped, bobbing his magnificent head at the adobe. His shrill sound echoed above the ravenous fire. In the next instant, the other horses emerged, snorting. With Paco in the lead, the animals dashed off toward the stream.

"What's going on?" Drake asked from the open door of the kitchen.

Jeff came out of the bedroom. "What's all the noise?"

"The barn was set on fire. The horses escaped." Relief lingered in Courtney's voice.

Beau closed the shutter and moved her away from the window. "What time is it?"

"Two," Drake answered.

As he stood, Beau's knees and ankles popped in protest. He winced "I'm getting too old for this."

Jeff grinned. "Aren't we all?" He raised his arms overhead, working the knots out of his body. "I brought Celina in the other day. You were right, Beau. Stover paid her to trip Lonie during that fight. She said Stover threatened to kill her if she didn't go along. I'm not sure what charges I can keep her on, but if she goes free, I'm running her out of Santa Fe."

Rubbing at the tension mounting in his shoulders and neck, Beau stepped over to the other window, ending any further conversation about Celina's duplicity. He inspected the rifles then went about checking all the weapons in the main room. "Stover's probably thinking he'll be close to victory with that fire."

"If we don't get help soon, we might not last the week," Jeff remarked. "What's to stop Stover from storming the house? We couldn't shoot fast enough to pick off every man he sends out."

"We've been in tighter squeezes than this. Where's your sense of adventure, Jeff?"

"Maybe I've lost my outlaw edge. All I know is, if we make it out alive, I'm hauling Stover in and going to the governor and make him listen. I don't give a damn anymore if it risks exposing who I used to be. I'm sick of men like Stover running my life."

"I can help," Courtney spoke. "My father will get you the best lawyer in the country to clear your name."

"Her father's rich," Beau commented with disregard.

"If money will save Sheriff Taylor's life, isn't that all that matters? God knows you're not in the position to pay for a good legal mind."

Beau shot a silencing glance at Jeff and Drake before bringing his heated expression back to Courtney. "Money is not the answer to everything. Jeff will be cleared, with or without your father's money." He left her alone and charged into the kitchen.

Courtney fumed. "He's so...impossible!"

A broad grin lit Drake's weary features. "Can't disagree there."

"Me either," Jeff chuckled, returning to the bedroom.

Even though her nerves remained tender, Courtney calmed down and fixed Beau's brother with a rueful look. "He told me, Drake. I know about his past. I see now why he tries to make people think he's unapproachable. What I can't figure out is how he can be so pigheaded and arrogant when he's capable of being tender."

Drake smiled perceptively. "Tender is one word I've never heard in the same breath with Beau's name."

As he walked toward the center of the room, gunfire erupted. A stray bullet flashed through the shutter, whizzing dangerously past Courtney's head, and slammed into Drake's left shoulder. Her "Oh, my God!" swiftly brought Beau and Jeff into the main room at the same moment Drake collapsed to the floor.

"Get down!" Beau ordered her, then snapped his attention to Jeff. "See to the bedroom window. They've opened fire again. We can't let them get too close." He knelt beside his fallen brother.

Drake clutched his shoulder in agony, blood oozing through his fingers. "Don't worry about me. It's not serious. Just hurts like hell."

Beau removed his shirt, tore it in half, and stuffed one of the pieces between Drake's wound and his bloodied shirt. He looked at Courtney. "Can you handle this room by yourself?"

She nodded in stunned silence.

CHAPTER THIRTY-ONE

Dawn broke across the land in a haze of colors. The sky was awash with shades of red and orange through the lingering fog from the smoke of the barn fire that burned out shortly before daylight. Dead men littered the yard, most seeming to be deep in slumber. The scene was eerie, Courtney thought as she turned away from the window. At least the horses got away. She was grateful for that.

Sitting on the floor with a weary sigh, she crossed her legs and rested against the wall. Exhaustion fatigued her body. She was sticky with sweat and edgy from the imprisonment Stover had created. The confinement grated on her nerves.

Across the room, Drake was sitting on the floor, his back leaning against the wall for support. His face was pale, but he was holding up fine, considering the gunshot wound and lack of proper medical help. Now and then he grimaced. All Courtney could do was look away, allowing him his pain in as much privacy as their situation permitted.

"I get the feeling there's more to your being at Rancho Ortega than visiting your brother." She observed the fleeting change in his eyes from weary to mild surprise.

"Beau sent for me. He had a gut feeling about what Stover was up to. I left my ranch to my foreman and rode down here as soon as I could."

"Where is your ranch?"

"Up Cheyenne way."

"I hope you're not going to tell me you raise cattle." She laughed wryly.

"He doesn't raise cattle," Beau grumbled as he walked into the room.

A gasp trapped in her throat. The sight of Beau shirtless caused her heart to flutter. When he knelt at Drake's side to examine his wound, Courtney let her gaze roam over his tattoo, then across the width of his shoulders and the length of his spine. Excitement fluttered deep in her belly. Resting her hands on the slight swell of her stomach, she smiled, missing Beau's dark scowl when he glanced at her over his shoulder.

None of it, however, escaped Drake's notice. "How's that baby holding up?" he asked, grinning when Beau spit out an unhappy curse.

In answer, Courtney lifted her smile to Beau's brother. She realized almost from the moment they'd met that Beau confided in his older brother. So she wasn't surprised or upset that he knew about the baby.

Beau pressed a clean piece of cloth to Drake's shoulder and pushed his shirt back into place a little harder than was warranted.

"Ow!" Drake yelped, drawing his shoulder back.

Beau stood, looking down coolly at Drake. "Feel good enough to shoot?"

"I can handle a gun." Drake struggled to his feet. "I hope my shoulder heals before I return home. Braden didn't mind seeing to business for a few weeks, but he might not take to running the ranch while I recuperate."

Courtney's attention snapped to Drake. Her mind groped for an explanation. Braden. Why did it sound so familiar? When she looked at Beau, alarm reared within her. Murder darkened his countenance as his eyes held Drake's.

"Beau, didn't the foreman from the Bar H go by the name Braden?"

He didn't acknowledge her. He was too busy bludgeoning Drake with silent hostility.

The Bar H, Courtney mused. The Bar... Hamilton! Her eyes flashed on Drake, then slid heatedly to Beau. In a blink, she was on her feet.

"You lying bastard. You went on and on about *stinking sheep* and all the while your brother is a sheep rancher? Why did you withhold the truth from me?"

"Beau likes to shroud himself in mystery."

"Shut up, Drake," Beau snapped.

"You're despicable, Beau Hamilton." Livid with rage, Courtney itched to pick up her rifle and shoot him for the deceitful bastard he proved to be.

"He's more than that," Drake commented, ignoring Beau's glare. "My brother can't seem to tell the truth to save his life. He's been lying for so long, he's forgotten how to be honest."

"You're goading me, Drake, and I don't like it."

"I don't give a hoot what you don't like. She has every right to know about you. If you won't tell her, I will."

Beau glowered now, fighting his foolish anger in silence. He rocked with indecision, though Courtney thought it was over punching Drake, wounded as he was. Beau turned abruptly and stormed off toward the kitchen. At the door, he spun around and pinned her with a flustered and vexed look.

"I'm half owner of the Bar H. And I could well afford a thousand lawyers for Jeff. And that night Manuelo's cousin challenged me to shear a sheep was no surprise. I've been doing it for years, and I haven't lost yet."

Courtney's mouth hung open in utter bewilderment. His admission caught her off guard, and she couldn't mutter one word. Not a single sound. It all clamored in her throat, choking her and strengthening her shock. Everything she'd noticed the day Beau began working for her made sense now. All of it had been a ruse, one big lie. He'd humiliated her and had been aware of doing it with every lie he spoke.

Betrayed by the man she loved, Courtney wanted to crawl into a dark corner and lock out the world. Feeling low, deceived, and hurt, her bottom lip began to quiver, and she couldn't even summon the will to stop the prelude to tears.

"I'm sorry," Drake said. He glanced to his right at Jeff, then tilted his head for him to check on Beau. "My brother rode out to the Bar H to tell me about the turn of events at Rancho Ortega. We agreed that buying some of your sheep would help you until a solution to the real problem could be worked out. Beau despised what your husband did to Manuelo and his family. You must know, my brother would lay his life down for Manuelo. I doubt Beau told you, but Manuelo and Paco are brothers."

Courtney moaned in misery. "What else has he been keeping from me?"

"Whatever else my brother neglected to tell you, it's not my place to say. Can't say I agree with all the lying he's done, but don't be too quick to judge his reasons."

Courtney set her plate on the counter beside the stack of others and leaned wearily into the cabinet. Fatigue pinched between her shoulder blades, making her neck stiff. Not knowing what Stover planned sapped all her energy and frayed what little nerves she had left. Cooped together for two days with three men and very little time for privacy didn't help either.

Someone entered the kitchen, but Courtney didn't turn around. She wasn't in the mood for conversation.

"Are you all right?"

Her eyes closed. She had hoped it wasn't Beau. The cold edge in his voice from earlier was replaced with concern. His moments of tenderness were rare, but knowing he was capable of caring burrowed deep in her heart.

"Yes, I'm fine." She used her fingertips to blot the moisture from her eyes. When she faced him, her heart wrenched all the more. His chest glistened with sweat, but she was captivated by the breadth of his shoulders and the strength of muscles she saw there. All the scars riddling his upper body belonged now. With his features subdued, his eyes appeared haunted by the pain of something more than his unpleasant past or, perhaps, by the lies he had woven. He shifted from one foot to the other, glanced down, then back at her again.

"This isn't easy for me to say," he began, his discomfort puzzling. "I...apologize for not being up front with you." He lowered his head and said no more.

"Beau," she called to stop him. But she couldn't say it. She'd thought about it all morning, debating fiercely within herself, still she couldn't tell him about their baby. "I want you to know that as soon as this is over, I'm going home to New York. I'll sign Rancho Ortega over to Manuelo. Don't be angry, but Drake told me about Manuelo and Paco. I fully respect your loyalty to the Ortegas."

"Beau! You'd better get out here!" Drake shouted.

Courtney followed on Beau's heels and waited anxiously while he stared out one of the windows in the main room. When he slammed his fist into the wall, she hurried to the other window and cautiously eased open the shutter.

"My God," she breathed, horrified.

Stover's men surrounded the ranch. The cattleman's patience had finally run out. He meant to end the standoff. Beau snapped orders to Drake and Jeff before he cast his grim sight on her. "Let's hope we can shoot as fast as they attack. Keep your head down between rounds."

His gaze swept over her with raw yearning. Courtney shivered from the intensity of it. A quirk curved his lips into a grin, and she distrusted the sudden humor in his eyes.

"Now that the barn's gone, you should have no trouble hitting something else."

She never got the chance to burn him with a retort. The men surrounding the adobe broke loose, shouting and charging. She slammed the shutter and poked the barrel of her rifle through the hole. Squeezing the trigger, she prayed to God to keep her and the men safe.

The noise in the adobe was deafening as the four rifles exploded repeatedly. The riders converging on them fell one by one. But then a shrill sound rent the air, followed by chanting of sorts, and a barrage of foreign sounds. Courtney listened with uncertainty. She glanced at Beau, perplexed to find him grinning like a man who had cheated death.

"Reinforcements," he quipped with an air of cockiness. He drew in a deep breath and released it with a heartfelt chuckle. "Drake! Jeff!" he shouted. "Hold your fire and look out your windows."

Reluctantly, Courtney dragged her attention away. Had he gone insane? She peered through her shutter and almost gagged on her shock. Indians! Rows and rows of Indians. She noticed a quick movement beyond. Scores of Mexicans raced over the hill toward the adobe, their leader the same man she had seen in the Sheriff's office and again on the hill watching over the ranch. She turned her befuddled expression on Beau.

"Merely a few friends dropping in to say hello." Relieved, he bellowed with laughter.

All Courtney could do was sink to the floor in joyful exhaustion.

Rounding up Stover and his army had been quite an interesting undertaking. Courtney's ears still burned from all the cursing. The dead were dragged to where the barn once stood. The wounded were gathered and roped together not far from the adobe.

The sight of so much blood unsettled her stomach. She rested a hand to it, hoping to control the mild nausea. Her friends in New York would never believe what she'd experienced here. They would faint dead away.

Standing beside Beau in the front yard, she held a handkerchief over her nose to help her breathe. Residue from the fire hung thick in the air. She watched in awe as Indians and Comancheros worked together. It was something she'd never, ever forget.

"What the hell took you so long?" Beau teased Raul Rivera as he gripped the Mexican's forearm in a strange handshake of gratitude.

"Assembling this many men takes time, *amigo*. And do not mouth off to me. Do you forget who taught you all you know about fighting and surviving?"

"No, *amigo*, I haven't forgotten."

"I thought Paco was your mentor?" Courtney gave Beau a skeptical look.

"He was, but Raul made certain I followed Paco's orders." Beau's charming grin and the twinkle in his eyes warned Courtney of his playful mood. "Raul's sister is Paco's wife," he added with a wink.

Courtney rolled her eyes in exasperation. "Are all these Mexican's related?" Raul's hearty laugh flooded her cheeks with a warm blush. She should have thought before speaking and hoped she hadn't offended him.

"No, *señora*. But we are *familia*. We stand together." Still smiling, he said to Beau, "We must be on our way. Paco is expecting us by next week."

"*Vaya con Dios, mi amigo*," Beau bid.

Raul nodded his acceptance, then turned a wicked grin on Courtney. "*Gringa*, you take care of this *hombre*." A spark radiated from his dark eyes. "He is *familia*, too. One day, I will tell you all about teaching this *testarudo*."

"I'd like that." Courtney smiled as she watched him walk away. In her mind, she couldn't picture Raul the fearless leader of the Comancheros. He had a genuine sense of humor. "Beau, what does *testarudo* mean?"

Beau's grin changed. He seemed suddenly shy. In a quiet voice he replied, "Pigheaded."

"Really? I see you haven't changed much." The sound of the Indian's laughter reignited her blush.

"Beau is our white brother. He spent many months in our camp, so I must agree with Raul." Cloud resumed his stoic mien.

"All right, that'll be enough of assessing my less than hospitable qualities," Beau said. Serious now, he clasped Cloud on his shoulder. "I am indebted to you."

"No, my friend. You have helped my people. It was our time to come to your aid. I will leave braves behind to see that no more trouble arises."

"Thank you, Cloud."

As the Indian moved away, his gait graceful and predatory, Courtney watched him. "You and Sheriff Taylor had this planned, didn't you?" She shifted her gaze to Beau. "That's the reason I saw Raul and Cloud talking to the sheriff in his office several weeks back. But how did you know when Stover planned to attack?"

"Remember those men we came upon?"

"The ones who used to work for Paco?"

He nodded. "When they hired on with Stover, they had no idea it was to fight against Manuelo. They stayed on to report back to me or Jeff."

"Well, then, I'm grateful to you and your friends for helping me."

Beau stepped closer until he stood a hair's breath away. "Is that all you're grateful for?"

"After all your lying, should there be more?" To her chagrin, he kissed her. Anyone lingering could have witnessed it. She pushed fervently at his chest, ending the kiss, but was helpless to stop her cheeks from turning crimson. At this rate, she might never stop blushing.

"I should get to work or my boss might bite my head off if she finds me dallying with the prettiest female here."

Courtney appreciated his humor. "I'm curious about one thing. If the money didn't matter to you, why did you accept my job offer?"

"Sweetheart, you wouldn't believe me if I told you."

Drake joined them, brimming with an amusing smile. Courtney groaned inwardly. He hadn't missed their searing kiss.

"I'm heading into town to have the doctor look at my shoulder."

"Why not have Carlita tend to it," Courtney suggested.

"Uh, no. I prefer a *real* doctor."

"Don't let Carlita hear you say that. She might shoot you in the other shoulder," Beau teased.

"Speaking of Carlita..." Courtney searched the yard.

"The Ortegas are fine," Drake assured her. "Manuelo is out comforting the sheep. Marcos and Eduardo are rounding up the horses. And Carlita"—he glanced over his shoulder—"is heading this way. I'll see you two later."

"Coward," Courtney gibed. Her lighthearted mood faded the instant her eyes settled on Beau. Her heart ached with the knowledge that she would be leaving soon, never to see him again. "Will you be going back to the Bar H?"

"In a few weeks. I'll help Manuelo rebuild the barn first. I also want to make sure Jeff doesn't need me here. He's got his work cut out if he's going to confront the governor."

"Were you serious about the Bar H merging with Rancho Ortega?"

"It was something Manuelo and I had discussed before Burgess came along. What about you? Will you be leaving soon?"

"Yes." The heat of tears rose quickly to her eyes. "Next week, perhaps."

Courtney was grateful for Carlita's interruption. She didn't want Beau to see her cry.

CHAPTER THIRTY-TWO

Courtney surveyed the yard from the porch. In the week since the fire, the rubble had been cleared and wood delivered to the ranch. Beau, Manuelo and Marcos worked on the new barn. Even Drake tried his hand at construction, although he was more of a hindrance.

"Dammit, Drake!"

Courtney laughed at the frustration in Beau's voice. Drake strode toward her, wearing a lopsided grin and his arm cradled in a sling against his stomach.

"I best stick to raising sheep. I never was real good with my hands. Got any lemonade left?"

"In the kitchen," she replied with a genuine smile.

Shifting her gaze to Beau again, Courtney's smile softened. Watching him do physical work stirred her feminine senses. He was unbearably attractive in her eyes, from the way he wore his Levis and dual guns, boots and hat, to his bare back glistening under the mid-day sun. The sight of his muscles gliding beneath his bronzed flesh scattered goosebumps over her arms.

Sadly, she would be on her way back to New York in three days. Now that Stover was no longer a threat, and Manuelo's ranch would be returned as soon as the papers were processed, Beau had no reason to want her to stay. Besides, he'd be heading for the Bar H right after they finished rebuilding the barn. She hated goodbyes, more so now that she was leaving the man she loved behind. Just thinking about it misted her eyes.

Two riders in the distance drew her out of her musings of Beau. It was the sheriff and her father. How nice.

Her father! What was *he* doing in Santa Fe?

Courtney stepped off the porch. Her sudden tension quickly turned her muscles into tight ropes. While she waited for her father to dismount, she glanced nervously at Beau. He was crouched down, hammering, seemingly oblivious to their uninvited guest.

Oh, dear. Her father wasn't happy. His features were besieged with anger, his eyes glowing, reminding her of a fire's fury against a dark sky. There was nothing giving about the man. Good Lord, he'd never listen to reason in his frame of mind.

Courtney turned to the sheriff. His apologetic expression told her everything she needed to know. Her father had been filled in about Stanley and Jared Stover. God help her if he had learned anything more.

"Hello, Father." She hugged him the instant he stepped off the wagon. She wondered if he felt her trembling. When she looked at him, she blanched. He was trying to control his temper. His cheeks always puffed out with the effort, as they were doing now.

"Were you afraid to write to me about Burgess' death?" he asked pointedly. Her father never dallied with words.

"I chose not to. If I had come running home, you would have given me your I-told-you-so lecture."

"For God's sake, Courtney. You're not accustomed to this lifestyle. Anything could have happened to you in this uncivilized part of the country."

"It's not that uncivilized here. Besides, I've made friends. Carlita and Manuelo took care of me like family."

"Yes, so the sheriff here said. Still, you had no business getting mixed up in a range war. That bastard husband of yours jeopardized your life."

"I'll give you that, Father. But as you can see, I came through it unharmed. Anyway, you wasted a trip. I planned to leave for New York in three days."

"Good," he grunted. His eyes lifted above her shoulder. She turned to see what had caught his attention.

Carlita joined them. "May I introduce Carlita Ortega. This is my father, Leif Danning." Courtney frowned when her father stiffly acknowledged the woman. "And this is Drake Hamilton."

"Hamilton?" Leif questioned.

"Uh, yes, sir," Drake responded uneasily. When his smile quavered, Courtney gave him a questioning look.

"Perhaps Sheriff Taylor will be kind and make you a reservation at the Exchange Hotel," she suggested, troubled by Drake's reaction to her father. The calculating shadow that settled into her father's eyes wasn't much comfort either. "I'll pack my belongings and finish business here. I should be in town and ready to go in a few days."

"I'm not leaving here without you, Courtney." His eyes kept drifting back to Drake. "Hamilton, don't I know you from somewhere?"

"No, sir," Drake answered.

Leif grunted again. "Pack your things now, Courtney. You're coming to town with me."

That demanding tone rattled her reserve. She positioned herself in an uncompromising stance and faced her father with determination. "This is exactly what I expected from you. Never a 'please, Courtney.' It's always 'do this' or 'do that.' Well, I won't. I'm old enough and responsible enough to make my own decisions. And we're not budging until I'm ready."

"Who's we?" her father demanded.

"Me and the baby, of course," she spouted indignantly then gasped, "Oh, no!"

Her father's face mottled with rage. "That bastard. That no good son-of-a-bitch. He gets his miserable hide murdered on your wedding night and manages to leave you with one more burden to bear."

"Stanley didn't leave me with any burden." She resented his referring to her baby as a ball and chain around her neck.

"You're pregnant, aren't you?" he shouted.

"Yes, but it's not Stanley's!" she yelled back without thinking.

Silence hung oppressively in the air. It felt as though a heavy hand pressed against Courtney's spine. Everyone looked stunned. *Oh, my God.* Her gaze shot to where Beau had been working. He was on his feet now, staring at her, his features twisted in a mire of emotions.

"Then who the hell is the father?" Leif demanded.

"I am." Beau tossed the hammer to the ground and walked across the yard, his eyes locked on Courtney's. He didn't notice anyone, didn't see the fire in Leif Danning's eyes. He finally remembered the night he'd gone to her drunk, but not so drunk he didn't realize something was different about her. She'd been tight, like a woman who had never been with a man. His eyes widened in disbelief. She'd been a virgin! She'd never slept with her husband.

Dammit. This blasted woman was going to leave without having the decency to tell him the baby was his. His gut coiled like a tightly wound spring.

A few feet away from Courtney, her father stepped in his path. Leif Danning stood larger than life and thoroughly peeved. Damn, but he looked like he wanted to hurt someone. Beau didn't doubt that someone was him. The man was a few inches taller, too many pounds heavier, probably a hell-sight stronger.

Beau rooted his boots to the earth. Foolish as it might prove, he met the hostility in Danning's eyes without blinking. His gunfighter's senses heightened, preparing him for the inevitable.

"Mr. Hamilton," Danning began stringently, stepping dangerously closer until they were almost chest to chest.

Courtney's gaze shifted from one man to the other. How did her father know Beau's name? As curious as she was, first she had to console her father's temper before he killed Beau.

"I can explain," she said, concealing the nervous edge in her voice. "I hired Beau to protect me when I discovered Jared Stover meant to harm Rancho Ortega."

Her father's incredulous features swiveled slowly to her. "*You* hired *him*?" He returned a venomous glare to Beau. "You two-timing bastard. Wasn't my money good enough? What the hell did you think I was paying you for? To service my daughter?"

"You paid him?" Courtney asked, aghast.

Neither man acknowledged her.

"Mr. Danning–" was as far as Beau got. The man's fist slammed into his jaw, and Beau stumbled backward to the dirt, dazed. He shook his head vigorously then replaced his fallen hat.

"Get up," Danning ordered.

You really did it this time, Hamilton. Beau complied, tightening his muscles. He took a punch to his lean belly, grunting from the impact. For a horrible moment, he thought he would lose his lunch. He clenched his teeth to combat the pain and slowed his breathing to compensate for the shock to his muscles.

"Fight me, damn you. Or are you too gutless?" Danning baited, jabbing Beau with another punch.

The only fighting Beau did was to catch his breath. His lungs were about to collapse from his efforts to take one lousy breath. His jaw throbbed, his stomach burned like hell, and his temper was on the verge of exploding.

"I won't fight you, Danning," he rasped. "I accepted your job offer and carried out my end of the deal."

"By getting my daughter pregnant? And taking money from her as well?"

"When she approached me with the prospect of working for her, I figured it would be a good opportunity to keep a closer eye on her." Beau inhaled, his breath trembling in his chest. "I didn't need the damn money. I did it so I could protect her better. When I discovered what Stover was up to, I had to do something."

"You got her pregnant!" Danning bellowed.

Beau glimpsed Courtney's flushed face. He didn't much care for the way her father humiliated her with his obsession over her condition. If he were in Danning's shoes, Beau knew he would have killed any man who lied and took his daughter's virginity. Still, his motives hadn't been without merit, and Danning should have dealt with his anger in private. Worried over Courtney's feelings, Beau didn't see Danning's fist until the man's powerful punch burst with more pain in his jaw.

"That does it," Beau gritted. He unbuckled his gun belt and threw it angrily to the ground somewhere near the hat that had flown off his head again. He raised his fists, effectively blocking Danning's next hit. If there was one thing Paco and Raul taught him well, it was how to defend himself in a fist fight. Unfortunately, they never explained what to do when he came up against an enraged father who was built like a bear.

Too quickly, Beau felt like Danning was using him for target practice. The man's punches were as sharp and quick as bullets hitting tin cans. He was damn sore and tired of being the object of the man's wrath.

Rustling up a lick of strength, Beau managed to duck the next blow, retaliating with a solid fist to Danning's cheek. Luckless in his effort, Beau took the brunt of Danning's next punch in his upper stomach. The air whooshed forcefully from his mouth. He doubled over as he dropped to one knee. Yet he refused to go down in defeat.

Slow in getting up, Beau knew the instant he was on his feet he'd be swallowing the man's fist. If God was merciful, He'd end his misery now.

"I'm not finished with you, Hamilton," Danning growled. Beau swore the man sounded as fierce as a rabid dog.

Courtney's father grabbed him by the throat and hauled him up. "Go ahead," Beau rasped. "Take your best shot."

"No!" Courtney shouted. "You'll kill him."

"Damn right I'll kill him."

CHAPTER THIRTY-THREE

The wretch deserved to suffer at the hands of her father. How dare he take money from her when he was already accepting payment from her father to ensure her well-being.

Courtney cringed. Her father's punches turned deadly. Beau wouldn't last, not against a man who had won a boxing title three years running at his men's club. She must end this foolishness before her father killed him. She retrieved one of Beau's Colts. Pointing it skyward, she fired.

Beau reacted like quicksilver, instinct sending him to the dirt. In the same motion he grasped his pistol and aimed it at her. He could have shot her, but she was too peeved to care.

"Fighting will not solve anything," she admonished the two of them. The disheveled and battered sight of Beau tore at her heart, but she refused to feel one ounce of pity for the dishonest rogue.

"I didn't start it," Beau snapped, sounding like a child caught in a schoolyard scuffle.

She shot him a damning look.

Frowning, ill-tempered and haggard, Beau got to his feet and thrust his hat on his head. When he strapped on his gun belt, Courtney noticed he was still riding high with agitation.

Beau swung his disgruntled expression to her father. "I quit. Find yourself another nursemaid."

Courtney huffed aloud. "I've never in my life seen a man quit so often. You're always running away."

"I don't have to listen to this crap." Beau started to leave.

"Beau Hamilton, if you walk away, I'll shoot you."

"Hah!" He threw a derisive look at her over his shoulder. "You need to learn how to hit a target first."

Courtney noticed her father's brows angle downward, clearly puzzled.

"What the devil are you talking about, Hamilton? My daughter is an expert marksman."

"Her?" Jabbing a pertinent thumb in her direction, he laughed cynically.

Red with fury, Courtney brought the gun up and, without taking the time to aim, squeezed the trigger. Beau swung around to the corral fence. The bullet hit a glass atop a post, shattering it into a spray of crystals and lemonade.

"If you think that was luck, watch the glass on that other post." Firing once again, she easily found her intended mark, shattering that glass as well. At this rate, there wouldn't be any drinking glasses left. But it was worth the satisfaction of seeing Beau stare in open-mouthed astonishment. Unfortunately, he was none too happy and nailed her with an unfriendly glare.

"Why the hell didn't you tell me you could shoot?"

"I tried many times, but you were too damn pigheaded to listen. Besides," she added, an air of nonchalance about her, "I didn't want to show you up."

"Show me–" The red on his face grew a shade darker. "Woman, that was an underhanded attempt to feed your own ego. Don't think for one damn minute that you can shoot better than me."

"Why not? Just because you used to be a hired gun doesn't mean you're the best," she countered. "And another thing. I should shoot you for the cold-hearted liar you are. How dare you accept my job offer when you were working for my father?"

His voice rose, matching hers in pitch and intensity. "I wouldn't have accepted your offer if you weren't such an incompetent rancher. You didn't know the first thing about sheep." He glared and deepened his voice. "Or men."

"Hamilton," her father barked. "I can't say I'm pleased with the situation here. Burgess wasn't good enough for my daughter. And I can't honestly say you are, either. I want to know what you intend to do."

"I intend to go back to Cheyenne to the Bar H."

"I hope you'll be very happy there with your *stinking sheep*," Courtney snapped.

"You're damn right I'll be happy. And so will you."

"What do you mean?"

"You're coming with me to Cheyenne."

"I will not!"

"Like hell you won't." In several long strides, Beau was face to face with her belligerence. He yanked the pistol from her grasp and shoved it into its holster. Clamping his fingers around her hand, he pulled her alongside him.

Courtney dug her boot heels into the dirt. "Where are you taking me?"

"We're getting married."

"Not on your life, Beau Hamilton. I will not marry you because of the baby."

He halted abruptly, hauling her against his length when she kept moving into him. "Then marry me because you love me."

His voice was suddenly husky, his eyes gazing down into hers with new hope. Ragged breaths fanned her face, but Courtney could only stare at him, shocked by his remark.

"That goes both ways, Beau," Drake gibed from the porch.

"I know that," Beau shot back. He touched her cheek. "Marry me because I love you."

"You do?"

"I fell in love with you when I watched you dancing on your wedding night."

"I should have suspected when you broke your vow, Mr. Hamilton. You know, the one about never going back for seconds."

Beau grinned broadly. "I fought it all the way. I guess I can't live without you. Or our baby." His features softened. "So, will you marry me?"

"On one condition."

He arched his brows dubiously.

"I don't have to shear another sheep for as long as I live."

A rousing laugh lifted Beau's chest, and he gathered her into his arms.

"I do love you, Beau," she whispered into his neck.

He pulled back, surprised. "You do? Honestly? But I...I didn't think a woman who's been accustomed to the finer things in life would ever fall in love with my kind."

"You grew on me." Her teasing grin caused him to smile again. "By the way, why did you accept the money from me and my father when you don't really need it?"

Beau glanced at her father, then his brother. "I was never able to stay in one place for long. So Drake ran the Bar H while I took on jobs, mostly like what you and your father hired me for. The money I earned, I sent back to Cheyenne to my mother. I set her up in business there. She runs a home for runaway boys."

"Oh, Beau, that's wonderful," Courtney said, tears welling in her eyes.

Her father stepped forward, scowling. "That's all well and good, young man. But my daughter's future and reputation are at hand here."

"I love your daughter, Mr. Danning. If she'll have me, I want to marry her. With your permission, of course," Beau added hastily.

Drake chuckled. "Never thought I'd see the day Beau Hamilton asked for permission to do anything. It's going to take some getting used to."

"All right," her father grumbled and pinned Beau with a dangerous look. "You had better be good to her, Hamilton, or I'll finish off what was started here today."

Beau ran a hand over his jaw. "I don't doubt that, Mr. Danning."

"And for God's sake, get a shirt on. There are ladies present."

Courtney held onto Beau's neck as he carried her across the threshold of the adobe and heel kicked the door shut. His eyes gazed lovingly into hers, and her heart skipped a beat. He loved her. Beau truly loved her.

"It was nice of Carlita and Manuelo to give us their home for our wedding night," she commented. She'd have to make up to the Ortegas all the wrong Stanley had done them. It wasn't until this morning that she learned Stanley had sold some of their furniture for gambling money.

"I wouldn't have cared where we spent our wedding night. Just as long as we're together, Courtney." Beau carried her into the bedroom and set her down beside the bed. His hands were all over her like tentacles of an octopus. She slapped them away.

"Don't be so impatient. We have the rest of our lives for this."

"Convince my body of that." He pulled her into his embrace, revealing the proof of his need when he pressed into her belly. He devoured her lips, stealing her breath.

Reluctantly, Courtney broke his delicious kiss. "If you love me so much, why didn't you object to me leaving for New York?"

"I didn't think I was good enough for you. My reputation and the life I led weren't good recommendations to hand a woman who grew up with propriety and wealth all her life. I thought I'd save myself the rejection." He grinned sheepishly. "And I was...uh, concerned about your father."

"My father?" Astonishment crept into her voice.

"Hell, yes."

Courtney laughed. "You were afraid of my father!"

"What's so humorous about that?"

"You were the one others feared. I guess I never thought *you* could be afraid of anyone, especially my father."

"The man paid me to protect you. I got my jobs confused, even though he'd warned me he'd come after me if anything happened to you. When I realized how I felt about you, I knew he'd kill me. I wasn't exactly his idea of a son-in-law."

"How do you feel about us now?" She leaned her hips into his. A thrill swept through her when he groaned.

"Like we were made for each other." He closed his hands around her thickening waist.

"How were we made for each other?"

"Hmm, Mrs. Hamilton. I'll have to show you." He lifted her onto the bed and stretched out beside her. "And I will have to keep showing you until I'm convinced I am indeed worthy of you. You know how hardheaded I can be."

Courtney molded her hand to the back of his head, drawing his lips down. "I'll prove to you that we were truly made for each other, Beau. Every day of our lives," she promised.

How very far their relationship had come. A few short months ago, she'd been intrigued by the mysterious, handsome ex-outlaw. Back then, she never believed anyone could tame his rebel heart. Now, Courtney felt as if she'd known Beau her entire life.

**Praise for *NO LAW AGAINST LOVE*,
Highland Press' Premier Book.
*Join the authors in their fight
against breast cancer!*
*Order at Amazon worldwide or
all online bookstores***

The lucky reader of NO LAW AGAINST LOVE
is hereby sentenced to laugh-out-loud
hours of enjoyment! Couldn't be better.
    - *Bestselling Author, Maggie Davis*

Funny, sensual and delightful...all in the name of
charity. Take 16 very talented authors; mix in some
of the most arcane and ridiculous laws that ever
existed (some still on the books today), mix them
all up, and you are in for an unbelievably rollicking
good time! Yet, the best and most important thing
to remember is that these wonderful ladies are
doing this all in the name of charity.
All proceeds will be donated to breast cancer
research and treatment.
    - *Marilyn Rondeau, The Best Reviews*

If you have ever found yourself rolling your eyes at
some of the more stupid laws, then you are going to
adore this novel. A stellar anthology that had me
laughing, sighing in pleasure, believing in magic,
and left me begging for more! Will there be a
second anthology someday? I sure hope so! This is
one novel that will go directly to my 'Keeper' shelf,
to be read over and over again.
Very highly recommended!
    - *Detra Fitch, Huntress Reviews*

You might forget Highland Press is donating
all of the proceeds from NO LAW AGAINST

LOVE to breast cancer research, but you will never forget the brilliant characters that come to life under the passionate pens of 16 romance authors. While reading this anthology, prepare to break out in a sweat, bust out laughing and break all of the molds as far as romantic short stories are concerned.
- Aysel Arwen, Author

This brilliant anthology has the unique ability to make you feel good. Firstly, the reader feels pleased that just by buying the book she is doing good, as all profits go to breast cancer research. Secondly, and more importantly, the reader is given a thoroughly diverse group of short stories to enjoy, all written by some talented authors! You will laugh, smile and nod your head in complete understanding as a whole bunch of true-to-life characters take you on some very crazy, but always entertaining journeys! Everyone should have a copy of this book!
- Anne Whitfield, Author

Romance lovers the world over can rejoice in this fantastic volume of short stories. Based on obscure and little known laws, each tale centers around one of the laws. It's a fascinating concept for an anthology and one guaranteed to spark imaginative scenarios! This volume runs the gamut of romance reading fun. Whatever your romance style, it's all here waiting for you. Get a copy today and curl up on the couch with it. Read it at the gym or enjoy it on a sunny day at the park-however you like to read, just get it and prepare to enjoy!
- Kenda Montgomery

Blue Moon Magic
Book 1 of the Once in a Blue Moon Anthologies

This magical anthology has something for everyone. Regency, historical, time travel, contemporary, futuristic, and even delves into the magical realms of faeries, selkies, vampires, and the supernatural. All the tales have one thing in common. Each revolves around a full blue moon and the magical wishes made upon it. I loved every second that my imagination was immersed into these tales. As you read each story, you WILL find yourself believing in magic. And I bet you will be checking your calendar to see when the next blue moon will be. Outstanding!
~ Detra Fitch, Huntress Reviews

Blue Moon Magic is an anthology of fifteen delightful short stories. Topics vary from tender love stories to time travel to a variety of paranormal tales. These are stories of love and magic, of lonely people finding their soul mates with the help of the blue moon. Every story held my attention and drew me into the aura of "Blue Moon Magic."
~ Florence Cardinal, Member of Calgary Association of RWA (CaRWA)

Blue Moon Magic is an enchanting anthology by 15 fabulous authors who based their stories upon the premise that a wish under a blue moon will be granted. With stories ranging from historical to the contemporary, readers will be drawn in immediately. So step inside the pages of this book to discover how BLUE MOON MAGIC works... This is an anthology that offers a bit of magic for

everyone. These fascinating and compelling tales of wishes fulfilled on a blue moon will convince even the hardest of hearts about the power of love. Kudos to all of the authors involved as this is one anthology in which every single story delivers a powerful punch!
~ Deborah Wiley, CK2S KWIPS AND KRITIQUES

Blue Moon Magic is an enchanting collection of short stories. Each author wrote with the same theme in mind but each story has its' own uniqueness. You should have no problem finding a tale to suit your mood. Blue Moon Magic offers historicals, contemporaries, time travel, paranormal, and futuristic narratives to tempt your heart. Legend says that if you wish with all your heart upon the rare blue moon, your wishes were sure to come true. Each of the heroines discovers this magical fact. True love is out there if you just believe in it. In some of the stories, love happens in the most unusual ways. Angels may help, ancient spells may be broken, anything can happen. Even vampires will find their perfect mate with the power of the blue moon. Not every heroine believes they are wishing for love, some are just looking for answers to their problems or nagging questions. Fate seems to think the solution is finding the one who makes their heart sing. Blue Moon Magic is a perfect read for late at night or even during your commute to work. The short yet sweet stories are a wonderful way to spend a few minutes. If you do not have the time to finish a full-length novel, but hate stopping in the middle of a loving tale, I highly recommend grabbing this book.
~ Kim Swiderski, Writers Unlimited Reviewer

Be sure to check out other books from our Highland Press Authors

Dawn Thompson
Deborah MacGillivray
Leanne Burroughs
Maggie Davis
Rekha Ambardar
Phyllis Marie Campbell
Christa Fairchild
Keelia Greer
Meagan Hatfield
Kimberly Ivey
Judith Laik
Isabel Mere
Cynthia Owen
Katherine Smith

Cover by Janet Elizabeth Jones

Printed in the United States of America

Printed in the United States
98638LV00005B/85-102/A